T0095324

MERIT THE GREYHOUND

THE RACING YEARS

by

J. R. Von Der Lohe

iUniverse, Inc.
New York Bloomington

Merit the Greyhound
The Racing Years

iUniverse books may be ordered through booksellers or by contacting:

iUniverse
1663 Liberty Drive
Bloomington, IN 47403
www.iuniverse.com
1-800-Authors (1-800-288-4677)

ISBN: 978-1-4401-1930-9 (pbk)
ISBN: 978-1-4401-1931-6 (ebk)

Printed in the United States of America

iUniverse rev. date: 02/20/09

This novel is dedicated to my friends and family.

Chapter 1

The Big Day

It was a clear crisp morning. True To Form called out to her puppies. "Come over here. I have something important to tell you."

Happily chasing chickens around the farm, the puppies looked annoyed at being summoned. But at her insistence, the three pups ran over to her, skidding to a stop. As they sat down in front of their mother, all panting for breath, the other farm animals fell silent. Everyone knew this was a special day.

True started to speak, and then stopped. Slowly, she looked over her pups and wondered what would become of them. She realized this was the last day she would ever see her pups. She had done her best to raise them, but in a few hours they would be on their own.

Each pup looked up at True. She barked, "You are special! You are Greyhounds!"

Hearing this, the pups sat a little taller. "You are the fastest dogs in the world!" continued True. "Your job is to *run*. Running will bring you joy! We are the world's oldest breed of dog! We were worshipped by the Egyptians!" Looking over each of her pups, True bent down and whispered. "Today is the big day. You are old enough to be on your own. Today, you will be selected by the people who will both guide you and determine your future."

True stopped, and then continued. "Soon, people will come," she said softly, "and they will pick you up. They will poke and pull at you to figure out what type of dog you're best suited to be. Will you make a good a racer, show dog or maybe you're suited to be just a pet?"

True composed her words carefully. "Racing dogs run against other greyhounds. They are trained to chase a mechanical lure around an oval racetrack. People watch the race and bet on which dog will win."

"I raced for four years until my owner brought me here to the farm. When I won a race I received praise and was treated well. When you race, running is your life. It is the only thing you live for."

"If you are considered to have potential to be a good racer," continued True, "you will be taken to a training camp. You will spend most of your time in a crate, but you will be trained to run as fast as you can."

Hearing this, one puppy's ears perked up. Merit, whose sleek coat made her look like a tiger, and who had always been a curious sort, looked confused. "What is a crate?"

True looked thoughtful. “It is a box of sorts,” she said. “It will be your private space, your den. You live in the crate and get let out to do your business, to eat and to run. You’ll get two meals a day and, if you’re lucky, you will get enough food to satisfy your hunger. Me, I didn’t mind racing. My trainer was a nice man. He made sure I was conditioned before each race. He always told me what was expected of me and looked out for me. When I won a race, I was treated well.”

True went on. “I never was a show dog, but it seemed like a nice pampered life. I met a few show greyhounds. They told me their owners took them into buildings where they paraded around. The judge examines the conformation and temperament of each dog. Looks, health and obedience are judged in these shows. Whoever the judge says is the best dog, is the best dog. From what I gathered,” she continued, “it doesn’t seem that much different from racing. You are trained, and then you live in a crate.”

True cocked her head to one side, thinking. “I was not raised as a pet,” she continued. “However, I think we are living as pets now and I like it here.” As she spoke, she looked over at all the other farm animals that had become her friends over the past year. In fact, all of the animals, except the chickens, had told her they would miss having the pups around. Their youth brought such playfulness and joy to the farm. As she saw the horses, cows and lambs gathered around her, she saw that they, too, were worried about her pups. She deeply inhaled their puppy smells. “Rest now,” she said, sighing. It’s going to be a big day. You will need your strength." As they lay down beside her, True snuggled them close, wondering what would become of their lives.

Blue was True's largest pup. Strong and pretty, he was solid gray with beautiful blue-gray eyes. He would make a good show dog, she thought. Merit, her second pup, was the fastest of all her pups and also had the build to be an excellent racer. Thin and sleek, her shiny blue fawn brindle coat made her look like a tiger. But True also worried: Merit was too sweet and seemed to lack the killer instinct essential to be a successful racer.

Della, the last in the litter, was a sweet, beautiful fawn pup. Since the veterinarian was worried about her hip, Della was going to live with a friend of the farmer. True knew that Della would be well cared for, although the family taking her lived far away. Drifting off to sleep True huddled closer to her pups, knowing she might never see them after today.

Soon, the loud rumble from a truck woke up True and her pups. Oh no! thought True, this is it! She looked at her pups intently, and then snapped. "*Sit up! Listen!* Whatever happens, I will *always* love you! Remember: you are greyhounds. Remember: you are special! Your speed can save you, but you will learn that it can hurt you as well. *Think* before you take off. *Use* your mind. *Use* your talent to..."

She was interrupted by her owner's call.

"Hey there, Miz True to Form! How is my ol' gal today? See you got your pups in line. You're such a good mom." True wagged happily at the kind words. The words went on. "You know today is the day lass. Your puppies are off to their new homes. Soon it will be just us again. The Watsons are here to get Della. They are taking her to their farm in Wisconsin." With that, he stopped and picked up Della. True just had enough time to give her youngest the quickest of kisses.

True looked at Blue and Merit, feeling a tear in her heart. "Della is going to be a pet," True told them. "She'll live on a huge farm." As she shared her visions of green grass and snowy winters, a shadow suddenly loomed over her remaining family.

Looking up, they saw a pair of hands come from the shadow, hands that then plucked Merit and Blue from their mother. True heard "What 'ave we got here? Some lil' greyhounds. Squirly lil' things. I think I like the blue one the best. He's rather handsome and I think he'd be a good show dog."

"Fine by me," said True's owner to a short plump woman. "He's yours for one grand."

"One thousand dollars!" the woman shrilled. "Are ye out of yer mind? How about eight hundred dollars?"

"Miss," replied True's owner, "he is worth every penny I am asking. Why, look at him! He is the best darn looking greyhound I've ever seen. Think of all the ribbons and trophies he could bring you." Putting Merit down, she looked Blue over. She lifted his ears, pulled his legs and examined his teeth, then asked, "What's the vet say 'bout 'em?"

The farmer said, "Come with me and I'll show you Blue's papers." The women put Blue down. True, Blue and Merit sniffed noses. Blue said, "Mom, she smells good, but she talks kind of weird." "Yes." True replied. "I've heard that although this woman is a little odd, she is also kind and gentle. We are lucky she has taken a fancy to you."

As their footsteps approached, True could tell the matter had been settled. True and Merit said their good byes to Blue. As the funny woman came and picked him up. Blue whimpered as he was carried away. True sighed.

Mother and daughter lay down together in the late afternoon sun, soon darkness would fall. Perhaps, True hoped Merit might stay.

It would be nice to have Merit around, to be able to watch her grow up, but she knew she should not think such foolish thoughts.

Merit looked at True.

"Mom," she said. "I'm scared. I don't want to leave." True tried to reassure Merit.

"This is nature's way of making pups grow up. If I were always near, you would never be independent. You need to go out on your own and have your own life. Whatever you do, just remember to do your best, and the best will come." As Merit started to feel a little better, the sound of an approaching car sent shudders down her spine. "It will be okay, Merit. You'll see," said True.

Car tires scrunched to a halt on the gravel driveway. The engine turned off and two feet stepped out. Merit hid her eyes and then tried to wriggle under her mother as the footsteps approached.

Merit heard the farmer say, "You must be Tom Coal."

"Yes, I'm Tom. Is that the pup we spoke about there?"

"Yes, that's Merit with her mom, True to Form. The fastest racing dog in the history of greyhound racing and Merit is built just like her."

Merit looked at her mom in amazement. She had never heard True described as a great racer. True realized that Merit was indeed going to be a racer. Intently, she looked into Merit's worried brown eyes.

"Listen. You are going to be a racing dog. Remember to train hard because you *must* win. You must run as fast as you can, every time you run. Just promise me you will train hard and run as fast as you can."

Merit looked at her mother's kind brown eyes, so full of worry. "I will, Mom. I will train hard and run fast. I want to be like you."

True spoke carefully. "Don't do it for me. Do it for you, because racing dogs don't always have the longest of lives."

True knew she was scaring her, but Merit needed her to know what was at stake. Merit looked at her mother as Tom Coal picked her up. "I love you, mom." Merit wrinkled her nose and sneezed, "He doesn't smell so good." True followed Tom as he put Merit into the car.

Merit looked at her mom through the window, and began to cry. "Mom, I don't want to leave you. I love you. When will I see you?"

As Merit howled, Tom interrupted her. "Now, now little pup, everything is okay." Merit cocked her head to one side and eyed Tom. Although he did not smell as good as the woman who had taken Blue, he had a much gentler voice. He was taller and skinnier than the farmer was, and he had kind brown eyes, just like her mother's. Merit decided to take a closer look. As she peered at him, he reached out and scratched her chin. He started up the engine of the car while Merit settled into his lap.

The car began to roll down the driveway when Merit heard her mother bark. Sitting and looking out the window by placing her paws on Tom's forearm, she watched as her mother ran alongside Tom's car.

"Everything will be all right," barked True. "Just do as you're told." Tom looked out the window and saw True running, then he chuckled. "If you can run as fast as your mom," he said, scratching Merit's chin, we'll be in hog heaven."

Merit wasn't sure what her new owner meant, but she liked how her mother looked running alongside of the car. She was sleek and her stride was sure. Her legs expanded and contracted in rhythmic harmony. She had never seen her mother run as fast as she did now. Merit barked, "Run ma, run!" As she reached the end of the driveway, True slowed down to a walk. Merit's last glimpse of her mom was of her panting, tongue hanging out as she turned back to the farm when the car turned onto the road.

Chapter 2

Going For a Ride

Tom looked at Merit. "Well little girl, it's just you and me now. We have a long drive ahead of us so you may as well get comfortable."

As he drove, he picked up a blanket from the back seat and put it next to him. Merit sniffed the blanket, walked a couple of circles on it and lay down. The sound of the car's engine and Tom's gentle strokes on her head lulled her into a deep sleep. As Merit slept she dreamt of the farm, and of chasing the chickens. Oh, how the chickens hated the little pups! As soon as a chicken started scratching for worms, Merit would run toward the bird as fast as she could. Merit laughed as the chicken used its useless wings to flutter its heavy body just out of her reach. A chicken once told Merit to "Go chase the cows." However, True told Merit that the cows were not afraid of the pups and they wouldn't run away from them. They would just kick at her if she got too close to them or their calves. As Merit dreamt, her legs quivered and she let out little grunts and whimpers.

Merit woke when the sound of the engine stopped.

Tom stroked Merit's fur. "Little M, we still have a ways to go on our adventure, but we need to get more gas."

What, Merit wondered, is an adventure?

"Would you like a drink?" Tom asked. Merit sniffed the bowl, took a tentative taste of water and then quickly lapped up the rest. Tom refilled the dish and Merit thanked him by wagging her tail as she took a few more sips. When she was done drinking, Tom picked her up and put on her leash. Merit was really excited, for she knew that when her leash was on, she would be led places she had never gone before. As they walked to the grass and under some trees, Merit thought to herself, *this* is what an adventure must be. To go where, you haven't gone before. And as she found the right place to mark, Merit decided that she liked adventures!

Tom put Merit back into the car. He reached into a brown bag and gave her a bone to chew. He filled the car with gas and soon they were on the road again. Sitting in Tom's lap, her paws rested on the window sill, allowing her to look out. As she watched the sun setting, she realized she was getting used to Tom's scent. He stroked her back from head to tail. He told her what a good girl she was. The food in her belly was making her tired so she curled back up on her bed and fell into another deep sleep. This time she dreamt of her mother running alongside of the car. She must have fallen into a deep sleep, for when she awoke she could not smell Tom and she knew she was no longer in the car. It was so dark she couldn't see anything. She sat up, stretched and yawned. When she got up and walked around she realized she was in a plastic container.

This must be the crate that mom told me about, Merit thought to herself. Feeling scared, she let out a long lonely howl. Then she heard something next to her crate wiggle.

"Hey, why don't you be quiet and let us sleep?" she heard a voice say.

"Who are you? Where am I?" asked Merit.

"Name's Gypsy," the voice replied, "and you're at the greyhound training camp. Now go to sleep!"

Merit sat in the dark. She strained to see as she sniffed the air. She could tell there were more dogs around besides Gypsy and herself. She let out another howl, saying, "Who's here and how do I get out?"

Gypsy answered. "You can't get out. Besides, even if you did, where would you go?"

"I'd go to the bathroom," replied Merit.

Gypsy whispered back. "You have to wait until morning. Whatever you do, don't go in the crate. They don't like it, and they'll push your nose in it and hit you."

"Who will?" Merit asked, "Tom?"

"No, Tom doesn't ever hurt us, but *they* will. And if we're not quiet we will be in big trouble if they have to come in here before morning. So please," begged Gypsy, "lie down and *be quiet*."

Merit was about to ask more questions, but then she remembered what her mom had said about doing what she was told. She lay down and tried to sleep. She wished someone would let her out of her crate so she could do her business. Merit did not like this place; she wanted to go back to the farm. Burying her head in her blanket, she tried to cry quietly.

As it started getting light outside, Merit could make out rows and rows of crates, some small like hers, others much larger. She tried to find a smell for each crate. As she sniffed the air, she heard a door open. She heard heavy footsteps approaching, then a voice call out, "Good morning Sunshine." Merit then heard but could not see a crate door open and a dog walk out. She heard the dog stretch and shake. The dog was led out the door.

Soon the person came back and let out another dog. The man said, "Good morning, Clark." She could tell by his voice and his walk that this man was not Tom. Merit had to go the bathroom so bad she started yapping and clawing at her crate's door. All of a sudden a man with an ugly expression was standing in front of her. "Be quiet little dog!" he yelled. With that, he held up a hose and blasted Merit with a stream of cold water. Startled and scared, Merit ran to the back of the crate. "That will teach you to be quiet," the man said, growling.

Merit heard Gypsy hiss at her. "I *told* you to be quiet. Now maybe you'll listen. You're lucky Joe is on duty today. If Linda was here, you would have been beat." Merit was not sure exactly sure what "beat" meant, but she could tell that she didn't want to find out. "They let all the big dogs out first," continued Gypsy. "They get taken out of their crate in the order in which they last placed. If they won a race, they get out first. Just be quiet and you'll learn all of this soon enough."

When Joe walked in front of Merit's crate, she sulked to the back of her crate. Until she noticed he was letting the dog in front of her out of his crate. Joe said, "Good morning, King." As the crate door opened, King walked out. Merit had never seen a greyhound as tall, sleek and muscular as King. He was solid black except for the tip of his tail; it looked as though it had been dipped in white paint. His dark gray eyes turned and looked up at Merit with a piercing hard stare. The fur on his back rose, he pulled back his lip and snarled. "What are you looking at?" As he stretched, she noticed a dark purple scar running down his left flank.

Joe spoke to King. "Knock it off King," he said as he bent down and placed an odd contraption over King's nose.

After Joe led King out of the room, Merit asked Gypsy, "What did Joe put over King's nose?" "That's a muzzle," Gypsy replied. "What's it for?" Merit asked. "It's to keep King from biting the other dogs," snapped her new friend. "Why would he bite other dogs?" Merit asked.

"King is not nice," explained Gypsy. "He came here only a couple of weeks ago and his last trainer beat him real bad. So Tom bought him and brought him here. They say King just needs time to adjust," added Gypsy, "but I think he is just plain mean."

"The first week he was here he got into a fight with a pup and killed her," continued Gypsy. "So now they put a muzzle on him. Tom should have never brought that dog here." Merit shuddered. It was all too much for her. Not only did she miss her mom but the dogs here weren't nice. Even Gypsy seemed tough.

Merit sighed and watched as Joe let four other dogs from their crates.

Two other dogs, Music and Speedy, needed muzzles as well. When Joe came by Merit's crate again, she instinctively bolted toward the back of her cage. Then Merit realized that Joe was letting Gypsy out, so ran to the front of her cage, straining to see Gypsy. As Joe handled Gypsy, Merit saw that he was white with black spots, much like a Dalmatian, and was not much bigger than she was. Merit smiled. She thought he was the funniest looking greyhound she'd ever seen.

Joe walked up to Merit's crate.

Shrinking to the back, Merit ran to hide. As he opened the door and reached in to grab her, Merit wiggled under her blanket. Joe grabbed her by the scruff of her neck. "Now, now little pup, settle down. It's time for you to go outside." Merit wanted to go outside so bad that she let him carry her from the safety of her crate.

But as they went out the door, the bright sunshine struck Merit's eyes, making it hard for her to see. Joe sat her down in front of the doorway on the cool, hard cement and walked away. Merits' eyes blinked, trying to adjust to the brightness.

The other greyhounds ran up to her, making her cringe into a little ball. Seeming to all sniff her at once, they all started asking questions.

"Where did you come from?" "How old are you?" "Who's your mom?" "What about your dad?" "Did Tom pick you out?" "Are you from a rescue group?" "Have you raced before?" All Merit could manage to say was, "I have to go the bathroom."

All of a sudden a voice rang out. "Leave the poor girl alone! She just got here. Don't any of you have *manners*?" As the crowed parted, Merit saw that this dog was a beautiful fawn color with a white blaze down her nose. She gently approached Merit. "Come with me, little girl," she said, "and I will show you around." As Merit and the dog walked off, Merit could hear Gypsy telling the others, "Tom brought her in last night..."

"What is your name?" Merit asked her new friend.

"Isabel," the dog replied. "Your's?"

"Merit."

"What a wonderful name for a greyhound! Do you know what it means?" asked Isabel.

"No," replied Merit.

Isabel laughed. "It means worthy of praise."

Merit liked the sound of Isabel's voice, soft and musical. As they walked through the yard, Isabel told Merit about her new home. "This is our yard," she said. "You will be allowed to come out here four times a day. And, we do our business over here."

Isabel led Merit over to a sandy area. "Whenever you need to go, you do it here. If they catch you going anywhere else you'll get into trouble."

"Why is everyone here so mean?" asked Merit.

"They're not mean, they're just strict," said Isabel. "You see, there are so many dogs for them to take care of that they've learned that it's easier if we follow their rules."

"How long have you been here?" Merit asked.

"With Tom, as long as I can remember," replied Isabel. "But we've only been in this place a few months now. Last year a huge storm, a hurricane, came through and destroyed our place. Tom was seriously hurt trying to save all of us. Unfortunately, two of his best racing dogs died; they got loose and ran away. One drowned in rushing water the other got hit by debris. It was a difficult time, especially for Tom. He hasn't quite been the same since. He has withdrawn from us. The hurricane not only ruined our home, but it left Tom in serious financial trouble."

Isabel was silent for a moment and then continued.

"Tom was in the hospital almost all of the last racing season. Although Joe did his best, well, he's just not the trainer Tom is. And, Joe had hired this woman, named Linda, to help take care of us. But she didn't always feed us, and she often lost her temper and hit us.

"Luckily for us, Carol the vet came one day to check on us dogs, and caught Linda hitting Clark. Carol told her she was fired and to leave immediately. We were all *so* happy! Then Carol took care of us until Tom came home from the hospital."

As Merit hunted for a nice spot in the dirt to do her business, she asked Isabel, "Do you race?"

"I used to," said Isabel. "But now I'm retired."

"Oh," said Merit. She couldn't think of anything else to say, so she just looked around the yard. The large rectangle grassy yard had a tall but sickly looking shade tree planted in the middle. Worst of all, there didn't seem to be anything she could chase. Suddenly, Merit was very homesick. For one thing, she had never been fenced-in before, and she didn't like the cold look of the chain link fence. It made her feel trapped.

Merit noticed all of the dogs gathered on the concrete patio in front of the door.

Merit once again looked at Isabel. "What's going on?"

"Oh," replied Isabel, "they're waiting for their dishes."

"Shouldn't we wait there, too? I'm awfully hungry," said Merit.

Isabel replied firmly. "No. Those dogs are *really* hungry. They will just take your food away, I'm afraid. Stick with me and I'll share with you."

Just then the door opened. It was Joe, carrying a large bowl of food. He started spooning out the food into a dish but when the dogs saw him, they started barking and jumping up on him.

Joe kicked out at the dogs and yelled, "If you dogs don't settle down, there won't be any food!"

Now it was King's turn to speak. "*Shut up!* If I have to miss a meal I will make *all* of you regret it!"

King's warning worked: the dogs quickly quieted down and stood patiently while Joe filled all of the dishes.

Merit had another question for Isabel. "Do their muzzles get taken off while they eat?" "No," replied Isabel. "Just watch. You'll see why. And make sure you stay by me."

Merit was confused, but she soon learned why Isabel had said what she did. For the larger dogs ate as fast as they could, and when they were done, they pushed the smaller dogs away from their dishes and stole their food. The smaller dogs who resisted were instantly squashed. Merit started to shiver. Isabel stared at Merit. "Come with me," she said. "I'll make sure you get something to eat."

Isabel led Merit to the side of the building. Isabel scratched at the side door, it opened and there stood Tom.

"Well, well," Tom said, "Isabel... have you made a new friend? Now I know why you wanted to go out into the yard with the others."

Merit followed Isabel into the room. The room was dark and cool. As Merit's eyes adjusted to the darkness, she noticed a desk and a couch in the room. The phone rang and Tom went to answer it.

Isabel looked at Merit again. "This," she said, "is where I get to stay."

Looking around, Isabel continued. "Once I retired, I didn't have to stay in a crate any more." She then led Merit to the kitchen where there were two large bowls. One was full of food; the other, water.

"Eat your fill," she instructed Merit. "Because when Tom gets off the phone he'll make you go back into the yard."

Merit wanted to ask her friend why she got to live in here and why the other dogs had to live in crates, but her hunger took over and she ate as fast as she could, inhaling and then choking.

Isabel chuckled softly. "Slow down Merit. You don't have to eat *that* fast. No one will take your food away from you in here." But Merit was so hungry and scared she couldn't slow down. She remembered what she saw outside and she knew she would have to learn how to eat really fast, or starve. Once Merit was done eating all the food in Isabel's dish, she belched and moved to the water dish where she rapidly drank her fill.

She was still busy slurping the water when Tom walked in and said to Isabel. "You know Izzy, we can't spoil her. She has to go out with the others or she'll never adjust."

With that, Tom bent over and scooped Merit up in his arms. "Come along lil' Mer'," he said, "You have to go back outside." As he carried her to the door, Isabel was right on his heels. She tried to go outside as well, but as Tom opened the door, he blocked her with his leg. "Stay in here, Izzy," he said.

As he bent down to put Merit down just outside of the door, Isabel spoke in a gentle voice to Merit. "Try to stay out of their way. Don't worry. I'll check on you later." Tom closed the door and Merit was once again outside, all alone.

Merit did not know what to do. Still, she felt safe where she was... so she curled up next to the door and feel asleep.

Chapter 3

A New Life

Merit woke to the sound of Joe calling her name.

He sounded so kind that she ran around the side of the building where he stood.

Scooping her up, he carried her to her crate. Once inside, Merit had just curled up to go back to sleep when she heard a voice.

"Well, aren't *you* a spoiled little dog? Did Aunt Lizzy take good care of the precious new pup?"

King was wickedly eyeing her. She tried to ignore him, but he snarled on.

"Poor little girl. Can't stick up for herself! You have to go hide behind Queen Isabel. "Someday Merit, Aunt Lizzy won't be there to protect you."

Merit was scared, but she was smart enough to realize that King could only get at her with his words, at least for now.

Perhaps if she said the right things to King, maybe when they were out in the yard together later, he would leave her alone. So she replied, "No, I don't need some old retired dog to take care of me. I can take care of myself!"

King chuckled. "Oh, sure you can. Let's see what happens later."

"Yes, you see what happens later, oh Mighty King," replied Merit.

King laughed. Merit could tell he liked being called Mighty King. So she said, "Mighty King, when we go out into the yard, will you teach me how to climb the tree?"

King laughed. "Of course!" Now Merit knew that she could not climb a tree because she had tried to chase a squirrel up a tree on the farm. But she continued their talk. "I can't wait for you to teach me!"

Merit settled in her crate and fell into a nightmarish sleep. She dreamt she was in the yard trying to get to her dish to eat but King would not let her near. Every time she tried, he growled and snarled every time she tried to come near. Her hunger made her foolishly brave. As she moved close to her dish, King picked her up by the scruff of the neck and shook her like a rag doll. She could feel her neck snap. Pain shuddered through her body.

When Merit woke, Joe was back in the room and had already started letting the dogs out into the yard. As King was let out of his crate, he looked up at Merit and snarled, "I'll see you outside." Joe told King to knock off his growling and reached down to see if his muzzle was secure. Merit shivered, she hoped her plan would work.

When Merit was led outside, King was waiting for her. The word had spread that King was going to climb a tree and all the dogs had crowded around the shade tree.

Clark beckoned to Merit. "I can't wait to see King try and climb the tree."

King first looked at the tree, then gave Merit an evil stare, then looked at the crowd. Then he spoke. "It's easy to climb a tree, you just need to get a running start. Now everyone, make room for me stand back." Separating, the dogs provided him a runway to the tree.

King delayed. "I have to do some warm up laps first." The big dog started running in a circle to the right, then ran a couple of circles to the left. One of the fastest dogs in the kennel, the other dogs watched King in amazement, how quickly and easily he changed direction! As King came around he said, "Here I go."

He ran straight at the tree. He ran clear up the side of the tree and than all of a sudden he lost his momentum and crashed to the ground. King let out a big horrible yelp. Gypsy ran for help. Merit stood there, what could she do?

King lay, crying and howling, "King," begged Merit, "are you alright?" Lying perfectly still, he didn't reply.

Joe and Tom heard the moans and ran out of the building. Kneeling by King's side, they tried to figure out what was wrong. "What happened?" Tom asked Joe. All the dogs except Merit barked, "King tried to climb the tree."

Tom stared at the dogs "Be quiet. Move away." Tom then picked King up and told Joe to call the vet. As Tom and Joe took King into the building, all the other dogs turned to Merit.

Gypsy spoke first. "Can you believe how high King got into the tree?" Speedy added, "And can you believe how far he fell?" All Merit could say was, "I hope he's not hurt. It's all my fault."

Sunshine looked at Merit. "It's not your fault. We all know dogs can't climb trees. King's arrogance got the best of him. That will teach him to be so pompous. King needed a lesson, Merit, and we're glad you gave it to him." All the dogs agreed. The dogs heard Tom's truck start up and they all knew King was going to the vet.

Merit walked away from the others. She couldn't help the way she felt. She knew that King was hurt, and that she was the one who had baited him. If I hadn't tricked King, she thought, he would still be in the yard. She felt really low. Merit heard a dog approach, but didn't look up. It was Isabel.

"Gypsy told me what happened," she said. "You should be proud of yourself for out- smarting that bully. Hopefully, if and when he comes back, he will be a different dog."

"What do you mean by *if*?" Merit asked.

"Well," replied Isabel, "he's a racing dog. If he can't race, who knows what will happen to him. In the past he was the fastest dog, but he is getting older now and his injury may be too serious for him to fully recover. We will have to wait and see."

Merit felt awful. "I don't feel well," she told Isabel. "I'm going to go lie down."

Merit went to the other side of the yard to be alone. She wanted to go back to the farm. She lay down and cried herself to sleep. She missed the farm. She missed her siblings but mostly, she missed her mom.

In a couple of hours the truck returned. Tom got out of the truck - King was not with him.

Chapter 4

Questions

All the dogs gathered around Tom as he walked through the gate. Barking out their concern for King, Tom ignored their questions and went inside the building. The other dogs walked over to where Merit lay.

"King must have been put down," said Gypsy.

"Did you see how Tom just ignored us?" added Clark.

"Yes," said Sunshine, "Tom looked so sad, King must have been put down."

Merit looked at the group of dogs that had gathered around and asked, "What do you mean, put down?"

"Boy, you're sure a naive little dog," snapped Gypsy.

Sunshine answered Merit. "When an animal is put down, it means they have been euthanized." Clark snarled, "Which is a friendlier word for killed." "*Killed*," Merit stammered. "But, but

... why?" Merit couldn't understand what the dogs were saying. Surely, they were just scaring her.

"When a race dog get hurts, it costs money and time for the injury to heal," explained Sunshine gently. "Sometimes," she continued, "the injury is not economical for the owner to fix, because the dog will not be able to cover its expenses if it can't race."

"Oh," Merit said. Although she pretended to understand what it all meant, Merit couldn't believe that someone would kill a dog simply because he could not race. She thought of Della and Blue. Both had found owners who would care for them, even though they weren't going to race. As Merit started to ask Sunshine another question, Isabel came out of the side door. Merit and Sunshine walked up to Isabel, who said, "I overheard Tom talking to the vet. King is out of surgery. He's doing well."

Hearing that, all the dogs ran over to Isabel to pepper her with more questions.

Gypsy asked, "What kind of surgery did King need?" Clark asked, "Will he be able to race again?" Merit asked, "When will King be coming home?" Sunshine asked, "How is Tom doing?"

"Now, now, one question at a time," said Isabel.

"King's hind leg was broken. They don't know if he will race again. Tom doesn't know how long King will be at the vets. Tom is okay, but he is concerned not only about King but how he is going to pay the vet. I overheard Tom and Joe discussing selling one of us to cover the expense."

"What!" the dogs yelped out in unison. "*Sell* one of us?" They all looked at each other. Clark was the first one to speak. "I certainly will not be sold. I've won my last three races." Sunshine added, "It will have to be one of the new pups, because they haven't put any money in training them yet." Merit and Gypsy looked at each other. Gypsy said, "Merit should go, she just got here and she's the one that got King hurt in the first place."

Isabel shook her head. "There's no use discussing this because no decision has been made. Who knows what will happen? We're *all* disposable. Any of us could be sold. I suggest you guys spend your energy preparing for training and racing and not waste it discussing which one of us may or may not be sold."

Just then, the door to the house opened and out walked Joe and Tom.

"Come here Izzy," said Tom. As she walked off, Isabel called out to the dogs. "I will let you know if I hear any more." Isabel went into the house; Tom closed the door, turned to the other dogs - looked them over and said to Joe. "Get the lures ready. Let's see what these dogs can do."

Merit's ears perked up. She turned to Clark. "What's a lure?" "It's something put in front of us to make us run," he said. "The one who gives best chase wins and is given a reward."

"Which dogs do you want to take to the track?" Joe asked Tom.

Merit suddenly had a new confidence. "I'm going to be the fastest," she thought. "That way, Tom won't want to get rid of me."

Joe called Merit and Gypsy to him. Merit looked over at Gypsy and said, "Race ya." With that, Merit took off toward Joe, running as fast as she could. She reached Joe in seconds and looked back to see Gypsy sitting in the same spot. He got up and trotted over to her. "Real funny, Merit," growled Gypsy. "Next time make it a fair start, and *then* we can really race."

"Come along now," Joe said to the pups. "Time to go to the track." As Joe attached her leash to her collar, Merit's tail wagged. As Joe put on Gypsy's leash, Joe laughed and said to no one in particular, "Merit sure likes her leash."

The dogs were then led out of the yard down a dirt path lined by shrubs, then led into a gate. Once they went through the gate, Merit and Gypsy found themselves in a small pen with another gate in front of them.

Merit heard Joe ask Tom, "What do you want them to do?" Tom replied, "Just show them the lure. Let's see who likes to chase it."

Merit looked over at Gypsy. He was watching a bird in the sky. "Have you ever chased a lure?" She asked him. Gypsy did not reply. Instead, he kept just looking around. After a minute, he turned to Merit and said, "Did you say something? I was daydreaming." Merit replied, "No. I didn't say anything."

As the gate opened, Merit saw a plastic bag scoot by her. She was off. She chased the bag around and around, running faster and faster. But just as she would catch up to it, the bag would be pulled further and faster way from her. In one last burst of speed, Merit lunged for the sack. The extra effort paid off! Leaping, she landed squarely with both front paws on the lure.

Merit looked up. Her tongue was hanging out of her mouth and she was panting for breath. Joe stood in front of her with a huge smile on his face. Tom came running up to them. He kneeled down in front of Merit and gave her a big hug. Tom looked up at Joe and they both gave out a loud hoot and a holler.

"Did you clock her? Joe asked Tom.

"Yes," replied Tom. "She ran the last lap in 29 seconds."

"That's the fastest dog I've ever seen," said Joe.

Merit looked around for Gypsy. He was still sitting in the pen, still looking at the sky. Merit barked at Gypsy, "What are you doing?" He barked back, "I'm watching birds fight over a nest." Joe and Tom looked over at Gypsy. Merit chuckled and told them, "I guess Gypsy would rather be a bird dog than a race dog." With no acknowledgement of what Merit said, Tom said "Joe, walk Merit to cool her down." Tom took the lure and walked over to Gypsy. As Merit and Joe walked around the track, Merit watched Tom trying to get Gypsy to chase the lure. Gypsy just seemed confused, and he just lay down.

As Joe and Merit walked around the track, Joe cooed praise on Merit. "You're such a fast girl! You're such a sweet girl!" Merit liked to hear the words, it felt good. For the first time since she arrived, she stopped thinking about the farm. Joe led Merit back up the path and into the yard.

As Joe undid her leash, he leaned over and patted her on the head. "Tonight you will get something special in your dish, little one." Merit wagged her tail and licked her lips at the thought. She walked over to Sunshine and said, "I got to chase the lure. It was fun."

"I like to chase the lure too!" said Sunshine. "In fact, when I was your age, it was all I looked forward to."

"But where's Gypsy?" Sunshine asked Merit.

"Oh, he is still in the pen. Tom couldn't get him to chase the lure. All he wanted to do was watch some birds fight over a nest."

"That's too bad" Sunshine replied. "He was such a nice pup." Sunshine then sighed. "It's just that if Gypsy won't chase the lure, then he won't make a good race dog and then Tom will probably get rid of him."

"Oh," Merit replied. "Where would Gypsy go?"

"I'm not sure," said Sunshine. "There are several places greyhounds go if they can't race. Some go to adoption agencies where they are placed into homes. Sometimes dogs are sold to other trainers to try a different training method. Other dogs are sold to industry for scientific research."

Merit shuddered. "None of those sound like good alternatives to being here."

Sunshine agreed. "I belonged to two trainers before I came here," she said. "Tom is certainly the nicest and fairest of the trainers. My old trainers did not give me enough food. My last trainer did not condition me before a race. He expected me just to be able to go out and race every weekend, even though I had been kept in my crate for the entire week. And they only let me out twice a day to do my business. We're lucky to be here, Merit."

Merit looked around the yard once again. Although it wasn't the farm, it was becoming familiar to her, and it didn't seem as scary as when she first came to the training camp. "I'm tired," she said to Sunshine. "I'm going to take a nap." Finding a nice place in the sun, Merit stretched out. Rolling over on her back, she let her legs stick straight up into the air, her tongue hang out the side of her mouth and her eyes roll back in her head. Soon, she drifted off into a dreamless sleep.

Chapter 5

Making Friends

Merit woke up, feeling a painful tug at her hind leg, she yelped. It was Gypsy. "What are you *doing*?" asked Merit.

"How did you know they wanted us to chase that stupid piece of plastic?" asked Gypsy.

"Because," said Merit, "Clark told me."

Merit could see that Gypsy was hurt that Clark had not told him as well.

"You see, I asked Clark what a lure was," Merit blurted out, "when Tom asked Joe to get them and he told me. I asked you if you had ever chased a lure when we were in that holding pen, but you were daydreaming."

Merit kept explaining. "Maybe if you spent more time paying attention on what was going on around you instead of living in your own little world, you would know what was expected of you."

Gypsy's face got all contorted and he started sobbing.

"I'm scared," he told Merit. "I like it here. I don't want to be sent away. I'd rather die."

Merit watched Gypsy. "I don't want you to die," she said. "Why would you say that?"

"Music said that Tom will get rid of me because I didn't chase the lure," replied Gypsy.

"But I don't want to leave. This is the only home I've ever had."

"Where did you come from?" asked Merit.

"I was born in a greyhound kennel," said Gypsy. "My mom was sick when I was born." He was crying so hard that Merit could barely hear him.

"I never got to see her! She died when my eyes were still closed! My brother and I were nursing, she was cleaning us and then she started coughing. Then she just put her head down, and died."

Gypsy was howling. "She died when I was only three days old."

Merit shuddered. She couldn't imagine such a thing.

"Oh, Gypsy," whispered Merit. "How horrible."

"I don't want to leave here," whined Gypsy. "After my mom died," he said, now sniffing, "Tom brought me here. Joe and Tom bottle-fed me. They're the only family I ever had." Merit felt sad for Gypsy. Now she understood why Gypsy had been so gruff to her.

Suddenly, Merit had an idea. "If you want Gypsy, *I'll* help you! We can practice together."

Gypsy looked up at Merit, still sniffing. "Thanks Merit. Please don't tell anyone I cried."

"It's our secret," said Merit. "Come on Gypsy, why don't we practice now? Then tomorrow, you can show them how fast you really are."

"Now," said Merit, "pretend I'm the lure and your job is to catch me. Catch me if you can!"

As she bounded away, Gypsy took off after Merit. They ran and ran all over the yard. Watching the race, the other dogs began yelling. "Faster Gypsy! You're gaining on her." Others yelled, "Faster Merit! Or he'll catch you." Acting as a sort of lure herself, Merit would slow down and speed up just as Gypsy was catching her. Being chased is as much fun as doing the chasing, she thought.

When Merit got tired, she stopped and turned to Gypsy. As they panted, trying to catch their breaths, Gypsy gasped. "That was fun. Thanks Merit." "No problem," she replied. "It was fun for me, too."

Just then Joe came out with their dishes. As all the dogs gathered around, Joe gave them each a dish. Joe gave Merit her dish last and it had a slice of bacon in it. Joe stood over Merit and cooed to her, "I'll make sure no dogs steal your food." Merit wagged her tail as she gulped down her food. As she choked on it, Joe laughed. "Slow down, sweet girl. No need to eat so fast." But Merit did not want the others to know she had received an extra treat, she did not want them to be jealous.

Later that evening as they settled into their crates, Gypsy talked to Merit.

"Tell me about where you came from. Tell me about your mother."

"I was born on a farm," began Merit. "The farm had lots of animals; cows, horses, lambs, pigs, chickens, geese and ducks. My brother and sister and I loved to chase the chickens."

When Merit told Gypsy that her mother's name was True to Form, Merit heard Clark gasp, then whisper to Sunshine. "She was the fastest greyhound in the history of racing…"

Merit pretended not to hear him as she continued telling Gypsy about her mom. "My mother had the kindest brown eyes," she continued. "She was a race dog before she had me." Then, although Merit told Gypsy all of the things her mother had told Merit about being a greyhound and the advice she had given her.

Merit purposely did not mention that her mother was the fastest dog in the history of greyhound racing. Merit felt that since Gypsy did not have a mom, the best thing to do might be to share some of True with him.

From that moment on, Merit and Gypsy became the best of friends.

Chapter 6

A Lesson to Learn

When Gypsy and Merit were led to the racetrack the next day, Merit spoke firmly to her friend. “Now it’s your chance to show them.” Once the gate opened and the lure started, both Gypsy and Merit ran for it.

Gypsy caught the lure. Joe looked at Tom. “Can you believe it?”

Tom was silent for a moment. “I didn’t think he had it in him.” Gypsy wagged his tail, knowing that he made them happy. He turned to Merit and said “Thank you Merit, for letting me catch the lure.”

Merit smiled. “Gypsy, I didn’t let you catch the lure. You caught it on your own.”

“Really? You’re sure you didn’t let me catch it?”

“No,” replied Merit, “You ran so fast I couldn’t keep up with you.” Gypsy beamed. Tom and Joe walked up to them.

Tom said to Joe, "Joe why don't you take Gypsy back to the kennel? I want to work a little more with Merit."

As Joe lead Gypsy away, Tom said to Merit, "Lil' M, we have to work on being competitive. You ran much faster yesterday. You have got to run the fastest *every* time."

Merit looked up at Tom. Although his voice was stern, she could tell by his expression that he wasn't mad. Merit remembered her mother's words echoing in her mind. "You must run as fast as you can, every time you run."

Tom interrupted Merit's reverie. "Let's give this another try M."

Tom led Merit back to the box. But when the gate opened this time, Merit ran after the lure as fast as she could. When she finally caught it, Tom praised her said, "I need you to run like that *every* time, regardless of *whom* you race against." Merit barked at him. "I will! It's just that Gypsy needed a boost of self confidence." Tom laughed patted her on the head. "Merit," he said, "you're a special dog." As he led her back to the kennel, he said, "I think it's time to see what you can do on the track. Tomorrow you'll race with Clark and Sunshine."

Merit stopped and looked at Tom. He tugged at her leash. "Come along M. You'll do fine. I just want to see you race against the veterans."

Both Merit and Gypsy both got an extra treat in their dishes that night. As they settled in their crates, Gypsy whispered. "Tell me some more about your mom."

"After you left with Joe today," began Merit, "Tom told me something that my mother told me, too."

"What is it?" asked Gypsy. "Tell me," he pleaded. "They told me," said Merit, "that racing greyhounds must run as fast as they can every time they run."

"I guess your mom gave you some pretty good advice," said Gypsy.

"Yes, I think it's advice we both should follow," replied Merit.

"Yes, I guess you're right," said Gypsy, sighing. "I'm tired. Good night Merit."

"Sweet dreams," Merit replied. As Merit curled up she overheard Clark tell Sunshine, "I wish I had a mom like Merit's." Merit smiled as she fell into a deep sleep.

Chapter 7

You Can't Please Everyone

Just before dawn, Merit woke up as her crate was being carried out of the building. Still trying to figure out what was going on, she found her crate placed in the back of Tom's truck between Clark and Sunshine's crates.

In unison, the two other dogs barked. "Hi Merit."

Yawning, Merit replied sleepily. "Hi."

"Today's your big day, right Merit?" asked Sunshine.

"I guess," Merit replied. "Where are we going?"

"To the race track," said Clark.

"Do you guys always race so early?" asked Merit.

"No," said Sunshine. "We're going in for special practice today because Tom wants us to show you around the track."

"Oh," said Merit. "But, I was at the track yesterday."

"Not our track, silly!" said Clark. "*THE* track! The greyhound race track in Corpus Christi."

"Oh," Merit murmured, suddenly feeling as if she wanted to throw up. As Merit grew silent, Clark said to Sunshine, "Say something to the poor pup. Look, she's shivering."

"Merit, said Sunshine. "Please don't be scared. We're here to show you the ropes. You have no reason to be afraid."

"Listen to her Merit," chimed in Clark. "She's telling you the truth. This is just another one of your adventures! Now try and get some rest. It's still early. We won't be there for a couple of hours." Feeling better, Merit curled up in her blanket, knowing that her friends Clark and Sunshine would be there to help her. As the truck's engine lulled her to sleep, she muttered, "I *do* like adventures."

Merit heard Clark calling her name – pulling her out of a deep sleep. She yawned and stretched. Tom came around the side of the truck and smiled at the dogs. As he opened their crate doors and put on their leashes, he said "Good morning Clark, Sun and M. How are my best dogs this morning?"

Merit looked around. Although dawn was barely breaking, she could make out a large building sitting in the middle of the huge parking lot. "This is it," Clark told Merit as Tom put their leashes on and led them toward the building. "We go in through the side door over there. Usually we'll be put in a crate until the paddock judge is ready to weigh us. After being weighed, we will be given an identification tag displaying the race we will run and what our position will be. We then have our muzzles and blankets put on, then we're led out to our post."

"But since this is not an official race," continued Clark, "I'm not sure what Tom will do with us." Tom led the three dogs through the side door. No one was around.

Sunshine looked at Clark. "It sure seems different when no one is here."

"Yes," replied Clark, "Usually there is so much noise and activity you can't even hear yourself think." Thinking about what Clark had just said, Merit smiled, then said, "Even though there's no one here, I can still smell dogs."

"Right, Merit," said Sunshine. "Even though we can't see any other dogs from here, a lot of dogs are trained on the premises and some are even boarded here." Merit nodded.

Tom led them into the lockout kennel and tied them to a post. Here, he placed a muzzle on each of the dogs. This was the first time Merit had ever had a muzzle placed on her and she tried to pull it off with her paw. As she struggled with the oddity, Tom said, "Merit, don't do that." Reaching down, he lifted her nose and looked her in the eye.

"The muzzle is for your safety," he said firmly. "All the dogs are required to wear one when they race. It protects dogs from other dogs. You see, some dogs bite when they get passed up during the race. Understand M?" He looked at her steadily now. "You're not being punished."

Merit looked at Clark and Sunshine. Their muzzles made them look fierce.

"How do I look?" she asked them.

"Like you," replied Clark. "Only you're wearing a muzzle."

As Merit rolled her eyes, Sunshine spoke up. "You look like tough competition, not at all like the little pup we came in with."

Merit stretched and said, "Let's go!"

As Merit walked off, Tom pulled her leash and said, "Wait a minute, you need your blankets." Tom put a blue blanket on Merit; a red one on Clark, and a white blanket on Sunshine. "I like the red the best," said Merit.

"Eventually you'll get to wear all of the colors," said Sunshine. "You see, the color you wear determines your post position. You're wearing blue, so you'll be second. Clark's in red, he'll be in the first lane. Since I'm wearing white, I will be in the third post."

Merit thought a moment. "Still," she said, "red seems like the fastest color."

"It will be today," said Clark, laughing. Being away from training camp and hanging out with Clark and Sunshine was fun, thought Merit.

Tom gingerly led them over to a scale. Clark stepped up first.

"Eighty-five pounds," said Tom. Clark got down and Tom said "Your turn, Sunshine."

When Sunshine got on the scale Tom said, "Seventy-one pounds. You've gained a pound."

Sunshine jumped off the scale and turned to Merit. "It's your turn now."

Lowering her head, Merit sniffed the scale as she timidly stepped up. "It's okay. It won't hurt you," said Clark.

Once Merit was fully on the scale, Tom patted her head. "You're a good girl," he said. "You weigh 65 pounds."

Clark and Sunshine laughed. "If it weren't for your jacket and muzzle," said Clark, "you wouldn't even weigh enough to qualify for a race."

Leading all three dogs out of the paddock, onto the track and into their starting boxes, Tom spoke. "M, good news!" he said. "You're going to get to eat more food." Merit wagged her tail and licked her lips.

Sunshine nodded at Clark. "Tom is going to give Merit a portion of your food, flabby!"

"Not if I win this race," said Sunshine. "He'll give her *your* food."

Clark growled as the door to the starting gates closed. A bell went off and the mechanical lure on the inside of the tack was in motion. Sunshine leaped out of her gate and Clark was right on her tail. As Merit left her box, she was pelted with the sand and dirt they kicked up. Merit was running as fast as she could, but it was all she could do to keep up.

As the dogs approached the first corner, Clark was on the inside and Sunshine was on her left. Sunshine slowed down and cut into the inside lane, tripping Merit. Merit tumbled and somersaulted two times end over end until the momentum left her sprawled out on her backside. As she regained her breath, Tom came running up to her. She could not make any noise. Tom knelt down, his concerned eyes gazing at her. He felt her legs, neck and ribs and said, "I think you'll be okay." Merit finally caught her breath just as Sunshine and Clark came running up to them.

"I'm sorry Merit," said Sunshine, panting. "I didn't realize you were so close. Are you okay?" "Yes," said Merit, breathing heavily. "I'm alright." With that, she got up and shook herself. Tom laughed. He liked the way Merit shook. A little right and left rotation starting at the nose, wriggling down throughout her whole body, whipping her tail around, nearly pulling her legs out from underneath her. None of his other dogs shook with Merit's enthusiasm.

"Can I try again?" asked Merit.

"Let's try it again," said Tom. The dogs looked at Tom, then each other. Clark said, "People never listen."

As they were led into their starting boxes, Clark spoke to Merit. "When you approach the first corner," he said, "you need to check your speed or your corner will be too wide and you'll end up on the outside. You see, it's hard to win a race if you're on the outside lane because it takes more speed to keep up with the pack."

"But," added Sunshine, "it's safer to run on the outside of the track."

"Why?" asked Merit.

"Most of the dogs are trained to be on the inside of the track," explained Clark. "It can get crowded and dangerous."

"Thanks for telling me all this stuff," said Merit. "I don't know what I'd do without you."

"Probably have a wreck," said Clark. "Just be careful. Too much speed can hurt you." Merit thought back to what her mom had told her. "Your speed can save you and you will learn it can hurt you. Think before you take off." Now, Merit waited for the gate to open.

There was no hesitation for Merit when the gate opened. Merit took off like a bullet.

Since she was between Sunshine and Clark, Merit knew she had to get ahead to move to the rail first. Concentrating on her rhythm and her breathing, her eyes focused on the lure. She did not smell anything. She did not hear anything. As she stretched out, she looked like a super hero flying through the air. As her legs contracted, her body seemed to almost fold in half until her feet sprang apart as they fleetingly touched the ground. All of a sudden, the lure stopped. It took Merit several strides to slow to a trot and then to a walk.

As she turned back she saw Clark and Sunshine cross the finish line. Although they looked toward Merit, they did not look at her, they looked through her.

The joy she felt moments ago was now deflated. The two more experienced dogs said something to each other, and then walked away. While Merit was trying to think of something to say to them, Tom ran up to Merit.

He had a huge smile on his face. Before Merit could move, Tom knelt down on one knee, scrubbed her down with a towel and said, "Why Merit - you've made me so proud! You're the fastest dog I've ever known. I can't believe you're mine. How did I get so blessed? Let's get you cooled down."

As he led Merit around the cool down path, he told her, "I don't think a dog has ever run that track in less than 25 seconds. I think you can set a new record, M."

But Merit didn't care about a record. All she knew was that her friends were not talking to her and that she felt lousy. She started to ask Tom why the dogs were mad at her when she remembered what Clark said about people never listening, so she decided to keep quiet.

For the first time in a long time, Merit's thoughts drifted back to the farm and her mother.

It seemed that no matter what she did, she could never please everyone. She racked her brain to try to remember some advice her mother may have said about racing and friendship, but she could not think of any. But Merit knew this: she had to find a way to show Sunshine and Clark that even though she was faster than them, she was still their friend.

Chapter 8

The Idea

As she walked with Tom rambling on, Merit thought, but how? The idea came to her in a flash. With a strong sense of purpose, Merit leaped forward and sprang into the air. Her leash slipped from Tom's unsuspecting grasp and Merit was free. She leaped as she ran toward the kennel, where she caught up to Clark and Sunshine.

Merit went panting up to them. "Hi guys, listen, I need your help. You have the knowledge and the expertise to win races. I have the speed to help you stay in top condition. If we train together, we can all win races and then Tom will have more then enough money to pay our vet bills and keep our training facility."

"Well, if we pull together we might be able to get Tom out of this jam," replied Clark.

"And we *do* owe him something for being so kind to us," Sunshine mumbled.

Clark thought a moment. "And Tom would sure receive some nice cash if we all placed. Okay, let's train together."

When the dogs were back in the truck, Merit looked sadly at Clark and Sunshine. "I'm sorry I made you mad," she said.

"We're not mad," replied Sunshine. "We know there will always be dogs faster then us. It's just, well, it's just we've been the fastest for so long it's hard to accept."

"Yes," added Clark. "It's hard to act mature when your time is up."

"But before you came to us, we talked about it," said Sunshine. "And, we decided that you need our help you or you'll end up getting hurt."

Merit was feeling better already. "You're right," she said. "I do need your help."

Chapter 9

Clark

"Will you tell me about your racing career?" Merit asked Clark.

"Sure," he replied. "I started racing when I was 18 months old. My first race, my maiden race, was at Hollywood Racetrack in Florida. I was placed in the starting box with seven other dogs. I was wearing yellow."

"You were in gate number seven?" asked Merit.

"Yes," replied Clark. "Personally, I like to run on the outside so number seven is a good gate. I got lucky with that draw. The horn sounded and I took off. All eight of us dogs, all running full speed just inches from each other. I couldn't believe how competitive we were. It is a good thing that we wear muzzles when we race. Not so much the maiden races but when you start moving up grades the dogs are more likely to cop an attitude if you try and pass."

"Can you blame them?" interrupted Sunshine. "You *have* to place. You know how it is. The smart dogs figure it out fast, the rest no longer race."

"True," said Clark. "You have to keep winning in order to move up the grades."

"Do you know how many races you have to win or place to race a top-of-the-line –an 'A' race?" asked Sunshine.

"Hmmm, not to mention that the dogs you're racing against are also training and running the same schedule," added Clark.

"How many races *do* you have to win?" asked Merit. "I mean to get to the 'A' grade?"

"At least five," said Clark. "And with each new grade, you compete against a better group of dogs. It's really hard not to lose focus."

"But you *have* to place," added Sunshine. "That means you must come in first, second, or third, because if you don't, after three races you drop a grade." Sunshine thought a moment. "Racing is hard work, but it's worth it. I mean, you know where you live, you know what's expected of you, you get food and shelter. And we're lucky, Tom likes us and takes care of us."

Sunshine paused, then continued. "Some trainers you see at the track will make you angry, but you have to remind yourself that your job is to win the race, *not* make friends. And you *have* to concentrate, even though other dogs will still try and distract you. You need to learn to see past them, past the kennel, past the starting box, into the first corner and the home stretch." Sunshine chose her next words carefully. "You see, Tom needs us to win, too. If we don't make money, he can't afford to buy us food, pay our vet bills and keep the facility."

Clark spoke up. "Some trainers," he said, "will risk their dogs to win a race. A few trainers will get so far into debt that the only way they can pay their bills is if their dog can win a race with a huge purse."

Merit looked puzzled. "What's a purse?"

"It's the money the dog earns if he wins," explained Sunshine. "The largest purse I ever won was $124,000 at Hollywood Racetrack."

Clark spoke up. "I've earned $215,000 in my career."

"And to think," mused Sunshine, "that our owners can get rid of us anytime."

"Or kill us," murmured Clark.

The dogs fell silent. Merit couldn't believe all she had already gone through today. It seemed like years since she had been brought here, not just a few hours ago. Laying down, she tried to sort it all out. She couldn't. Her head hurt and her muscles were sore and cramped. As her body twitched, she fell asleep.

Chapter 10

A Day Off

It was a few days later, and Merit couldn't believe that today she was the fourth dog to be let out of her crate. Putting her leash on her and walking her down the trail behind the house, Joe spoke softly. "You'll only race three times a week," he said. "So, we have to work on your overall condition by taking long walks on your off days."

The sandy warm soil felt good under Merit's paws. The sun warmed her back. As Merit lifted her nose and smelled the air, a cool breeze brought her good smells of cattle and horses. She was entering the woods, loving the instant cooling of the shade, the darkness and the silence.

Suddenly Merit's ears perked, they stood fully erect. Joe noticed Merit stalking forward, her nose and paw pointed toward a small squirrel off the side of the trail. Joe yanked on her leash but he could not get her attention. All of a sudden Merit took off after the squirrel. Joe tried to keep a grip on the leash but he tripped and slipped. The rope burnt his palm as it was forced from his grasp.

"Merit! Merit! Come HERE!" Joe yelled.

She ran from tree to tree sniffing, smelling leaving her mark, Joe picked himself up, blew on his palm and called out. "Merit, come here Merit." But as she moved deeper and deeper into the forest, Merit ignored him.

As she trotted down a small trail a tiny rabbit darted out, crossing right in front of her. Taking off into the brush after the rabbit, Merit was jumping over a small shrub when her leash got tangled in some underbrush. With no warning, Merit crashed down into the shrub, the branches ripping her thin skin. All she could do was yelp in pain.

Joe heard Merit's cries, but he couldn't find her. He called to her, but Merit could not hear because she was crying so hard. Finally, Joe stumbled across the trail Merit had taken and found her in a deep thicket of shrub several feet off of the trail. He looked for a way through the branches and plunged in. The shrub cracked and shook as Joe invaded it and brought Merit out.

"Merit," said Joe. "Are you alright?" Your eyes look bright Merit, but you're breathing kind of strange. Let me look at you."

Turning her over, Joe let out a low gasp, a huge gaping wound covered her left side.

"Oh girl," he said. "What did you get into? We need to take you to the vet."

Grabbing Merit's collar, Joe led her back to the kennel. "Tom," he called out. "Come here, *quick*." Tom came out of the house. "What's up?"

"Merit's got a wound on her side, she'll need stitches."

"Put her in the truck," said Tom firmly. "I'll call the vet's office and let them know we're on our way."

Merit winced in pain as Joe placed her down on the seat. "You'll be okay Merit," he said. "Be brave."

Merit looked at Joe weakly. Smiling at her, he patted her head and then closed the door. Stretching out, Merit tried to lick her wound, but she couldn't reach it because it was just behind her shoulder blade. Sighing, she let out a soft cry as she put her head down on the seat.

The door opened and she looked up as Tom scooted in. He fired up the truck and away they went.

Chapter 11

Dr. Carol

Merit only wanted to fall asleep. The sound of the engine and the gentle rolling of the cab lulled her. But just as she was just about to doze off, Tom shook her nose.

"Merit," he ordered, "you *can't* go to sleep. I don't want you to go into shock and die."

But Merit only wanted to sleep. And she was getting cross at Tom's constant barrage of chatter, petting and shaking. All she wanted to do was sleep. Growling, she curled up into the smallest ball possible, and as far away from Tom as she could get.

Tom chuckled. "Come on Merit, we're here."

He got out of the truck and walked around to Merit's side. Opening the door, he gently lifted her out and stood her on the ground, then led her into a small building. As soon as Merit entered, an overwhelming antiseptic smell filled her nostrils, making her sneeze. The blue glare from the florescent lights and the tile floor didn't help, it made the room feel cold and uninviting. She was about to leave when Tom patted her head. "Merit," he said, "you're going to meet Dr. Carol. She'll take good care of you."

A young girl suddenly appeared behind the reception desk. "Hi Tom," she said, in a squeaky voice. "Is that the dog you called about?"

"Yes," Tom replied. "Seems she got away from my handler and got tangled up in a thorn bush. Tore her side; here." He pointed to Merit's flank.

"Why don't you take her into the examination room?" said the girl. "And I'll tell Carol you're here."

Merit was led into a little room with a door on the far side, one table and a chair. As Tom closed the door behind them, Merit whined. She suddenly realized she was trapped in this unfamiliar room and began to tremble from fright.

Tom spoke softly. "Merit, take it easy, it will be okay."

Merit looked up at him but thought, "I don't like this place. It gives me the creeps."

But just then, the other door opened and in walked a woman wearing a white lab coat. She was almost as tall as Tom and had blond hair pulled back into a ponytail. Merit cocked her head to one side as she said, "You must be the dog that had the incident with the thorn bush."

And although Merit was still unsure of this place, she liked the women's voice, she spoke softly and in a low and even tone. Merit wagged her tail, and Tom said, "I think Merit likes you, Carol."

"How have you been?" Carol asked Tom.

"Things are going good," he replied. "Merit is one of the fastest pups I've ever had, so things are looking up."

As Carol walked up to Merit and started the examination, Tom asked, "How has King been doing?"

"Well," said Carol, "I'd say recovering nicely. The infection is clearing and you should be able to take him home in a couple of weeks."

As the vet looked at her teeth, lifted her ears and took her temperature, Merit thought back to that day when King fell from the tree. "Well," said Carol, "the tear looks pretty nasty. It will probably take about 14 stitches."

"That many?" asked Tom.

"Yes," replied Carol. "You see, I'm going to have to pull the skin back over the wound, like this."

"How much will this cost me?" asked Tom.

"With antibiotics, about a hundred dollars," replied Carol. The room was quiet, and Merit could only think about what Clark had told her about dogs being put down when they got hurt and their vet bills became too expensive. Her heart was beating loud and fast.

"Okay," said Tom. "Let's do it."

Tom was silent for a moment. "I can't believe my luck though," he said. "First King, now Merit."

"Yes, they're fragile dogs," Carol said. "I'm going to have to put Merit under to give her the stitches. Do you want us to clean her teeth at the same time?" Tom reached down, and pulled back her lip to look at her teeth. "Sure." he said.

"Tell you what," Carol said, chuckling. "We'll throw that in for free."

Tom smiled. "Thanks."

Merit noticed that Tom's voice was different when he spoke to Carol. He spoke more slowly and his voice almost trembled.

"Why don't you let us keep her overnight and you can come back and get her?" said Carol.

"Okay," replied Tom. "Guess I'll swing by about 10 tomorrow morning to pick her up and settle our bill. Thanks again for letting me make payments for King. I had no idea his surgery was so expensive."

"Yeah, when you brought him in we didn't discuss figures, did we?"

"Nope. And it's just as well because I wouldn't have been able to justify the surgery. But I'm sure that King will make good breeding stock."

"Yes," agreed Carol. "He's a fine dog. It's sad he won't be able to run as fast as he used to. And there's the chance that he'll develop some arthritis as he ages, but it would have been a shame to put down such a fine young dog." Carol thought a moment, then smiled. "Let's hope that no more of your dogs get hurt for a while. I don't need the business *that* much."

Merit saw that when the vet spoke to Tom she leaned closer toward him. It was odd, she thought, how differently they acted with each other.

"Well," said Tom. "Guess I'll see you tomorrow."

As Tom turned for the door, Merit tried to follow, but Carol had her leash.

"See you tomorrow," she called back. "And Merit, you come with me."

Merit was led through the back door and down a long hallway. Merit saw they were walking into a room full of large crates with small crates on top. In the last crate she saw King.

As they walked by, King lifted his head.

"Merit! What happened to you?"

"I got a cut from some thorns," she replied.

"Oh," said King. "Well, that's not as bad as what I'm going to do to you when I get out of here. If it wasn't for you I wouldn't be here."

Merit had no chance to reply because she was being led into a small room.

Except for a large stainless steel table in its center, the room was completely bare. A counter with a sink lined one wall. There were no windows. Merit shuddered. Carol pressed a button on an intercom and a voice sprung from the box, startling Merit.

"Yes?" said the box.

"Could you let Vernon know I need a hand in the operating room?" said Carol. "I have a greyhound here that needs some stitches." Carol closed the door and turned on a bright light over the table. The door opened and in walked a young man. Merit looked at him as he said, "What's up?"

"This is Merit," said Carol. "She has a tear in her side and she's going to need some stitches. Could you take her and weigh her?"

"Sure," he said, leading Merit outside the door and to a scale. She stood on the scale and thought back to her day at the track.

"I weigh 65 pounds," she told Vernon. But as usual, no one ever heard her.

Vernon led her back in. "She weighs 65 pounds," he told Carol.

"Why don't they listen?" thought Merit.

"Why don't your prepare the anesthesia for a 50-pounder," said Carol. "That way we'll be sure not to give her too much."

"Is it true that greyhounds are different from other breeds?" asked Vernon. "I learned that in school."

"Right," said Carol. "You have to be really careful medicating these dogs because they have no body fat. Plus, their metabolism is so high it doesn't take much for them to overdose."

"Charlie told me that King almost had a seizure coming out of surgery," said Vernon.

"That's right," Carol said. "We didn't want him coming out while we put the pins in his knee, so we probably gave him a little too much. We'll give Merit a little bit and if she needs more, we can give it to her."

Merit watched Vernon as he opened a couple of drawers. There was a syringe, a needle and a vial. As Merit watched him insert the needle into the vial, he grabbed a cotton ball and put some alcohol on it. Approaching her with the needle and the cotton ball, Merit turned and scratched at the door, maybe it would open.

Vernon spoke softly. "It's okay girl. Come here."

Merit turned and looked at him. Tail between her legs, she skulked over to him.

Swabbing the ball on her front leg, Vernon kept talking. "Oh! You're such a good girl!" The needle went in and Merit winced. All of a sudden, she was drowsy. She tried to lick her warm nose, but her tongue was dry and felt like sandpaper. As Merit lay down, she put her head on her paws. Her eyes rolled back in her head and her thick tongue hung out of her mouth. "Vernon," she said, slurring his name. "I feel funny."

Chapter 12

Learning New Skills

Merit woke up.

She was in a steel crate. Her head pounded. She tried to remember what had happened.

Slowly, the smell of the room and the glow of the florescent lights reminded Merit of where she was. She glanced at her left side. There, she could see tiny black stitches in the shape of the letter C. As Merit put her throbbing head back on the pillow, she heard a familiar voice growl.

"How are you feeling Merit?" It was King.

"Not so good," she said.

King snarled. "Well, *you* haven't gone through nearly enough pain."

"The vet said you had pins put in your leg," said Merit. "What are those?"

"The 'pin' you refer to goes from my hip down to my paw," said King. "It's holding my leg together so the bone can grow back. When I fell, my entire leg was shattered."

"I'm really sorry King," said Merit.

"Not as sorry as I'm going to make you," replied King.

Merit did not know what to say so she just repeated herself. "I'm sorry, really sorry you got hurt King. I had no idea you would hurt yourself."

Just then Vernon walked in.

"Oh, Merit you're awake." He knelt down and looked at her. "You should sleep girl. You look like you're still pretty groggy." He leaned over in front of King's crate and said, "Well King, ready to go for your walk?" As he opened the door to King's crate, Merit heard an eerie metal rubbing against metal sound. She looked over to see King wincing as he crept out slowly and gingerly. His hind leg had a metal brace on it. Metal rods seemed to come out of King's leg in every direction. Vernon knelt down and gently inspected it.

"It looks like the inflammation has gone down considerably, King. Come on, you six million dollar dog. Let's go for a walk."

As King was led out the back door, Merit put her head down and closed her eyes. She could not get the sight of King's leg out of her mind. It was so grotesque. Poor King. Once again, Merit felt guilty for King's injury.

Vernon soon led King back and put him into his crate. "King, I had no idea you were hurt that badly," said Merit.

Merit sounded genuinely concerned, King calmly explained "Merit, you have no idea what I've been through," he said.

"There have been a lot of times that I wish that Tom had just decided to put me down. My leg always aches now. I have sharp pangs of pain running from my paw through my hip, then down my spine. And I can hardly go the bathroom because my leg can't handle my weight."

"I'm sorry," Merit said, "You should be glad though that Tom likes you enough to spend six million dollars fixing you up. He seemed to not want to spend the hundred dollars on my stitches."

"My surgery didn't cost six million dollars!" exclaimed King. "Where did you get that idea?"

"Well, Vernon called you the six million dollar dog," replied Merit.

"Oh, he called me that because of a TV show he used to watch where they rebuilt this man with machine parts," said King. "And Vernon told Carol that the external pin system they put in my leg reminds him of the Bionic Man, the star of that show. He always says, 'We can rebuild him....'"

"Oh," Merit said weakly. And because she couldn't think of anything to say, Merit just lay in her crate and stared at the floor.

She was startled when King asked her, "What has been going on at the camp?"

"Not much," replied Merit. "Gypsy and I have been chasing lures."

"Well, race season is going to start soon," said King. "When is your maiden race?"

"I don't know," replied Merit.

King sighed as he lay his head on his paws. "I'll never race again," he said. "I'll be lucky if I'll ever be able to run. I can't even walk right."

Merit glanced up. "Well, won't you ever get those pins out of your legs?"

"The external pins, the ones you see, will be removed in a couple of weeks," said King dryly. "But one inside pin will always stay in my leg."

"Oh," Merit whispered. "Does it hurt?"

"It doesn't really hurt anymore," replied King. "More like, it stings, aches and itches. I can't get comfortable no matter how I lay down. I wish Tom *had* put me down!"

Merit snapped back. "But how can you say that King? How do you know you'll never run again? You haven't even healed! You haven't even gotten that contraption off of your leg. It's just been a few weeks. Remember King, you had surgery! You're the only dog I know that has had an operation. That already makes you special!"

King sighed. "Yeah right, I still wish I was dead."

Merit lay down, once more, she couldn't think of anything to say. She was just beginning to drift off when King spoke again.

"Merit, will you tell me a story? I can't sleep."

"Sure," replied Merit. "Give me a moment to think of something." Her mind whirled. What story could she possibly tell King? What could she say that would be intriguing enough to keep his mind off his leg?

Slowly, Merit began to speak. "Once upon a time, Old McDonald had a farm. And on this farm he had a..."

"Wait a second," King loudly interrupted. "This sounds like the song 'Old McDonald' to me."

"How do you know that song?" asked Merit.

"When I was a pup I was raised around a bunch of little kids and they used to sing it all the time," replied King.

"Okay, but this one is different," explained Merit. "It just starts out kind of the same, but it *is* different. You see, there's a greyhound," continued Merit. "And this greyhound was always hungry."

"Aren't we all," interrupted King.

"King," said Merit, sighing, "I can't tell you a story if you keep interrupting."

"Sorry, Merit. It's just that, well, of course, a greyhound was always hungry. Greyhounds are hungry, period. Even after eating a nine-course meal a greyhound can always find room for more. It's like saying that ice is cold."

"Fine!" Merit snapped. "If you're so good at stories, you tell me one."

"I guess I will *have* to!" replied King haughtily. "Okay then. It was a cold dark night as the pup entered the world. The pup was the last of the litter. He was the smallest pup. He was the runt."

Merit interrupted. "The runt is always the smallest, oh great King of story telling."

"Wise guy!" replied King. He continued. "He fought for air as his mother tore his sack. With one great breath, he entered the world. And as his mother was cleaning him, he thought, 'I'm going to *be* someone!' And as he was drying off, nestled among his siblings and nursing, he thought how great it was to be alive. To feel his brothers and sisters wriggling over his body. To taste his mother's sweet warm milk. To smell his mother and brothers and sisters. To know the wonderful sensation of his belly being filled."

King stopped for a moment. "Then all of a sudden he was pulled from his mother by two cold claws! His eyes would not open. He could not see! He tried to open his eyes but he couldn't! Afraid, he started yelping but his mother would not come. He yelped louder and louder. Still his mother did not come for him. He could not see he did not know where he was."

"Then he was placed against a soft surface, the cold claws stroking him from head to tail. It was like his mother, except this touch was dry and cool. He quieted down as he inhaled, trying to determine what it was. Just as the new smell was becoming faintly familiar, the pup was placed back against his mother. He started to drink. He was thankful to be back where he belonged. The end."

"That was a nice story King," said Merit. "Was it about you?"

"I was certainly never a runt," replied King.

"I guess not," said Merit. "What were you like as a pup King?"

"Oh, like most pups. I liked to chew things up and get into mischief."

"What sort of mischief?"

"You know, learning how to open the cupboard door, and then helping yourself to food."

"How can you do *that*?" asked Merit.

"Oh, there's always a way," said King, mischief dancing in his eyes. "All you have to do is this: closely observe the people to see how they open and lock the door. You can learn how to open it yourself, or if you always pay attention, you can get in when they are careless. But there's one important trick, Merit. You can never leave a trace that you've gotten into the food. Once they know, they'll make your access harder and harder until you're completely at their mercy for every scrap."

Merit cocked her head. "I'm still finding it hard to believe that you can open doors and break into cupboards to get food."

King smiled. "Oh yeah, watch this."

King nuzzled up the latch on the crate, then bit at it, next got his tongue on it and then lifted it off the catch. Next he reached up with his front paw until he got his nails caught in the latch and pulled it loose. King then pushed his crate door open and silently snuck out of his crate. Walking over to the closet, he slid its door open with his paw. Bending down, King put his nose in the box on the floor and removed a bone. Silently, he finally crept across the floor, and handed Merit the forbidden prize.

"Be quiet," he whispered.

King returned to the closet, removed another bone and silently crept to his crate. After putting his catch down, he returned to the closet and closed the door, then returned to his crate. King grabbed the crate door by his teeth and pulled the door shut as he backed in. First replacing the latch, he then ate his bone and said. "See what can be done when you put your mind to it?"

Merit looked at King with new wonder. "You are the smartest greyhound I ever met!" she exclaimed. "Thanks for the bone."

"You're welcome," said King.

Merit finished her bone quickly. "King, can I have another?"

"Sure," he said. "Get it yourself."

"I can't possibly get myself out to get a bone."

"Have you ever tried?" asked King.

"Yes. I mean I've tried to get out of a crate before."

King kept pushing Merit. "You may have tried but did you really put any thought into it, or did you just try to muscle your way out?"

"Oh! I see what you're saying," replied Merit. "I may have tried, but I just haven't used the right technique."

"Correct. Why don't you give it a try? If you get stuck, I'll help you."

"Okay," agreed Merit.

"But just be quiet Merit! You don't want to get caught, or they'll lock you in so you won't *ever* be able to get out."

"Okay," replied Merit. "But this is kind of scary, King."

"Yes Merit," said King patiently. "Most things in life worth doing *are* a little scary."

Merit stared at her crate door, wondering how she could lift the latch. She already knew that she had seen a lot of crate doors latched and unlatched. So, in her mind, she visualized a movement of a hand. It suddenly made sense: just put her nose through the wire, then lift the latch with her tongue, then use her paw to slide it over. Pushing against the door, Merit was free again! She was so excited she started running circles around the examination table.

King growled. "Stop running! Settle down!"

All of a sudden the door opened, Vernon walked into the room. Merit froze. King groaned.

Vernon stared at Merit. "Girl, what are you doing out of your crate?"

Merit just stood and looked and then lowered her head in shame. Vernon next walked over to her crate and inspected both the door and the latch. Looking puzzled, he said, "Merit, come here, girl." Merit trotted up to him. He examined her stitches. "I guess you're fine. I must have forgotten to latch your door."

With that, Merit went back into her crate and lay down. Vernon then closed the door and replaced the latch. Walking across the room, he then walked over to the closet and took out two bones. Giving one to Merit and the other to King, Vernon next turned out the lights as he left the room. "Night, dogs. See you in the morning."

"*That* was a close call," said King. "You're lucky he thought he forgot to latch your crate. Did you see his face? It was like he knew he latched you in, but he couldn't even comprehend the alternative. It's just as well."

"Well," replied Merit, "I got another bone, so there you go."

"Good night Merit."

"Night. King."

Chapter 13

Tom and Carol

It was early morning and, just coming awake, Merit heard King getting a bone.

"King," she whispered. "Will you bring me one, too, please?"

"Sure, just be quiet, King hissed."

As he was returning with the bone, King paused. They both heard voices. Pricking up their ears, they strained to hear. King quickly scrambled to his crate, then closed and latched the door. King and Merit knew that one of the voices belonged to Tom.

"King, can you make out what's saying?"

"No, but have you noticed the way Tom's voice drops when he talks to the vet?"

"Yeah, and he stands differently, too."

"I think Tom likes her," replied King.

"Really?"

"Well," explained King, "men act silly in front of women they like."

"Oh," said Merit. "How do you know?"

"Well there have been a couple of girls Tom has been interested in and he always acts goofy when he's in front of them."

"You'd think they'd notice the difference," said Merit. "But maybe they don't know him well enough to know that's not how he always acts. They probably think he's just a clumsy, dimwitted guy because he stutters and drops things around them. Come to think of it, maybe that's why none of the girls seem interested."

"That's too bad," answered Merit. "Poor Tom."

At that moment, Tom walked in with Carol. As they came toward the crates, Tom brushed up against the counter and knocked off a clipboard that had been lying there. Then, just as he reached down to pick it up; he hit his head on the table.

"I see what you mean," said Merit. "What a goof."

Rubbing the back of his head and then putting the clipboard back, Tom turned to Carol.

"I guess I better take Merit home," he said. "I mean, before I break something."

Carol laughed. "Let me get her for you."

As Carol approached Merit's cage, Tom walked to King.

"Can I let King out?" he asked.

"Sure. Just keep the leash on him so he won't run out, and hurt his leg."

As Carol opened Merit's crate, she walked out. Stretching, she found that the stitches pulled, and winced in pain. When Tom opened King's door, he limped out. Merit could only stare at all of the steel protruding from his hip and down his leg. Tom patted King on the head. "How's my boy today?"

While Tom talked to King, Merit looked at Carol, who was watching Tom. She had a strange look on her face. When Tom turned to look at her, she blushed and quickly turned away.

Tom pointed to King's leg. "How much longer until this contraption can be removed?"

"Two... I mean... three weeks."

Noticing how flustered the vet acted, Merit and King exchanged knowing looks.

"Looks like she's fallen under his spell, too," said King. "Maybe Tom's actually found someone that will like him back."

"Looks like it to me," said Merit.

As Tom put King back into his cage, King glanced at Merit, who was being led out.

"I'm sorry you got hurt, but it was good to see you," he said.

"It was good seeing you, too, King. I really *am* sorry you have to go through so much pain with your leg. But it sounds like you'll be home soon. Hang in there."

Carol spoke to Tom. "You know, I'll be at the track on Thursday. It would be convenient for me just to stop by your place to take out Merit's stitches then."

Tom stammered. "Uh, that would be okay. I mean, great. I mean, okay then. I'll see you."

Back in the truck, Merit noticed Tom taking a deep breath. When he exhaled, she could tell he was getting back to his normal self. Merit pawed at Tom's sleeve, begging him to roll down the window. Looking over at her, laughing, he said, "Okay girl! Here you go." All the way back to the kennel, Merit kept her head out the window. It felt great, her tongue was hanging out and her eyes turned into little slits by the wind.

Chapter 14

King

When they reached the kennel, Tom led Merit over to the yard. There, all of the dogs gathered around. They all wanted to hear what happened to her. Merit first told them about her run-in with the bush and then having to go see Carol. But when she started to talk about King, Music spoke up.

"Who cares about that bully?"

"Yeah, Tom should have put him down," added Speedy.

"He thought he was so tough," said Gypsy.

Merit wanted to tell them that King had frightened her at first, but they had become friends. But she knew how the other dogs felt about King, and that they wouldn't understand what he had gone through... and how it changed him. Merit looked at Gypsy and thought: "Boy dogs don't like other dogs to know that they have feelings. I better keep King's feelings to myself. "

Still, Merit told the dogs about King's brace and how it had to stay on his leg to keep all the bones in place while the injury healed. She told them how it stuck out of his skin and how the flesh around each hole smelled rotten from infection.

Clark startled Merit. "The poor guy, it can't be pleasant having that kind of thing sticking out of your leg."

"Well, it gives me the creeps just hearing about it," said Music.

"When will King come home?" asked Gypsy.

"Two or three weeks," said Merit.

"Are those two still sort of crazy for each other?" asked Sunshine. "Last time I went to the vet, I thought they were going to stare at each other for hours before giving me my shot."

"You think they would have gotten together by now," added Clark.

Isabel walked up to the group. "Are you guys busy gossiping again? I can't believe you. Every time some one goes to the vet, all everyone can do is talk about Tom and Carol. Really, don't you dogs have more important things to be doing–like training?"

"And by the way," she continued. "Tom was talking to Joe about the vet bills. King's surgery cost more than $1,000. And Merit," added Isabel, "do you know how much your stitches cost?"

"One hundred dollars," said Merit quietly.

Isabel turned to all of the dogs. "If you all want to stay here, you need to think about how you're going to earn your keep during racing season. You dogs are being ridiculous!"

Tom then called for Isabel and she walked off. Gypsy made a sour face and mimicked her. "Don't you guys have more important things to do..."

Clark interrupted. "She's right, you know. Tom is going to have to pay for King's surgery and Merit's stitches, not to mention our upkeep. So we better concentrate on winning races, not on Tom and his friend."

Merit looked at the other dogs, and no one looked as worried as Gypsy did.

"What are you thinking?" she asked.

"If Tom sells a dog, I'll be the one to go. I'm not as fast as you are and I don't have the experience the others have. I can't live like this. Every day is uncertain. They're driving me crazy. I'll *never* know about tomorrow."

"But Gypsy," said Merit, "no one knows about tomorrow. I mean, any one of us could be hurt or sold. You can't worry about what hasn't happened. You can only face what faces you, not what *might* face you. Think of all the time and energy you've wasted on all of those 'what ifs.' Instead, just enjoy *today* and do your best *now* to ensure your best future. If you worry too much, that worry will paralyze you."

Merit looked over to the other dogs. "Could someone get Gypsy moving?"

"Get Gypsy!"

Clark, Sunshine, Music and Speedy took after him, and it was all he could do to keep one step ahead. Watching them run around and around after a few laps, Merit next yelled out, "Gypsy, change direction!"

Gypsy ran in between Sunshine and Music, bearing left. Music and Speedy fell in behind, followed by Clark and Sunshine. Merit chuckled, it was fun to watch the two fastest dogs bring down their pace in order to keep them from running over the slower dogs. After a few more laps, all the dogs began to walk. All were panting, tongues hanging out.

"Listen, Merit," said Clark. "I think that Gypsy is finding his racing legs. He's getting faster."

Gypsy came up, laughing. "Well, I was afraid you were going to run me over."

Merit chuckled as well. "Gypsy, you should always run fast. Something is always scaring you."

"Very funny," replied Gypsy.

CHAPTER 15

Back Home

It was Thursday afternoon when a big truck pulled up the driveway. All of the dogs except Isabel were outside.

"Well," said Clark, chuckling to Sunshine, "Looks like the Missus is here."

As Carol came got out of the truck, Tom came out to of the house. "Hey Carol," he greeted her and then called Merit. As Merit ran up to Tom, he put her leash on and led her out to the truck.

"Hi Tom," said Carol. "How's Merit?"

"Just fine. She didn't pull out any of her stitches." Merit couldn't help but notice how Tom's voice shook.

Reaching into the back of her truck, Carol took a small pair of scissors out her toolbox. She clipped the stitches. Got a pair of tweezers and pulled out the thread. Merit quietly laughed, because it tickled. "That's it," said Carol. "Good as new."

"Not even much of scar," mumbled Tom.

"Nope, you can hardly tell she got cut." Merit watched as Tom and Carol's eyes met. They seemed to stare at each other for a long time, until Tom finally broke the silence.

"Carol, uh, would uh, you like to go get some, uh, lunch?"

"That would be wonderful," replied Carol.

"Uh, great," said Tom. "Let me go put Merit away." Tom led her back into the yard, she, and all of the other dogs, strained to look through the fence to observe Tom and Carol's exchange. They all laughed as Tom stammered as he asked Carol, "Um, Um, which truck should we take."

"We'll take mine," said Carol. Tom nodded and got in her truck. With that, the two drove off.

"I think Carol was afraid to let him drive," said Clark.

"I can't believe how shy he is around her," added Sunshine.

"Why can't he just be himself?" asked Gypsy. "Why does he act so strange?"

"Well, humans *are* strange," said Speedy. "There's just no explaining their behavior."

"Guess we should do some stretches while it's still warm out," said Sunshine. But all of the dogs lay on the grass, sunning themselves. Merit rolled on her back and let the sun warm her belly. Her tongue rolled out of her mouth, over her nose, the tip resting in the dirt.

Today, thought Merit, is a good day.

Chapter 16

Training

With each passing day, each dog trained as hard as possible, each one focusing on increasing its speed around the track. And with one another's guidance and support, they all increased their speed, and came up with better game plans for running both a clean and fast race. As each new day grew longer, Sunshine would announce the days until opening day.

Three days before the first race, Isabel came outside and walked up to Merit.

"Tom told Joe that he's going to bring King home today."

"It will be nice to have him here," replied Merit.

"Why do you say that?" asked Isabel. "Of all of us dogs, I thought you'd be the most nervous about King coming back."

Merit smiled. "I can see how you would feel that way, but when I was at the vet, King and I had a chance to discuss things. He really isn't all that bad once you get to know him."

"The accident must have changed him," said Isabel. "I mean, before, he was the meanest, scariest, most intimidating dog I've ever met. You weren't here then Merit, but King *killed* a pup when she got too close to his dish. I've never seen anything like it. I do hope you're right. I hope he *has* softened. I don't want to be around a bully."

"Yeah," Merit said, "King was an intimidating dog. That's why I tricked him to climb the tree. I was afraid he'd hurt me and I wanted to make sure he couldn't."

Isabel was silent for a moment, thinking. "Well, we'll have to wait and see what happens when he returns."

"Do you think I should tell the others how he's changed?" asked Merit.

Isabel again fell quiet. "Hmmm. Maybe you should wait for them to realize it by themselves. I don't think they will believe you, after all, no one liked King. He'll have to work hard to gain their trust, and I'm afraid if you tell them he's changed, they will be harder on him if he doesn't live up to their expectations.

"However," continued Isabel, "*I* will give him the benefit of the doubt. I promise I'll be nice to him when he returns."

"That," replied Merit, "will mean a lot to him."

Chapter 17

King Returns

King and Tom came home later that day. All the dogs were silent as King was led into the yard. He kept his head down and favored every small step. Merit broke the quiet first.

"Welcome home!"

"It's good be out of that hospital," moaned King. "That place is depressing."

All the dogs watched King as he limped slowly through the yard and into the house.

"Did you see how badly he limped?" Sunshine asked no one in particular.

Gypsy went up to Merit. "Why did you talk to King?"

"Can't you see," explained Merit, "that King is not the dog he used to be? He'll probably never be able to run again. Why, he can barely walk. He certainly is not a threat to anyone now."

Clark spoke up, "He always said he was sorry and regretted snapping at that pup. That he didn't mean to kill her. I know that almost of his adult life he has worn a muzzle, he did not realize how much damage he could do when he snapped at that pup. Tom and Joe made a bad call by not putting on that damn muzzle and you know it. I don't want to hear anything more about it. It was an accident. He certainly would not behave that way again. He has learned how bad his bite can be."

"Poor King, imagine the guilt he must feel," Speedy said. All the dogs nodded.

Sunshine spoke up. "I know he's hurt and all that, but I don't know why he got to go into the house and not the kennel."

"Maybe he's retired now and gets to live with Isabel," replied Merit.

All the other dogs just looked at Merit. "Well," Sunshine said, "I wouldn't want to be King. Isabel is pretty territorial. I don't think she'll allow King to just move in like he owns the place."

"Yeah," jumped in Speedy. "Remember when I snuck in once when the door was left ajar? She nearly bit my head off. I didn't even get to look around."

"I have a feeling everything will be fine," said Merit. The others just looked at Merit.

Just then, Joe came out the back door and whistled for the dogs to get their dishes. The dogs tore off as fast as they could. After eating, they were led into their kennels. As night fell, the dogs all were lying quietly as they heard King cry out in pain. All strained to listen. After some time of silence, Clark spoke up.

"King probably tried to make a move on Izzy," he said.

"Ick," replied Sunshine. "Clark, you're disgusting. Shut up and go to sleep."

Chapter 18

A New Coach

While the other dogs were eating the next morning, King and Isabel came out of the house.

"Good morning gang," said Isabel.

The dogs said good morning to both Isabel and King, but King didn't reply.

Merit looked closely at King. She noticed his eyes were bloodshot and puffy. "King, are you okay?"

King stared at Merit, then dropped his head and slowly shook it side to side, "No."

"What's wrong?" asked Clark. King lifted his head glaring at both Clark and Merit. King silently walked away.

Isabel tried to explain. "He's still in a lot of pain. And he's having trouble adjusting to the idea of retirement."

"I would love to retire!" exclaimed Gypsy. "Why can't he adjust?"

"He feels useless," replied Isabel. "He just doesn't know what to do with himself. He feels he has nothing to live for."

"Poor chap," said Clark. "I hope he's finds something to lift his spirits."

"Well," Sunshine said, "enough worrying about King. We should start training. Only two days until opening day."

"We should train hard today and have tomorrow off to rest before the race," added Clark.

"You know," said Merit, "we could use some guidance today with our training session. Why don't we ask King if he can help us with our drills today?" Isabel looked at Merit and smiled. "I think," she said, "that *that's* a great idea!" Nodding, Clark ran over to ask King. As he trotted off, Isabel turned to Merit. "You know Merit, you're a special dog. You're always thinking of ways to make everyone happy."

"Well," said Merit, "no sense in having King mope around when we can use his help."

"You're right!" replied Isabel.

Clark now returned with King. King looked at them with a steady gaze. "Clark says you guys want my help. Is this true?"

Except for Sunshine, all of the dogs barked an enthusiastic "Yes!" Instead, she remained quiet, staring at the ground. "Well Sunshine?" said King. "I guess you don't want my help?"

"You see," Sunshine murmured, "we've been training on our own and we've been doing just fine. I don't see how you can help us get better in one day."

"Hmmm," replied King, thinking. "I know I haven't been around for some time, but if you guys run like you did before I left, let me tell you, you need help. Maybe not from me, but you guys don't get out of that starting box fast enough. And if you can't get out of the starting gate, you'll never win the race."

Clark was thoughtful. "You were always the fastest dog out of the gate and we *know* that's one of the reasons you were so successful," he said. "Could you maybe give us a few tips on getting out of the gate quicker?"

"Of course!" barked King. "Let's go down to the track and work on it."

The dogs looked at him like he was crazy. Then Isabel spoke. "King, how are we going to go to the track? Joe and Tom are gone, and we can't get out of the gate ourselves."

Knowing what King could do, Merit smiled slyly. "King will get us out of here. Won't you, King?"

King shot Merit a look and snarled. "Be quiet Merit." Then he ordered the other dogs to move aside. Next, King limped up to the gate and lifted the latch with his nose, then pushed the gate open.

"Hooray!" yelled Gypsy. "We're *free*!" Then he ran for the open gate, but just as he was about to go through, King moved into Gypsy, knocking him to the ground. King winced and growled. Gypsy tried to stand up, but King stood over him.

"Wait a minute," instructed King. "This is *not* a free for all. We must all stick together and walk to and from the track as if we were on leash. If anyone doesn't want to go train, stay here. Isabel, how long until Tom and Joe get back?"

"You've got about two hours," replied Isabel. "Okay," continued King. "It will take us about 15 minutes to get to the track and back home, so we'll train for about 45 minutes and we'll still be back in plenty of time. We'll walk down single file," he went on. "Merit, you bring up the rear. There will be no talking. We can't afford to draw attention to ourselves."

"Please be careful," pleaded Isabel. "There won't be enough money to get you all out of the pound."

Pound? Merit thought, what is a pound? But King roared back. "*Enough* worrying Isabel. Let's go!"

All the dogs did exactly as King had instructed. As Merit went through, King told her to close the gate. Doing as she was told, she silently trotted up to the others. The dogs were eerily silent as they walked toward the track, and made it there without incident. But when they reached the gate to the track, they noticed it was locked.

King turned to the others and, with his head, gestured that they should go back. The other dogs nodded and silently turned back to the kennel. But Merit shook her head no, and ran straight to the gate. The dogs couldn't help but gasp as Merit sailed over the gate in one quick leap. Merit then turned and looked at them through the fence. At that moment, she suddenly had a realization: there was no way King could ever execute such a jump. The look in his eyes held much pain.

But all a sudden, Gypsy came down with a thud, just inches from Merit. "Watch out," she yelped, "You can hurt someone."

Merit walked up to King. "Can you coach us from there?" she asked.

King sighed, then spoke. "Yes," he said.

With that, Clark, Music and Speedy jumped the fence.

"Why don't you go first?" King asked Merit.

"Okay," replied Merit, "but what do you want me to do?"

"First go into the starting box," said King firmly. "Then have Clark run the gate. When the gate opens I want you ready. And when you're in the gate, stand like so." King knelt down. "See how I can use my legs to spring?"

"Yes –"

"Well, I want you to stand in the box just like this until the gate opens," continued King. "And then, I want you to *spring* out."

Merit then ran over to Clark. "Let's go to the starting boxes, I need you to open the gate," she said.

"Okay," replied Clark. As the dogs reached the starting box, Clark said, "Get in."

Clark looked over at King. King quickly gave Clark a signal to open the gate. Merit sprang out and was around the track in no time. She trotted over to King. Although winded, she managed to say "*Wow*, great technique, King."

King did not seem impressed. "Do it again!"

So Merit got back inside and once again, crouched down. Again, Clark closed the gate. But this time when Clark looked at King. King shook his head no. Instead, after a few moments went by, he nodded at Clark to open the gate. But this time when the gate opened, Merit walked out and looked at Clark and King.

"What's wrong?" asked King. "Why didn't you spring out?"

Merit was upset. "My legs are *killing* me! How do you expect me to crouch down for so long, then have the strength to just spring out?"

"Well," King replied airily. "Don't you see? *That's* the trick. If everyone could do it, it wouldn't give you an edge, would it? What you'll need to do, Merit, is practice squatting. That way, no matter how long you wait in the box, you're ready to go."

Clark chimed in. "There really *is* no way to tell when the gate will open, you know. We *do* know the clue is that right before the gate opens, the announcer says something like, 'Here comes Wishbone', or whatever the track calls their lure."

"But," interrupted King, "you won't be able to *hear* the announcer when you're in the box, since a lot of the other dogs bark and claw at their gate."

"The dogs get so excited to race they kind of lose their mind," added Clark.

"Well, none of the dogs I've trained with before use King's technique," said Sunshine.

But for the next hour, all of the dogs practiced crouching and springing out of the starting box. When it was time to go home, the dogs started jumping back over the locked gate. Then, as Gypsy jumped, his left hind leg got caught. Letting out a small yelp as he landed head first on the ground. Before any of the dogs could say anything, he sprang back up and said, "Let's *go*."

The other dogs stared, it had all happened so fast.

"Are you okay, Gypsy?" asked Sunshine.

"Yeah," said Gypsy. "We need to get back."

Quietly, the dogs once again walked single file. As King rounded the bend, he saw a big fluffy brown dog walking toward them. "Here comes another dog," he said. "*Don't* talk, *don't* stop, and keep your head down. His owner is probably not far behind."

Sure enough, an old woman came into view. As she spotted King, she smiled. "Hey there, aren't you a beauty."

But her face fell when she spotted the other greyhounds following King. She quickly caught up to her dog, grabbed its collar and pulled it to the side of the path. The woman and the dog stood quiet and still as they passed. As they walked away, the dogs heard her exclaim, "I've never seen such a sight, have you Frank? It's not every day you get to see a parade of greyhounds!"

The dogs continued silently up the trail toward the kennel. King then opened the latch. Next, Merit closed and latched it behind them. "Whew," said Isabel. "It's good to be safely home." The other dogs murmured their agreement.

But King wasn't finished. "You guys do some stretches before your muscles tighten up. Then get some rest."

Turning to Isabel, he looked at her steadily. "I'm going into the house, want to come?"

"Sure," replied Isabel.

As they walked off, Merit turned to Clark. "I think Isabel is starting like to King. She's looking at him a little differently."

"I didn't notice anything," snapped Clark. "Let's go stretch." The two went to join Gypsy, Sunshine, Music and Speedy on the lawn.

Chapter 19

Insomnia

Something awoke Merit.

Groaning, she woke slowly from her deep sleep. Lying in her crate, listening to the other dogs breathing deep and heavy, she realized that the kennel had become much quieter since King had left. His snoring was so loud that it had nearly echoed off of the stone brick walls and concrete floor.

Then Merit remembered: in a few hours she would be running her first race. She was apprehensive. On one hand, she wanted to win. But she didn't want to crash and get hurt, and she certainly did not want to make a fool of herself. I know what is expected of me and how it should go, she reasoned, but, I'm still nervous. What I really need to do is pace.

Gently, Merit lifted and slid the crate latch open. Silently she jumped down, then crept pass the dark row of crates. Around and around she went, but no dog stirred. All were sound asleep.

Pacing and worrying, she then realized that the kennel was starting to fill with sunlight. Quickly, she jumped back up in her crate and latched the gate.

Clark opened his eyes. He had been woken by Merit's latch. Sitting up, he cocked an ear and looked around. But hearing nothing more, Clark curled back up. Merit put her head on her paws, sighed and told herself to get some sleep. But few moments later, Sunshine shook in her crate and howled. "Wake up everybody, today is *RACE* day!"

Eyes heavy and dry, Merit lifted her head. She felt nauseous. All the dogs started chattering at once. Merit thought she might throw up. Gypsy looked over. "You don't look so good."

Merit stared back, her brown eyes like dull stones. "I'll be okay," she said. "I just didn't sleep well."

"I hope you'll be alright," replied Gypsy, "I mean, you trained awfully hard for today. It would be a shame to have wasted all that work on one bad night sleep."

Merit looked over at her friend. "You're right."

When Merit was let out of her crate, she spent so much time stretching and yawning that Tom even remarked on it. "Come on girl, or we won't make it to the track in time for the first race."

Knowing what she had to do, Merit dragged herself to the truck and crawled into her crate. As soon as the truck fired up, Merit fell fast asleep and did not stir until they arrived at the track. But she was still so groggy that the scene seemed like a dream.

As Tom put a muzzle on her, Merit could only stare off into the distance.

"You don't look so good," said Tom. "Let me take your temperature." Turning to Joe, he continued. "Get me the thermometer. Merit might not be fit for racing today." As Joe brought the implement over, Merit tried to tell Tom that she was just tired. Of course, she wanted to say *I want to race!* But by now she knew that people never really listened.

Clark looked over to Merit. "Well, if you want to race you better pull yourself together. The judges will take one look at you and deem you not fit. Then you'll just sit in your crate all day, while the rest of us get to *run*." Merit knew that was not an option: she took a deep breath and shook as hard as she could. At this, Tom and Joe both laughed, watching Merit twist her body from nose to tail as she wiggled and flapped. Next, Merit leaped into the air, pulled on her leash and loudly barked, "I want to *RACE*!"

"Well," said Tom, "Guess Miss M got her second wind. Put the thermometer away."

Chapter 20

Merit's First Race

As they made their way into the track, Merit could see at least 40 other greyhounds being led around, she had never seen so many different kinds. Most of them were smaller than she was. Next, she was led into a kennel where a handler took her to get weighed and put her blanket on. Here, Merit saw that she was number three. A lucky number, Merit said to herself.

While tied in the holding area, she leaned up against the fence and yawned. The big greyhound next to her said, "Hey Sally, look at the tough competition."

Merit ignored them and closed her eyes. Instead, she saw herself springing out of the gate and running the track. She shut out all the noise around her. Then, Merit suddenly felt a sharp tug on her leash. She hadn't even noticed the handler approach and was not aware of being untied. Merit blinked. She was led into the bright sunshine and onto the track.

In the racing area, Merit first looked to the left and saw bleachers filled with people and heard children squealing. Led to the starting box, she was placed in box number three as they lowered her gate. Merit crouched down. The other dogs were barking and clawing at the gate.

All of a sudden the gate lifted, and Merit was off! Running swiftly around the track, she didn't stop until the lure did. Waiting for the handler to come get her, Merit heard the big greyhound grumble. "What an act! That dog acted dead tired, then flew around the ring. There's just no way." Silently, Merit stretched and yawned as the handler put her leash on.

Back in the kennel, Tom retrieved Merit from the handler. "You're the fastest dog, Merit," he said, patting her head. You're the *fastest* dog." But Merit was so tired she could barely wag her tail in response to his praise. Tom led Merit to her crate and put her away, Merit slept until they reached home.

Chapter 21

Back Home

As Joe brought Merit back into the kennel, he looked at Tom. "Do you think something is wrong with her?"

"I've heard greyhounds need about 16 hours of sleep a day," replied Tom. "She's probably just a little tired and stressed from all the activity. Let's see how she looks in the morning."

Sure enough, Merit was her normal peppy self when she woke the next morning.

Stretching, she shook and flopped as she was led into the yard. Joe laughed at her and said, "Looks like you're feeling better M."

Tom walked out. "Joe, I talked to Carol and she's coming out to look at Merit."

"But Merit's okay. Why did you call the vet?"

"I didn't," replied Tom. "She called me to find out how opening day went. I mentioned Merit was under the weather and she offered to come out before lunch."

"I see," said Joe. He smiled and looked away.

"What's that supposed to mean?" said Tom.

"Oh," said Joe, still smiling. "It seems our vet is a little smitten with you. Better watch yourself before you find yourself tied down with a wife and kids."

"And what," snapped Tom, "would be so wrong with that?"

"Nothing, I guess," replied Joe. "I just can't imagine you catering to a woman. I mean, you know you're pretty headstrong. And women can be hard to please."

"Enough," said Tom. "Leave it alone. Go clean the kennels, will you?"

Merit looked over at Clark, and they tried to keep their laughter to themselves.

Tom looked at them and growled. "What are you two smirking about? Why don't you both bug off!"

Merit and Clark trotted over to the shade and lay down. Once they were out of earshot, they laughed and rolled around. "Tom thinks he's so tough," said Merit, giggling.

Clark wiggled around. "This grass feels good today. It's nice and damp." They both laid down and sighed.

"Life is good," said Merit. Just then, King and Isabel walked up.

"Merit," said King, "we heard Tom and Joe talking about the race."

"Good job," said Isabel.

"How are you feeling Merit?" asked King.

Merit looked back. "Good. No strains or sprains."

"Then why is the vet coming out?" asked Isabel.

Merit and Clark looked at each other and started laughing again.

Clark spoke first. "After Merit raced yesterday afternoon, she looked dead on her feet. Actually, before she raced she was practically in a coma. We all thought she was sick."

Merit interrupted. "I was just a little tired. I didn't sleep well, that's all."

King looked over at Merit. "Did you leave your crate and go on one of your adventures?"

Merit looked down sheepishly. "I did, I couldn't sleep. I thought if I walked around it would help me sleep."

"Yes Merit, exhausting oneself usually lends for a decent night's sleep, but it's tough to race the next day if you spend all night walking around," said King sternly. "I know it's hard to sleep the night before a race, but it's the most important thing."

"I kept telling myself to go to sleep, but it was no use."

Isabel spoke. "When I was racing and couldn't sleep, I used to concentrate on clearing my mind. I would think of nothing. Then I would visualize the track with no sound, just the image. I would start with the large and work down to the details. I would concentrate on every color, every smell. Without all of the noise, without the sound, the track actually becomes a quiet and familiar place. Before you know it, you'll be sleeping peacefully."

King looked at Isabel. "I used to do the same thing." Isabel smiled. Merit and Clark looked at each other and rolled their eyes as Carol's truck pulled into the driveway.

Coming out of the house, Tom called for Merit. She quickly trotted over to him.

"Well, she looks sound," said Carol, getting out of her truck.

"Yeah," said Tom. "She seems to be as good as new now."

Carol came in the gate and gave Tom a hug, "It's good to see you."

First, Tom just stood. Then he awkwardly tried to return the hug. "Yeah."

She looked at him, puzzled, and then knelt down to inspect Merit. Merit thought that Carol smelled nice. As Carol looked into her eyes, Merit smiled.

"She's such a sweet dog," said Carol. "Where did you get her?"

"From Joe Greene. He breeds greyhounds, but he doesn't race them. He buys his dogs from the track, spends a lot of money on buying the best. Gets one litter from them. After that he spays the females and neuters the males. Then he trains the retired racers for domestic life and makes sure they go to good homes. He was one of the people who helped start the whole greyhound adoption network."

"Thank God for people like him," said Carol. "When I first moved here after school a lot of my clients were into dog racing. During my first week, a trainer asked me to euthanize several dogs. None of the dogs had anything wrong with them. I told him I wouldn't do it."

"Two days later," continued Carol, "that same trainer reported them missing. Eventually the dogs washed up on the shore of the river. They'd been shot."

"I heard that you testified at his trial," said Tom.

"Yes. I just told the jury that he had asked me two days before the dogs disappeared to put them down, but ethically I couldn't do it because the dogs were in fine health. That and some other evidence got him six months in jail."

"*Six* months for killing *four* dogs? That's a weak sentence."

"Yeah. After that I avoided working with racing greyhounds," said Carol. "I mean, I just felt that the whole industry was cruel. But then I met you and a few other trainers. The ones who truly love and care for their dogs. And I know how the dogs love to race and compete. You can see it in their eyes."

As if on cue, the dogs got up and stretched and chased each other around the yard. Each one was barking, "Get Merit! Even with his slow gallop, King fell in line. Carol and Tom laughed.

"Look at them go!" exclaimed Carol.

"They don't know they have the day off," added Tom.

"Ah, greyhounds!" said Carol. "They *do* love to run!"

Chapter 22

Another Day

The next day after breakfast, the dogs were led down to the track. No breeze blew and the morning was growing warm. The dogs were panting.

Speedy looked at Merit. "It's hard to run in the heat."

Merit looked back. Speedy's tongue was hanging out the side of his mouth, looking thick and dry. "Speedy, how are you feeling?"

"Fine," he replied.

Merit stopped walking and looked again. "Speedy, you really don't look right. Are you sure you're okay?"

"Yes, I'm fine." He sighed.

"Well, make sure you take it easy" said Merit. "Don't strain in the heat."

Speedy mumbled his reply "I won't."

Clark walked up to Merit. "Is Speedy alright?"

"He *says* he is," replied Merit. "But I don't think he *is*."

"Well," commented Clark, "he's a grown pup, he can take care of himself. If he says he's okay, you can't worry about him."

"I know," said Merit. "It's just, sometimes even though someone says nothing is wrong, you know there really *is*. And it's frustrating that they won't or can't tell you what's really going on. It's just so fake."

"Yeah, but sometimes we need our space and it's better just to let it go," replied Clark. "If you badger the dog, all it does is upset you and him. I mean, if the dog doesn't want to discuss it, you can't either."

"I guess you're right," said Merit.

"Of *course* I'm right." Clark chuckled.

Just then, Sunshine walked up. "What are you two talking about? Looks like you two are up to no good, if you ask me."

"Oh, we're just plotting how to take over the world," replied Clark. Merit giggled.

"Well," said Sunshine. "It's time to practice. Come on."

The dogs first walked around the track and then entered the starting boxes. The gate opened. They all trotted in behind the lure. It wasn't going very fast, in fact, they easily made two laps in a slow easy jog. Then, as the lure sped up, and their speeds increased, each of the dogs started stretching their stride making their bodies dip lower and lower, faster and faster.

It happened quickly.

Just as the dogs came down the back straightaway and around the corner to the inside bend, Speedy collapsed. The fall came so suddenly that Gypsy had to jump over his body to keep from trampling him.

"Something's wrong with Speedy!" yelled out Gypsy. He ran back to Speedy.

Gently sniffing at him, Gypsy called out at the same time. "Are you okay, Speedy? Speedy?"

There was no reply. Gypsy pawed at Speedy but he just lay still. At this point, the other dogs rushed up, followed by Joe. "Move back!" yelled Joe. Kneeling down, he looked at the completely still dog. Joe's face turned a pale gray and his mouth trembled. No words were necessary, his reaction said it all.

Speedy was dead.

"Must have heat stroke," murmured Joe. "Damn." Merit saw tears steaming down Joe's face as he softly stroked Speedy. Merit glanced over looked at Speedy. His tongue was blue, but other than that, he looked as if he were sleeping. However, he smelled different, something that puzzled Merit.

"Hmmm, poor chap," said Clark.

"He died doing what he loved to do," Sunshine said.

Merit gazed at the other dogs that were all standing in a cluster. They were all the same, but Speedy lay on the ground. Why? She was confused. Speedy was a nice dog. Merit became sad, realizing that she would never get to joke around with him ever again. No longer would Speedy be picking on her either. Why?

Tenderly, Joe scooped Speedy into his arms and headed back to the gate. When the dogs followed, he firmly but softly said,

"Stay back." As Joe closed and latched the gate, he turned around. "I'll be back. Stay, and be quiet."

The dogs silently looked on as Joe carried Speedy up the trail to the kennel. When he was no longer in sight, Gypsy muttered softly. "What a bummer."

Merit flopped down in the dirt. "I should have tried harder to make him rest. He looked sick."

"Oh Merit, it's not your fault," said Sunshine.

"It's the way life goes," added Clark.

Music spoke up. "I'm going to miss him," she said, whimpering. Merit looked at Music, who looked sad. She felt worse knowing that Music was upset.

Merit decided to walk over to Music. "I'm sorry. I know he's your best friend."

Music looked at her, then looked down and sniffed. "He *was* my best friend."

Merit said, "Do you want to hear the last joke he told me?" asked Merit.

"Yeah," said, Music, looking up.

"What did the mountain lion say when he was tired of chasing the rabbit?"

"I don't know," Music said, now half smiling.

"I hate fast food," said Merit. All of the dogs laughed—a quiet, respectful laugh for their friend Speedy.

Joe came back to the track, this time with Isabel and King.

Then, turning them loose, he walked back to the kennel. The dogs stood, watching. Half way up the trail Joe turned and yelled. "Stay!" He then continued to walking up the trail. Once Joe was out of sight, Isabel and King joined the other dogs.

"We saw Joe bring Speedy back," offered Isabel. "Tom's not home so we don't know what's going on."

"Joe is really upset," added King. "He's crying and carrying on."

"Kind of strange seeing him so emotional," said Isabel. "But he did raise and train Speedy himself."

"I think he considered him his special dog," added Gypsy. "He always got better rub downs and more food in his dish."

"Kind of like Isabel and Tom," said King, rolling his eyes. "She can get away with murder. She can get on the couch and he doesn't even notice her. Me? I get busted in 10 seconds."

Isabel stared at King. "Are you done?" she asked. Then turning and looking at Merit, she asked just one question. "What happened to Speedy?"

Merit could only look down with a look of guilt, so Gypsy spoke up. "He just fell down dead. Joe said it might have been heat stroke."

"I know he didn't look well," said Merit quietly, "but he said he was fine."

"Well," replied Isabel, "you'll learn there is only so much you can do for others."

King spoke up. "We have to be really careful in this heat."

"What is 'heat stroke'?" asked Merit.

It's when your body overheats and stops working the way it should," explained Clark. "Sometimes you just faint, but other times, it can lead to serious problems. You can die."

"How do you prevent this heat stoke?" asked Gypsy.

"You just have to stay cool, drink lots of water and know when to rest," said Clark.

"How can you tell if you have it?" asked Music.

"Your tongue gets swollen, and hangs out of the side of you mouth," said Clark.

"And your breathing is heavy and shallow. Lots of panting," added King.

"Well," said Isabel. "It's getting hot. Let's move to the shade." All the dogs gathered under the big tree near the edge of the fence. All were quiet, thinking of Speedy.

Joe and Tom came down the path just as the sun was high in the sky. Tom called to the dogs and when they came, all of their leashes put on. Joe led Isabel, King and Gypsy, and Tom led Merit, Sunshine, Clark and Music up the path and into the forest. The cool shade felt good. First they stopped by the stream and the dogs drank, then they slowly made their way down the trail. No one spoke. A rabbit darted out of the bushes in front of Joe and the dogs ignored it.

Joe turned to Tom. "I think the dogs are sad, too."

"Of course they're sad," said Tom, sounding more than a bit weary. "Don't you think they have feelings? These dogs are emotional *and* smart. They understand more than we'll ever give them credit for. I think we should give them a few days off from training and skip the races this weekend." Joe nodded in agreement.

"I hope you appreciate how good Tom is to us," said Sunshine to the others. They all agreed. They returned to the kennel, and were fed their dishes. Afterwards they lay around the yard until late into the night. Merit enjoyed lying on her back while looking up at the stars. Gypsy rolled over on his back, too. "What are all those lights in the sky?" he asked.

Merit rolled her head to one side. "Stars," she said. "Gypsy, have you never seen stars?"

Clark offered, "How could he? He's lived in the kennel his whole life and we are usually put away long before the stars even come out."

"These stars are neat, but what exactly *are* stars?" asked Gypsy.

"I've heard that stars are suns that are far away," said Sunshine.

"The stars move in a pattern," added King. "And if you know the pattern, you can always figure out where you are, and never get lost."

"I wish we could stay out all night," said Gypsy.

"It's so nice on a night like this that we're allowed to be out, but it can get really cold. And it's sure hard to sleep when you're shivering." Merit replied.

As the moon rose out of the horizon, Gypsy gasped. "Look at *that* star. It's huge!"

"That's not a star, Gypsy," explained Isabel. "It's the moon! I think the moon is a planet."

"A planet? What's a planet?" asked Gypsy. No dog answered.

"I guess we don't really know what a planet is," offered King. "We've just heard the term. It's hard being a dog, isn't it?"

"It's hard to learn things, it's hard to communicate with people, and you can't do what you want," said Merit.

"Yes, but I imagine, it's hard being anything," said Isabel. "All creatures seem to have their limits and hard times."

"Everything except birds," added Merit. "They seem to always be so carefree. Must be nice just to take off and fly."

Just as the evening was starting to cool down, Gypsy spoke again. "I see what you mean about it getting cold."

"It actually gets colder just before dawn," said King. And at that moment, Tom called all of the dogs to their crates.

Chapter 23

The Beach

The next morning was hot, with a warm breeze blowing from the south. Joe and Tom gathered the dogs after their breakfast. "Okay dogs, we're going to be taking a few days off from training," announced Tom. "And since it's so hot, we're going to the beach!"

"The beach?" said Merit and Gypsy, who didn't even know the word. Meanwhile, Sunshine howled and danced. "The beach! The beach! I love the beach!"

Laughing at Sunshine, Joe loaded their crates into the back of the truck. The dogs jumped up and hurried inside. As the truck started off down the road, Gypsy asked, "Um, okay. What's a beach?"

As King started to speak, Clark chimed in. "Don't tell them, let it be a surprise."

"Well, it can't be *all* bad," reasoned Gypsy. "I mean, everyone seems pretty excited. So as long as there is nothing to be scared of, it's okay with me.

"We're off to another adventure!" added Merit.

When the truck stopped Merit smelled the air. She didn't recognize any of the scents the breeze carried. At the same time, she heard a low rumble in the background. Gypsy seemed to be getting scared; the unfamiliar surroundings caused him to start trembling.

"Gypsy" said Sunshine. "Believe me, there's no reason to be scared."

"But I don't know where we are, and what that noise is," said Gypsy. "And everything smells different."

"Gypsy, why do you always expect the worst?" said Sunshine. "Just because you don't know something doesn't make it bad. Wait and you'll see. The beach is a great place."

As Joe opened their crates and put leashes on everyone, Merit and Gypsy timidly looked around. There were all sorts of things they had never seen before. Once they hit the sand, Joe removed their leashes. "You dogs stay close," instructed Tom. "It's early enough in the day so you can run loose, but keep together. And don't get into any mischief."

As soon as those words were out of his mouth, Sunshine barked loudly. "Last one to the water is the loser!" Then she took off, and without thinking, Merit and Gypsy ran after her, as well as King, Isabel, Clark and Music.

When Merit and Gypsy reached the water's edge Gypsy stopped, but Merit plunged in after the others.

Gypsy stood at the water's edge. "Get out!" he said. "You'll all drown!"

But the dogs ignored Gypsy and ran back and forth, happily dodging waves. Merit stopped and drank some of the water, then shook her head. "It's salty," she said.

King knelt beside her. "Don't *ever* drink the water. It will make you sick."

The two watched as Sunshine led the others in a big circle in and out of the water, jumping and playing in the waves. A big bird sailed overhead and screeched. "What a beautiful white bird," said Merit.

"It's called a seagull," replied King. "They have web feet and can land in the water."

"It's so *big*," said Merit. "This beach is full of wonderful creatures."

"Whenever I get to come here, I always see an animal I never knew existed," replied King.

Merit looked over at Tom and Joe, who were both sitting on a blanket but still keeping a close eye on all of them.

"Let's go buzz them," said Merit.

King looked over at the men. "Okay, but don't get too close. If we shower them with sand, they'll get mad and might take us home."

"Okay," replied Merit. Running fast, she came up to the men. Just as she was ready to touch the blanket she turned sharply, and sprayed sand all over Joe. Tom laughed.

King yelled at Merit. "What did I tell you?!" But Merit only laughed and said, "Let's go find some beach animals!" Then she took off down the beach. Chasing her, King bellowed, "Wait up!"

Suddenly, Merit stopped at the edge of a cove where there were all kinds of birds with long beaks. Panting, King came up alongside her. "Those are sand pipers," he explained. "They use their beaks to pull things they like to eat out of the sand."

Merit watched them chase the waves out, dig and then, as a wave came back to shore, they would retreat. "They must not like to get wet," observed Merit.

"Yeah," replied King. "They're strange little birds." Just then, King looked away.

"Oh, here come my favorite birds," he said. "I think they're called pelicans. They have a scoop in their beak that they use to catch fish."

Merit looked at the large birds as they glided by on top of a wave. "The beach is great," she said. "Can we keep exploring?"

"Better not," replied King. "Joe and Tom will be upset if we disappear, and if we get into trouble they may not bring us back here again."

Merit looked over at Joe and Tom. Sure enough, they were walking toward them. "I think they're calling to us," said Merit. "But I can't hear them over the waves and wind."

King gave Merit a sly look. "Race ya!" With that, the two took off toward the men.

When they reached Joe and Tom, the dogs noticed they were in a serious discussion and didn't pay much attention to them.

"I think it's nice of you to offer to get me my own pup," said Joe. "But it's too soon. Speedy was special, I don't think I should to try to replace him yet. Why don't we wait until next spring when there will be more puppies to choose from? You never know. I mean, Isabel and King may have a litter and I would really like to have one of theirs."

Merit looked at King. "You and Isabel are going to have puppies?"

"Well we've been trying," said King. "But it hasn't happened yet."

"It would be so neat to have puppies around," added Merit.

"Yes," said King. "It would be nice, but we'll just have to wait and see."

At that moment, Joe and Tom noticed Merit and King. "Okay. Time to go get the other dogs," said Tom.

"I think," Merit said to King, "that Joe doesn't want to replace Speedy right now."

"He really liked that dog," replied King. Tom and Joe next gathered and leashed the dogs.

When everyone reached the truck, Clark groaned, "Now it's time for the bad part."

"What?" said Gypsy, who panicked quickly. He started to shake with worry.

Sunshine laughed. "Gypsy, will you calm down? We're just going to get the salt and sand rinsed off of us." With that, Joe led the dogs to a shower and rinsed them off; next, Tom toweled them dry and put them into their crates. As Merit was being led to her crate, she looked back at the beach and noticed that it was now filling up with people.

Tom followed Merit's gaze. "Looks like we got done just in time. I don't think those sunbathers would like a bunch of greyhounds tearing around throwing sand all over them." He patted Merit on the head. "I hope you enjoyed the beach." Merit wagged her tail and shook. As Tom put her into her crate, she then gave him a quick kiss to show her joy." Tom laughed. "Merit," he said, "you're a special dog."

Curling up, Merit and the others fell into a deep sleep on the way home. Her dreams were about all the ocean birds and the smells she had seen and experienced that day. When they got home, Merit awakened quickly. "That was the best adventure yet!"

Everyone agreed.

Chapter 24

The Day After

By the next morning, the dogs could sense it was back to business.

First they were let out of their crates at the crack of dawn and then fed their breakfast. After an hour or so, Joe led them out of the yard, down the path and into the forest. The dogs were quiet as they walked the trail. They could tell Joe was lost deep in thought. Sensing that he was still sad, they were on their best behavior.

Gypsy looked at Merit and whispered, "Look. Music's crying."

Merit walked over to Music and whispered in her ear. Music looked up at Merit, then sniffed and smiled. "You're right Merit," she said. "Speedy *does* live in my heart. I feel Speedy is still with me." Joe looked down at Music, then smiled and patted her on the head. He took a deep breath and said, "Let's start heading back." With that, Joe turned and led the dogs back toward home. Led into the yard, then released from their leashes, they trotted off freely. Each realized how lucky they were to be greyhounds, how lucky they were to be with Joe and Tom, how lucky they were to be alive.

"I'm going to see what Isabel is up to," said Merit.

Merit walked up to the door and scratched at it. Tom opened the door and laughed. "Merit, did you come to visit? Come on in."

She trotted into the room and stood there, letting her eyes adjust to the darkness. Isabel was lying on her bed. "Hi, M. What are you up to?"

"Well," replied Merit, "I wanted to see what you're up to."

"Just lying here being bored."

"Want to come outside and lay in the sun?" asked Merit.

"Sure," she said. Watching Isabel struggle to get up, she noticed how stiff her friend was. Working hard, it took her a while to get her long legs underneath her. Even then, she wobbled as she stood. Merit watched her shake slowly, then stretch. Watching Isabel stretch, she could hear Isabel's joints creak and pop.

As they walked outside, Merit didn't speak. She could tell Isabel was in pain, but she didn't want to bring it up and embarrass Isabel. "I think I overdid at the beach yesterday," began Isabel.

Tom came out of the house. "Isabel, come here," he said, then gave her a pill.

"That should help," said Isabel, slowly walking back to Merit.

"What did he give you?" asked Merit.

"Some medicine that will help my pain."

"Oh," replied Merit. "Do you hurt like this often?"

"Most mornings," replied Isabel. "It's not usually this bad."

King sauntered up to the two. "How are you feeling?" he asked Isabel.

"Pretty stiff. But Tom gave me some pain killer and I should be feeling better soon." King gave Isabel a kiss. Embarrassed, Merit turned and walked away. She walked over to where Clark was lying down. Joining him, she sighed.

"What's up?" Clark asked Merit.

"Well, look," said Merit, gazing at Isabel.

"Yeah, I noticed she was hurting. Did Tom give her anything?"

"Yes," replied Merit. "It's that hip of hers. The last race she was in, she got tripped up in the pack and nearly broke her back. She retired after that. It's a good thing that she's so fast. She'll make good breeding stock."

Merit looked over at her friend. "I don't like that we're only kept alive as long as we're a benefit to our owners. I mean, doesn't anyone have a dog, just to have a dog?"

"Yes, Merit, and they're pets," said Clark patiently. "In some ways, they're lives are very different from ours. And in some ways, so much the same." For some reason, Merit thought of her mom True. "My mom told me there are race dogs, show dogs and pets," said Merit. "She thought being a pet was the best."

"Yes," said Clark. "But no matter what kind of animal, it all depends on the owners. I've met loose dogs in the woods that were pets; they'd been beaten and starved by their owners. For dogs it's not what you do, but who you belong to. There are some mean people in the world."

Merit stretched out. "I feel grateful today. I'm alive. I'm not in pain. Tom is good to us and we get to go to the beach."

Clark laughed. "Yes Merit, it's nice to look around once in a while and remember how lucky we are."

"So, when do you think we'll start training again?" asked Merit. "Probably tomorrow," replied Clark. "Better rest up while we can."

Just then, Gypsy walked up, snickering to the resting dogs. "Tom just called Carol and asked her to come over and look at us."

"Will you grow up?" replied Clark.

"Stop gossiping. It's not polite," added Merit.

"Boy, are you surly today," said Gypsy. "You guys better get some more sleep." With that, he sulked away.

Clark chuckled. "Tom called Carol? Tom called Carol."

"You're as bad as Gypsy," said Merit teasingly. With that, she rolled onto her back.

Later that afternoon, a truck pulled up and all the dogs ran to the gate to meet Carol.

Tom came out of the house, making his way through the sea of tails and noses. He reached the gate laughing. "Some fierce watch dogs I have, huh?"

"Well, we know they're not vicious. But so many loose dogs *are* intimidating."

"Thanks for coming out," offered Tom.

"No problem." Carol smiled warmly. "I'll look them over to make sure they're healthy." Do you want me to do some blood work?"

"Yes," replied Tom. "Check to see if they have heartworms."

"I'll check them out to make sure they're in good order."

"Which one do you want to see first?" asked Tom.

"Is Isabel still limping?" asked Carol.

"Yes, but I gave her a pill."

"One or two?"

"One," Tom replied.

"How long ago?" Carol asked, looking at Isabel.

"This morning, I'd say around eight o'clock."

"Well let me check her out. Then you can give her another. Poor girl. You can tell by the way she stands that she's in pain."

Tom looked over at Isabel. "It's hard for me to tell. She is such a stoic."

"That's a dog for you," said Carol. "Everyone thinks they have this high threshold for pain. However, being pack animals, they feel vulnerable demonstrating any weakness." Carol looked Isabel over, listening to her heart and her lungs. Next she examined her eyes and teeth, and took her temperature. She finished and stood up and looked over at Tom.

"She looks a little dehydrated. Has she been drinking water?"

"Some, not as much as usual. Maybe because all she's done lately is sleep all day."

"Try moving her water bowl by her bed," suggested Carol. "Give her another pill. And it might be a good idea that the next time you take her to the beach, you limit her play," she sternly added.

"Okay," mumbled Tom.

"Hmmm," observed Clark. "Seems like this visit is all business."

"We'll have to fix that!" said Merit, grinning. As Tom and Carol kept talking, Merit spun around, hitting Carol in the back of the knees, which caused her to fall into Tom. Catching her in his arms, they looked at each other. Tom turned red and started stuttering. "I uh, I uh, uh, Merit. *Bad* dog." Blushing, Carol regained her balance and stood up. "Hmmm, *quite* the dog you have there." Merit moved to the back of the pack, lying low.

Tom spoke next. "Come here Merit." Merit approached, but put her tail between her legs at the thought of being scolded.

"Well Carol," said Tom, "I guess she wants to be looked at next."

As Carol examined Merit, Tom spoke. "You should have seen her on the beach yesterday. She had so much fun jumping in and out of the waves and running up and down the beach. She really is an unusual dog. It's like she understands the joy of life."

Finished with Merit's once-over, Carol spoke. "Well, she is certainly fit and strong. Her heart and lungs sound healthy. And she's big for a female. She should make an excellent racer."

"Just like her Mom," said Tom.

Merit smiled and stood proud. It was nice to think that someone thought she was as good as her mom. Clark whispered to Merit. "Oh! Please! Deflate your ego a bit."

Tom looked down and said, "Clark's next." Merit snickered.

After Carol was done looking at all the dogs, she spoke to Tom. "Well, all your dogs are healthy. But King and Isabel need to take it easy. They should be put on restricted activity and should go on slow walks on leashes. If you run them, it should only be for a short period of time." Carol paused. "You know, these dogs have a tendency to run themselves into the ground because they don't know their limits. It's in their genes to run."

"Okay," mumbled Tom. Carol looked at him, but he adverted his eyes. "Is something wrong?" she asked. "Well," said Tom, "I feel bad for letting Isabel go to the beach and getting her exhausted." Carol nodded. "Well now you know that she really needs to take it easy. Especially if you're planning to breed her."

Gypsy laughed, but the other dogs glared at him and told him to be quiet. He just walked away singing "Isabel and King are going to have puppies." Isabel blushed and Clark chased after Gypsy. "You better run," said Clark, "because if I catch you…"

"What's got into them?" asked Carol.

"Don't know," replied Tom, "but maybe we should move inside so we don't get run over."

Once they were inside with the front door closed, Gypsy skidded to a halt. "Merit!" he yelled. "Save me!"

"You are on your own," replied Merit. "You wouldn't need saving if you'd learn to mind your own business and keep your mouth shut."

"That's right!" said King, growling. "Let's go inside, Isabel." The two walked over and scratched at the door. It opened, they went in.

At that moment, Joe came out of the side door and yelled, "Suppertime! Come get your dishes!" Each dog went to his own dish while Joe stood guard to make sure no stealing would take place. As usual, Merit ate her food as fast as she could. Joe laughed and said, "Slow down Merit. Really, you don't need to eat so fast."

Chapter 25

Pressure

It was back to business the next morning.

After being let out of their crates, the dogs were fed a small dish, walked and then taken to the track. Knowing she was going to race, Merit got excited; she loved to run. She tried tugging at the leash to make Joe walk faster, but he quickly pulled her back "*NO*, Merit! If you pull on me, I'll take you back, and then we can practice walking on the leash all day." Merit fell in line and decided that she would mind her manners while she was on her leash.

Once they were at the track, Joe put muzzles on them and put them into the starting gate. The gate flew open and the dogs leaped out. They ran around the track and when the lure stopped, they stopped, and waited for Joe to come to them. He praised them and put their leashes on and put them into a pen. "Go be good dogs," he said. This, the dogs had learned, was a cue meant to tell them to do their business. Once that was done, all were given a treat.

Merit looked at Clark. "Why is going to the bathroom a part of our training?"

"After you're done racing here, they take a urine sample to test it for certain drugs," replied Clark.

"Really?" said Merit.

"Sure," replied Clark. "Some people will try anything to get any advantage to win the purse."

"Oh," said Merit. "But, what happens if they're caught?"

"Depends," said Clark. "You can be scratched from the race, or the trainer gets fined, or he may not be allowed to race any more."

"Hmmm, why would anyone risk that all?" asked Merit.

"Well, if your livelihood depends on winning a purse, desperate trainers will try anything," explained Clark. "Sometimes they're able to hide the drugs by using unusual drugs. Sometimes the whole thing is rigged, so whoever collects the sample exchanges the dirty urine with clean urine. It's not as common now as in the past. They have so many people watching to make sure everything is above board."

Once all the dogs had finished, Joe put their leashes on and led them back to the yard.

"I can't *wait* to race again!" exclaimed Merit.

"Yeah it *is* fun," said Sunshine.

"We should be racing this weekend," added Clark.

"Which track do you think we'll be at?" asked Sunshine.

"Well, it's early in the season," said Clark. "So we'll probably just go to Corpus."

Merit had been listening patiently. "Do you think I'll be able to race then?" she asked.

Clark looked over at her slyly. "No, Tom has just been training you and paying your room and board because he likes you."

"*Of course* you'll be racing," said Sunshine.

Music thought a moment. "I wonder if you and Gypsy will be racing together."

"There's no way I can ever beat Merit," said Gypsy. "What if I lose and Tom gets rid of me?"

"I thought we had heard enough of the 'What ifs'… just do your best," said Merit.

"Yeah, none of us can beat Merit," added Clark. "She'll win the race for sure."

"Merit's competition makes us faster," said Sunshine.

Already feeling pressure to win, Merit was getting a knot in her stomach.

"Enough already! Who *knows* who will win? I'll just do my best." With that, she walked off.

Isabel came out of the house and went over to Merit. "What's up?"

"Nothing."

"I heard Tom talking to Carol," said Isabel. "Tom asked if she could wait until after this weekend to get the bill paid. He's hoping one of you will bring in some cash. And he hasn't paid Joe for a couple of weeks either. It's stressing him out." Merit groaned as her stomach tightened. Isabel looked at her. "Are you okay?"

As Merit stammered, Clark spoke up. "*I'll* be racing this weekend."

"I wouldn't have said anything if I thought you were racing," said Isabel thoughtfully.

"I don't mean to pressure you. Don't worry about the bills. That's Tom's responsibility. Yours is to run."

"I know," replied Merit, "but we need to run and win so we can *live*. I'm surprised any of us can handle this pressure. Look what it's done to Gypsy. I worry for him."

"Is he racing this weekend, too?" asked Isabel.

"Who knows? Clark seems to think so."

"Well, I'll try and find out for sure. Merit, you just rest and focus on your routine. That's what I did before a race. Live in the moment and don't let your mind wander."

Merit lay down in the shade and curled up. "Sleep," she said, laughing, but she took some deep breaths and dozed off. She woke up in the late afternoon, feeling much better. First yawning, then stretching, she got herself up and shook. Joe called her to dinner; tonight there was beef and vegetables. Inhaling the food, Merit realized how good it tasted.

Chapter 26

Race Day

When morning came, the dogs realized that the sun had been out for quite a while before they were let out of their crates. "It's about time," grumbled Clark, walking past Joe. Joe seemed much more reserved today, perhaps, thought Merit, he was tense. As they were being let out of the kennel, Gypsy then stepped on Sunshine's toe. Letting out a yelp, Sunshine snapped at Gypsy. Luckily, Gypsy managed to move just out of the way of her bite.

"I'm sorry Sunshine," said Gypsy. "Please settle down."

Merit could tell that everyone was on edge. It was race day. Clark looked at Merit and stretched as he yawned. "It's a big day Merit. Are you nervous?"

"No," said Merit. "I mean, I'm not thinking about it. It will come when it comes, no use in fretting about it. I'm saving my energy for running."

"Of course," replied Clark. "I can't wait to see you at the track with all the strange dogs and people around. Just try to stay focused, Merit. I wish you all the best." At that, Clark walked away. Sometimes, Merit thought to herself, I don't really understand my friends.

A little while after breakfast, Merit was called to the kennel. Walking into the darkness, her eyes blinking as she tried to adjust to no light, Joe led her onto the scale and made a notation in his notebook. Merit tried to get his attention by looking at him and wagging her tail, but today, he was all business. Joe then scooped her up and put her onto the metal table. He trimmed her toenails, and then looked at her gums and in her ears. He took her temperature. As he started to rub her down, Merit lowered her head and her tongue drooped out.

Finally noticing her, Joe spoke. "Oh Merit. Does that feel good?" Once done, he gently placed Merit back on the floor, and then took her out for a short walk in the forest. When she came back, Joe let her loose in the yard and called in Music. All of the dogs got Joe's special treatment that morning.

In the afternoon, the dogs watched Tom load their crates into the truck. Joe came out and started leading the dogs into their crates. No one said anything. The dogs just watched as Tom and Joe went about their race day jobs. Soon all were on the road. Merit sighed. The tension was getting to her. Taking a few deep breaths, she kept telling herself to stay calm and focused. But with each exhale, doubt, fear and intimidation began to creep in.

As the truck came to a stop, all of the dogs perked up their ears to see if they had arrived at the track. But Merit knew. She could hear the jingle of leashes, collars and harnesses that other dogs were wearing. Lifting her nose, it wiggled as she sniffed.

"Ahhh," said Clark, who seemed to be reading her mind, "The smell of a hundred greyhounds."

Tom came around to the back of the truck. "Joe," he said, "I'll go check in. You tend to the dogs." When Joe gave them each a small bowl full of water, he looked at Merit. "Don't you drink it too fast, girl. You'll get sick after you run. I know how you are, lil' one."

Just then, Tom returned.

"Merit and Gypsy are in the first race," he announced.

Gypsy groaned. Tom continued. "Music is in the third race, Sunshine is in the fourth, but Clark is not racing until the twelfth race. It's going to be a long day." Joe sighed.

"Well," said Tom, "let's take Merit and Gypsy on in."

With that, the two were brought out of their crates, muzzled, leashed and led into the building. Although Merit had been in the room before, she wasn't expecting so many people or dogs. Tom then walked her over to a crate. Once inside, she stood looking out of the grated door. The dog being placed next to her was a black female. Her owner called her Action as he closed her door. A white and tan brindle female named June was placed in the kennel on the other side. Merit watched as dogs of all colors soon filled all of the other crates.

Gypsy was three crates down from her. But once the dogs were inside their temporary homes, Merit could no longer see anyone. She could, however, both smell them and hear them. One dog was grunting "Let's go, let's go…" Merit only told herself to stay focused, and to run as fast as she could.

In fact, Merit was concentrating so hard on ignoring everyone that she was startled when her crate door finally opened. A boy reached in and led her to the scale. "Seventy-two pounds!" a man boomed. Right after that, a blue jersey was placed on her. Second position, thought Merit, second lane... second lane… second lane...

Merit glanced behind her and noticed that Gypsy would be in the seventh lane. His face was wrinkled with worry, but Merit caught his eye and winked at him. He lifted his eyebrow and tried to wink back. Merit could see that she had eased her friend's tension a bit. She also knew that she needed to stop worrying about Gypsy and focus on the race.

The dog directly behind her was still mumbling, "Let's go! Let's go!" Merit blocked him out as they were placed in the starting box.

Then the bell sounded, the door flew open, and Merit literally ran for her life.

She passed the dog coming out of the first box, hugged the rail and never slowed or looked back. She could feel her lips and cheeks vibrate and shake with every pounding stride. Soon she overtook the lure and couldn't decide if it was time to stop, so she kept running. It wasn't until someone stepped out on the track in front of her that Merit realized she needed to stop. The boy put a leash on her and patted her head. Merit looked around. She was the only dog on the track and the roar of the crowd was deafening. They were hooting, hollering, applauding and stomping their feet.

Taken off the track and led to the sand paddock where she was asked to do her business, she looked over at the other dogs. Gypsy was smiling at her and said, "Way to go, Merit!"

As they were led out of the yard, respective owners claimed their dogs. Joe grabbed Merit and Gypsy and led them out by the truck. Joe rubbed Merit down and Tom rubbed Gypsy down. Merit was confused by their silence; she and Gypsy were simply put into their crates. "Joe, you stay here," said Tom. "I'll see to the other dogs."

"Sure thing," replied Joe. "We don't want anyone snatching the fastest dog we've ever trained."

Gypsy laughed and Merit looked at him. "What's going on? What happened?"

"You set a new record Merit!" explained Gypsy.

"Hmmm," Merit murmured. "I did?"

"Yep," beamed Gypsy. "And *I* got second place."

It was Clark's turn to speak. "Good show, you two. Let's hope Sunshine and Music do as well. Then we can really celebrate."

Hearing that, Merit and Gypsy stretched out and fell asleep. They didn't wake up until Tom returned with Sunshine and Music. "How'd you guys do?" asked Clark. "Came in third," said Sunshine, sniffing.

"That's respectable, how about you?" asked Clark.

Music smiled. "I got second."

"Good for you!"

Tom looked at Joe. "Why don't you take Clark out to stretch his legs? I'll look after these two." Just then, a compact man walked up to Tom. "The greyhound that ran in the first race, is Merit her name?"

"Yep," replied Tom.

"Interested in selling her? I'll give you $50,000 for her."

"Nope," said Tom. "Not interested."

"Well, then," said the man, "if you ever change your mind, let me know. Here's my card."

"Thanks," replied Tom, "but I don't think I'll ever sell Merit."

"Your choice."

Gypsy sputtered. "Fifty thousand dollars, that's a *lot* of money."

"It is," agreed Merit. "But I'm glad that Tom isn't interested in selling me. I don't want to run for anyone else."

Joe came back to Tom. "Did I see you talking to Chris?"

"Yeah," replied Tom. "He wanted Merit."

"Not surprising," said Joe. "That guy has built a good kennel with one strategy: buying dogs that have proven themselves. How much did he offer?" asked Joe.

"Fifty grand."

"Jesus. What did you say?"

"That I wasn't interested."

"Oh. Well, that kind of dough *would* get you in the black."

"I know, but Merit has the potential to earn a lot more than that. And he knows it."

"Well," Joe said, "I'm fond of Merit. I'm glad she'll be around."

As the day went on, more and more people came up to ask about Merit. They wanted to know her lineage and where Tom got her. Predictably, a few more wondered if he was interested in selling her. Tom's reply was always a quick no.

Finally, it was Clark's turn to race. But when they came back, Clark was limping and had his foot wrapped.

"Oh Clark!" said Sunshine. "Did you break a toe?"

"Yeah."

"What did they wrap your foot with?" asked Gypsy.

"Just Vet Wrap."

Joe spoke to Tom. "What happened?"

"Clark got tangled up at the finish line with another male. It was pretty ugly. He's lucky all he hurt was a toe. The other dog needed stitches."

"Ouch!"

"Yep," replied Tom. "Clark still managed to get second place."

"Wow," said Joe, patting Clark and putting him in his crate.

"What a day," said Tom. "All the dogs placed, that's some record. Let's get them home and call Carol. I want her to look at Clark's foot. The track vet was pre-occupied," continued Tom, "by the other dog that needed stitches. They didn't x-ray his foot; he just wrapped it up and sent us on our way."

"Okay, then," said Joe, smiling. "Let's go." Exhausted by their day, all of the dogs slept deeply. Arriving home, they were fed, rubbed down and put away for the night.

Chapter 27

Good News

The next morning, Merit was let out of her crate first, followed by Gypsy and then Music.

Merit was just finishing her business when Isabel trotted out of the house toward her.

"Hey M," she said. "Congratulations on setting a record! Pretty exciting, huh?"

"Not really," replied Merit. "I mean, I just *ran*."

"Well," said Isabel, "they'll *all* be watching you now. You're the favorite! Whatever speed you did yesterday will most likely put you in the A class. Now you'll be racing against more experienced and faster dogs. So you'll have to be careful. Some of the dogs will try and trip you up. Remember to keep your space."

"When will I race again?" asked Merit.

"Tomorrow, I think."

Clark came limping up. "How's your foot Clark?" asked Isabel.

Clark shrugged. "Not too bad."

"Carol's coming around 10 this morning," said Isabel. "Tom called her last night." Isabel gave everyone a big smile. "You should have heard him. He was all business, but after he said goodbye, he said out loud, 'I can't wait to see you.' Then he laughed."

"He has it bad for her," observed Clark.

"Well, I just hope they get together soon," replied Isabel. "I can't believe he won't just get on with it."

"Why," asked Merit, "is he so scared?"

"People can be weird," offered Clark. "They act so differently around certain people. Look at how Tom deals with Joe, and then look at how he deals with Carol. He's more relaxed and certain with Joe. In front of Carol, he can't even talk."

"Clumsy, too," said Merit with a chuckle.

Joe suddenly called out. "Merit! Gypsy!"

"See ya guys!" said Merit. Running up to Joe, she could tell they were going to go for a walk in the woods. After all, Joe had on hiking boots. Yipee, she thought, I hope I see rabbits! Joe laughed when Merit suddenly stopped right in front of him and hopped up and down. "Let's go! Let's go!" she barked happily.

Attaching the leash to her collar, Joe instructed Merit to say still. Oh, how she loved the sound the clink of the brass snap against the silver ring on her collar made! With that, Merit glanced at Gypsy sauntering over to Joe. "Slow poke!" she snapped. "Get over here so we can go!" Gypsy glared. "Make me." Merit was not happy, she lunged at her friend. But Joe pulled her back. "Knock it off!" With that, Gypsy's leash was fastened and the dogs moved side by side, walked out of the gate in front of Joe.

"Do you like racing?" asked Gypsy.

"Yes," Merit said. "Never really thought of it before, but I guess I *do* like it. It's fun to stretch out and feel your heart pounding. And I like feeling my claws in the sand or in the grip of grass underfoot. Do you?"

"No," replied Gypsy quickly. "It makes me sore and tired. I don't like competing. I mean, running is one thing, it's kind of fun. But I don't want to have to run *all* out *all* the time. And I don't like having to get so close to other dogs all going full speed.

"You're lucky, Merit," continued Gypsy. "You were way out in front the whole race. It's harder when you're stuck in the pack."

"But you finished second," offered Merit. "You did well."

"You're right, but only because I was scared. I thought that if I didn't pull out of it, I would get sucked up by the dog behind me."

"Well," said Merit, "fear can be the best motivator. And whatever your motivation was, you were successful. I'm glad you weren't hurt."

"I know," replied Gypsy. Poor Clark."

"Yup," said Merit. "First race of the season and he breaks his toe."

"How do you think they'll treat it?" asked Gypsy.

"Hard to say. I mean, Clark's been a good, fast dog."

"Yeah, but he's raced a while. Maybe they'll retire him?"

Both dogs stopped in their tracks, with their ears flying up as they spotted a rabbit sitting in the middle of the trail. Just as Merit was getting ready to spring, Joe took the end of the leash and lightly swatted her on the rear. "Move *on*!" he said sternly.

Merit turned to look at Joe as the rabbit hurriedly skittered into the underbrush. "You're no fun!" said Merit with a low growl.

Gypsy could only laugh. "What, you want *more* stitches, Merit?"

Merit ignored him - instead keeping her eyes looking forward in case there was anything else to chase.

Carol's truck was in the driveway when they returned home.

First leading them in, Joe turned both dogs loose.

Next, the dogs walked up to Sunshine.

"Where's Clark?" asked Merit.

"In the house with Tom, Carol, Isabel and King," replied Sunshine.

Just then the front door opened, and King came strutting outside.

"Look at him!" exclaimed Sunshine. "He looks as though he's the happiest dog in the world."

"Hey King," asked Merit. "What are you so happy about?"

King trotted up to them and did a little hop. "Isabel and I are going to have a litter of puppies!"

"Hooray!" squealed Merit.

"Congratulations!" exclaimed Sunshine. "Sure will be nice to have some little ones running around!"

"Good news!" offered Gypsy. "Little puppies, how fun!"

"When are they coming?" asked Merit.

"In about nine weeks," said King, beaming. The door opened then; perhaps Isabel would be coming out. Instead, Clark hobbled out on three legs.

"Oh no," whispered Merit. "What's happened to Clark's foot?"

"Carol just put a brace on it to keep him from putting any weight on his foot," explained King. "He should be okay in a couple of months."

"*Months*!" exclaimed Merit. "How is he going to manage on three legs for that long?"

"Oh they'll take the bandage off in about 10 days," said King. "They just want the foot to set right."

"But he looks like he's in a lot of pain," said Gypsy.

"I think he is," King said. "They didn't give Clark any medicine because Tom and Carol want to prevent him from using his foot. They're afraid if they gave him a painkiller, he would hurt himself running around. So he'll be let out just to do his business."

Clark limped up to them. "Did King tell you the good news?"

"Why yes," said Merit. "It's pretty exciting, but we're sorry to see you hobbling around in pain."

"I'll be okay," said Clark. "I mean, Carol did a nice job setting my toes, so they'll heal right. She's awfully tender. It's nice to have a woman for a doctor. Men can be so rough sometimes."

The door opened then and Joe walked up and caught Clark "Time to go inside buddy! We don't want you standing around any more then you have to. Let's go lay down inside."

"Talk to you later," said Clark. "And congratulations again, King."

As he was led away, King spoke up. "With all this excitement, I think I'll go take a nap."

"Wow!" said Sunshine. "So many changes."

"I wonder how many pups Isabel will have?" asked Gypsy.

"Greyhounds usually have small litters, but she may have as many as four," replied Sunshine. "Or it could be less. It will be weird to see Isabel's belly all big and round. She won't look much like a greyhound anymore."

Gypsy chuckled. "No, I suppose not. But then again, she doesn't have to worry about staying in racing shape."

"She's already put on some pounds since she retired," added Sunshine.

"So has King!" said Merit, with a chuckle.

All of the dogs looked over at a sleeping King, "Yeah," said Sunshine. "He sure filled out. I can hardly believe he used to be nothing but bones and muscle. That's what a lack of exercise will do to you."

Merit looked at Gypsy and Sunshine's well-toned bodies and wondered if her ribs and spine were as visible as theirs. "Are we too skinny?" asked Merit.

Sunshine spoke first. "Well, not compared to some greyhounds. I think we're just really fit. Joe always fills our bowls and gives us treats."

"Well, I'm always hungry," said Gypsy. "I'd like *more* food."

"Yes," agreed Sunshine. "But I think when you're a greyhound and train hard you're going to want more food. I remember that once Joe didn't close the food bin and King got out of his crate and ate and ate. He ate for about an hour straight. You should have seen him wolf down almost all of the food, he just got sick and threw it all up.

"Joe never forgot to close the food bin after he had to clean up that mess," added Sunshine. "So even though we *want* more food, maybe we can't handle eating our fill." That said, the dogs lay down, then stretched out and took a nap.

Chapter 28

A Special Treat

When they awoke it was almost dark, and Carol's truck was still in the driveway.

"Hmmm, I wonder what's up?" said Gypsy, yawning. They also noticed that Joe's car was gone.

"When did Joe leave?" asked Sunshine.

"I didn't hear anything," Merit said, stretching.

"Me neither," said Sunshine, sleepily scratching her ear. "Hmm, King's not in the yard either.

"Wow," said Merit. "We must have slept pretty hard. Hey, let's go see what's happening in the house."

Merit lightly scratched on the door, which took a few minutes for Tom to open.

"Oh wow! I forgot about you guys. Why don't you come in and join our little party?"

The dogs were puzzled and could only look at each other. "It's okay," reassured Tom. "Come in."

"I've never been in the house," said Gypsy warily.

"Me neither," replied Sunshine.

Merit stood tall. "You heard Tom. Come on in." Timidly, Gypsy and Sunshine followed Merit inside. First they walked up to Isabel and congratulated her. Tom suggested they lie down next to her, so they did. It felt good; the house was warm and smelled like beef. Something good was cooking and Gypsy's stomach started rumbling loudly.

Clark laughed. "Gypsy, do you have a drum in your belly?"

Had Tom heard Gypsy? "Oh, you guys haven't had your supper yet. I told Joe he could go home, and I almost forgot all about you. Good thing you came to the door."

"Can they have some meat?" called out Carol.

"Sure," replied Tom. "It's a celebration." At that, Carol and Tom walked into the kitchen.

"Wow. Do you guys have it sweet or what!" said Sunshine. "You get to be in the nice warm cozy house, we get our little crates in the cold kennel."

"Stop whining!" snapped King. "You *know* we paid our dues for this, or we wouldn't be in here."

Tom and Carol returned with four dishes, all brimming with meat, rice and gravy.

As Merit, Gypsy, Music and Sunshine rose to eat, Clark spoke up. "If you guys have any brains, you'll eat slowly and enjoy every bite. You won't be getting as good a meal as this for a long time."

But Merit's anticipation was so great that she began to choke, before she could even take a bite. Tom looked at Carol with concern, but she just laughed. "I think Merit's salivating too much. And it certainly was a good meal you fixed Tom," said Carol.

"I was hoping you'd like it," said Tom. "It's all I know how to cook."

"Strictly a meat and potatoes kind of guy, are you?" asked Carol.

"Not really. I just never learned to cook anything else. I mean, usually I'll just have a sandwich or something for dinner, nothing fancy. It's no fun cooking and eating alone." The two were silent.

The dogs tried to eat slowly but couldn't. They were finished before they knew it and began to look around for scraps. "Well," Tom said, "I guess I should put the dogs in the kennel before they get too used to being house pets."

"Yeah," said Carol. "I should get a move on myself, before I get *too* comfortable."

Tom stared at her. "Well thanks for staying for dinner. I enjoyed your company."

"It was nice," replied Carol.

They stood up and looked at each other for a long time. Finally, Carol said, "Well..."

"Let me walk you out," said Tom. First opening the door for her, he then gently closed it on the dogs that were trying to follow them out.

"Can you hear anything?" asked Gypsy.

"No," replied Sunshine.

Clark, Isabel and King were still lying in their beds. "Will you guys stop eavesdropping?" said Clark.

"We just want to know what's going on," replied Sunshine.

But Merit had something else on her mind. Lifting her head up, she smelled the air. "I've never been in a kitchen," she blurted, then took off. Clark and King yelled at her. "Dogs are not allowed in the kitchen!"

Merit wasn't listening. Skidding into the kitchen and eyeing the counter for nibbles, she spotted a plastic bag on the counter. Standing on her hind legs, she pulled it down and ripped the bag open. "Mmmm bread," Merit said, moaning happily as she ate. Just as she was looking for another treat, she heard a familiar voice. "Merit! *No*!" Tom was standing in the doorway, his hands on his hips. In the background, Merit heard Clark chuckle. "Busted."

Tom wasted no time. Grabbing her by the collar, he pulled her out of the kitchen, then out into the yard, then into the kennel and finally into her crate. "*Bad* dog! In your crate!" Merit just burped, while Tom glared. It wasn't long before Tom came back out with Gypsy, Music and Sunshine. After the trio was put into their crates, he gave them a treat "You're good dogs, not like Merit." Tom then walked out of the kennel and turned off the lights.

"Boy did you make him mad," said Gypsy. "I'm glad we listened to Clark and King. When they tell you something, *listen*."

"Say what you will," replied Merit. "Me? I got bread."

"Yeah, well not only did Tom give us a treat," added Gypsy, "but we got to do our business *before* we were crated. It's going to be a long night for you, Merit."

"Right," snapped Merit. Already her bladder was filling and already she was uncomfortable. Merit tried hard to sleep, but her overly full belly and bladder were making her very uncomfortable. She began to panic. But just then, the kennel door opened. "Come on Merit," said Tom. "Let's go be a good girl." Merit had never so happy to be let out of her crate.

It was a beautiful night, but she wasted no time finding a spot to do her business. More than anything, Merit did not want to risk upsetting Tom again. "Good girl," she heard him say. "Let's put you back so you can get some sleep. Tomorrow is race day." As he bent over to open the door to her crate, Merit gave him a quick, soft kiss. He laughed. "Merit, you're a special dog. Just stay out of my kitchen." He patted her head, put her in her crate, latched the door and left. Merit sighed in relief and fell fast asleep.

The door opened early the next morning, and the lights snapped on.

"Race day for Sunshine, Merit and Gypsy!" called out Joe. "Rise and shine, rise and shine!" Gypsy groaned and rolled over, while Merit got up and tried to stretch and shake in the confines of her crate. Sunshine yawned. "It's too early; we must be going to Gulf."

"What," asked Gypsy, "is Gulf?"

"Oh, Gulf Greyhound Park in La Marque," replied Sunshine. "It's the world's largest greyhound racing operation. It's huge! They have the largest kennel you've ever seen."

"Come on," said Joe. "It's time to load up". He started loading their crates in the truck while they went out to do their business.

Merit stopped to drink some water from a bowl. "Why are we going to *this* greyhound park instead of racing in Corpus?" she asked Sunshine.

"Probably a bigger purse."

Gypsy moaned. "Oh no. That means tougher competition."

"Why isn't Music coming?" asked Merit.

"Don't know," replied Sunshine.

Just then, Isabel came out of the house with Tom. Striding purposefully up to the dogs, she seemed to have something important to say. "You guys are headed to Gulf Park today."

"Yeah, I figured it out," replied Sunshine.

"Do you know why?" asked Merit.

"Yes," said Isabel. "There's going to be a big race happening there. Not today, but Tom and Joe want you to train at Gulf to get used to the track. Tom mentioned to Carol that since he only has three racing dogs left in his kennel for a good part of the season, he's going to have to commute to La Marque in order to compete for the bigger purses."

"How far is it from here?" asked Merit.

"About five hours."

"What about Music?"

"Tom sold her," said Isabel flatly. "He felt that she was not ready to move to the larger track, and that he couldn't compete at both tracks."

Gypsy was very quiet. "Oh," he said.

Just then, Joe called the dogs to the truck. As they ran around the yard taking care of business, Isabel called to them just as they were going out the gate. "Good luck!" "Thanks!" they all replied, then jumped into the back of the pickup. As Joe closed the door to the crates he looked at them. "You guys get some rest. It's going to be a long drive." With that, Tom closed the gate and he and Joe got into the truck. The dogs settled in and napped.

After a while Merit woke. She could tell some time had passed since the sun was high and it was getting hot. Merit looked over at Gypsy; he, too, was awake, but panting. Lying in her small space, Merit watched the saliva drip off of Gypsy's slim pink tongue, then gather in a pile between his front feet. Merit then heard Sunshine whimper. It seemed as if she was chasing rabbits in her sleep. Lying on her back, her eyes were fluttering under her lids; her paws were digging in the air.

Merit stood, stretched and shook as best as she could. "How did you sleep?" whispered Gypsy.

"Fine," replied Merit. "Do you know how much further we have to go?"

"Not a clue," said Gypsy. The pair sat silently, watching the landscape change from an arid brown to an inviting green.

Merit spoke after a while. "I wonder when we'll stop. I have to go."

"Me too," replied Gypsy. Suddenly, he let out a long howl, "Heeeeyyyyyy ggguuuyyysss, don't forget about us."

"Do you think they can hear us back here?" asked Merit.

"Probably not," replied Gypsy. "Or they would have told me to be quiet."

Merit chuckled. Sunshine opened her eye then and rolled over. "Hey Gypsy, what's the deal?"

"Merit and I have to go, and they don't seem to be stopping."

Sunshine got up, looked around and sniffed. "We're still on the interstate, not too many places to stop. I'm sure we'll stop soon." Stretching again, she lay back down and sighed. "I could use a drink," her eyes closing. Merit and Gypsy watched as she drifted off to sleep and into another dream.

Finally the truck veered off of the highway, down a side road and pulled off. Merit looked but had no idea where they were. "Hey, Sunshine, wake up. I think we're here."

Sunshine woke up, yawned, stretched and sniffed. "Nope, we're not at the track yet." Joe then opened the truck doors. "How are you dogs doing? Want to stretch?" With that, he opened their crates, put on their leashes and led them to a grassy area. Tom then came walking up with a large bowl of water. While Sunshine drank and Gypsy did his business, Merit couldn't decide which to do first, so she just stood there.

Tom reached down and patted Merit's head. "Merit, are you okay?" Looking up at him, she sensed his concern for her. In answer, Merit just stretched and yawned and shook. Tom laughed. "Oh you're just a sleepy girl, are you?" With that, Merit drank her fill of water and then went to take care of business. Joe spoke as soon as she finished. "Let's go for a walk and stretch your legs." All of the dogs then walked around the perimeter of the lawn before being led back to the truck.

"Load up!" said Tom. "Let's get on the road." Hearing this, the dogs jumped up and got into their crates. As the truck pulled back onto the highway, Merit looked at the group. "Might as well sleep." As she was drifting off, she could hear Gypsy questioning Sunshine about Gulf Park.

Merit woke up shivering. She was cold and it was dark. "Where are we?"

"We're at the track," said Sunshine matter-of-factly. "Joe and Tom went in to find out where we'll go."

"Oh, it's so cold."

"Yeah, I hope they get back here soon."

Getting up, Merit rearranged her blanket, first pulling it up into a large pile, then spinning around a couple of times, then lying down and sighing. Just then, she heard Tom and Joe's voices and her ears perked up. She could hear Tom first. "Well it's not too shabby," he said.

"Should be the Ritz for what you're paying," replied Joe.

"You're right. But if the dogs do well, it will be worth it."

"Let's hope," said Joe.

"Why don't you walk the dogs back and I'll take the truck?" said Tom. "I bet they could use a good stretch."

"Good idea," said Joe. "If it wasn't so cold we could turn 'em out in the paddock." As the men got closer, Merit stood up and wagged her tail. Joe opened their crates and put on leashes, then led them across the asphalt and over to some grass, where they stopped. "Let them clean this up, we're paying for it…" mumbled Joe. Next, the dogs walked through a doorway. It felt good there. It was warm, and they all lingered a moment.

Merit watched a man approach Joe. "Hi," he said. "My name's Cesar. I've been expecting you. You know where your dogs go?"

"Yes." replied Joe. "Name's Joe. The dogs are supposed to go there, right?" Joe pointed to some empty crates.

"Yep, those are yours. First time here?"

"Sure is."

"Well Joe," said Cesar, "the wash racks are in the center, over there and across from the restrooms." Merit saw him open a door. "And here's your office. I've got to go make my rounds, but I'll be back if you have any questions." As Cesar walked away, he glanced over his shoulder. "Guess I should mention that you're on candid camera. We've got security cameras on 24 hours a day."

Merit heard Joe mutter under his breath. "I guess I can't even pick my nose around here."

"What is this place?" Gypsy said.

"Just our new home away from home," said Sunshine. "I bet we'll be staying here for a while."

"Wow," said Merit. "This is some place."

It was Joe's turn. "Come," he said, giving them a light tug. He took the dogs over to a row of creates. "This is our spot." Further down the row, Merit could see more crates, most of them with dogs inside. She could also smell them and hear them. Merit, Gypsy and Sunshine looked at one another.

"It'll be okay, Gypsy. We're right here," said Merit. Reluctantly, Gypsy climbed into the crate between Sunshine and Merit. As Joe walked away, Sunshine whispered. "I think it would be best if we stay quiet until morning." Merit and Gypsy silently nodded in agreement. But someone did stay up. Every hour, Cesar walked down the row, shining a flashlight in every crate and then looking each dog over.

As dawn broke, the dogs awoke to a loud commotion.

Someone was letting dogs out down a hallway. Merit couldn't see anything. "What do you see, Sunshine?"

"Nothing at all," she replied.

Merit then heard a man's voice. "Come on now doggies, time to go outside. Good doggies." She next heard him putting muzzles and leashes on at least five dogs, then leading them outside. Soon he came back in and got another group of dogs and then another.

"He has so many dogs," said Sunshine. "I wonder if they're all his?"

"Probably not," said Merit. "I mean, he doesn't call them by their names." The man was walking toward their section. "Hi doggies, time to go outside. As he had done with the other groups he uncrated them, placed muzzles and leashes on them, and then started leading them outside.

"I wonder where Joe and Tom are?" asked Gypsy. As the dogs walked down the corridor to an outside door, they next came to a group of paddocks. They were all turned out together in a large fenced area. An empty paddock separated them from the other dogs.

As he let them loose, the man gave a simple command. "Go run." The dogs could only stand there as he closed the gate. Merit turned away first, looking around the sandy paddock. It was, she noticed, almost as big as their yard at home. The dogs next smelled their way around the paddock area.

"Gosh, how many dogs do you think have been in here?" asked Gypsy.

Sunshine spoke with authority. "Hundreds and hundreds."

Meanwhile, Merit was trying to see the other dogs, but none seemed to pay her any attention, although she could hear many of them playing. She was thankful, she thought, to have Sunshine and Gypsy with her. She sauntered up to her two friends. "I wonder when we'll race."

"Well, I need breakfast before we do anything," said Gypsy.

"I'm sure Tom and Joe will give us time to train before we race," said Sunshine. "Bet we won't do that for probably a couple of days."

After a while, the same man walked back out past their kennel and once again started collecting dogs.

"Here doggies, come here."

"I think these dogs will be led right by us on the way back in," said Sunshine. "*Please* don't say anything when they go by." Merit and Gypsy nodded their assent as the man led a group of five dogs toward them. All were tall, thin and muscular dogs, and all ignored them as they passed.

"Did you *see* those guys?" asked Gypsy. "They looked *mean*."

"No, they looked serious," corrected Sunshine. "This is not a social event, this is racing. Everyone is the competition. It's hard to race against your friends so you shouldn't make any."

Gypsy did not seem to understand. "Why not?"

Sunshine explained gently, "If you don't win, it's bad news. You can't worry about anyone's future but your own."

"Doesn't seem right," said Merit.

"It doesn't, it isn't, but it is what it is," replied Sunshine.

Just then, the man returned with another group of dogs. As these dogs passed, a large brown male looked Merit directly in the eye. "Hi, there."

Startled, Merit murmured a quiet hello and looked away. Gypsy laughed, "Hey, Merit. He likes you."

Sunshine looked at Merit. "This isn't good. You should have ignored him, Merit. You can't encourage behavior of that sort."

"All I said was hello. What's the big deal?"

"You'll see," said Sunshine, gently scolding Merit. "Time will tell. When we go back in you'll have to walk right by his crate. And he's going to say something. Then it will turn into this little game. I've seen it before. One of you will end up getting hurt when it's race time."

Merit pouted. "I don't think it hurts to be friendly."

The man came and got them "Here doggies, come here."

As Merit, Gypsy and Sunshine trotted up, he put their leashes on. Meanwhile, Sunshine begged Merit not to speak. But as Merit was led into the building and down the aisle, she suddenly realized that she didn't even know which crate her new admirer was in. She had to try hard not to look, and to keep her eyes straight ahead.

"Hi again. First time at Gulf?" It was difficult, but Merit was silent and kept walking. "See ya." When they reached their crates, the man took off their muzzles, gave them a treat and put them away.

"Hey, when do we get breakfast?" asked Gypsy.

Sunshine ignored the question. "Merit, I'm glad you didn't talk to that dog. He obviously does not follow track protocol."

"Maybe he's just being nice," said Merit. Sunshine moaned.

"I'm hungry!" said Gypsy, who was getting increasingly cranky. "When do we get our dishes?"

"Be quiet!" admonished Sunshine. Just then, the man returned. He opened each crate and gave every dog a dish. "Don't worry,' said Merit. "Food's coming."

After eating, the dogs took a nap. Next, the same man returned and took them back out into the paddock. Gypsy got Sunshine to chase him by slamming his body into hers. "Come on Sunshine," growled Gypsy. "Don't bother," said Sunshine. "Merit's too busy staring at her boyfriend." Merit blushed; was she that obvious? "I'm *not* staring," she stammered.

"Then stop looking over at him and *play*."

That was all Merit needed to hear. "That's it! I'm gonna get you!!!" Chasing Gypsy and Sunshine around the paddock, she frolicked until the man came to get them. With a sinking heart, Merit then realized that she had been so preoccupied that she had missed her new friend being led back into the kennel. What was his name?

As they were led into the building once again, Merit saw his crate. "You're pretty fast, what's your name?" He asked.

Sunshine groaned, Gypsy chuckled, while Merit replied. "Merit. And this is Sunshine and Gypsy."

"Nice to meet you," he called out after them.

"What do you think his name is?" said Merit.

"Who knows? I'm calling him Stupid," replied Sunshine. "All the other dogs know how to behave, he's *so* rude." Not wanting to hear any more, Merit curled up in her crate.

Just then, Joe and Tom walked up. "Come on, time to try out the track." said Joe, opening their doors. As Merit walked out, she looked down the aisle to see if she could glimpse her friend, but couldn't. Gypsy laughed. "What are you looking for Merit? Your boyfriend?"

"Shut up!" As Tom and Joe led them to the track, Merit exclaimed, "Whoa! This is impressive. Look at that building."

"That's called a grandstand," replied Sunshine. "Wow!" said Gypsy. "Look like it holds a lot of people."

The trio was then led into the building next to the track. There, they were weighed and had muzzles and blankets put on. They were led in front of the grandstand to the starting gate. Merit sniffed the cool breeze; it was going to rain soon. When they reached the starting gate, Merit was placed in the third box.

The bell rang! As the gate opened, Merit flew past Sunshine, and never did see Gypsy. After she ran the one lap, Joe came and got her. Rubbing Merit down, he kept saying, "Good girl, good girl," and then led her back to the box with the others. It started to rain. Hard.

Joe spoke first. "I guess we got lucky. This'll give us a chance to run a wet track." "Yeah," replied Tom, pulling his hood over his head. "Let's lead them around the track first, so they can get used to the feel. It's slopping up fast."

As she walked the track, Merit could feel the mud sucking at her paws. "This should make for interesting races," said Joe.

"Yeah," said Tom. "I can't believe they race here rain or shine, year-round. We'll have to see how they run on this wet track."

Gypsy seemed shocked. "We're supposed to *run* in this? It's way too slick and sludgy."

"I've never run in mud, have you, Sunshine?" said Merit.

"Yes, but it's not easy. Your paws slide until they grip. It's hard to keep your balance and momentum. I always slow it down to be safe. You can't run a fast race without the risk of tearing something."

"Why do they make us race in the rain?" said Gypsy, becoming huffy.

"I'm not sure, but at this track races go on every day and three nights a week, too."

"Does that mean that we're going to have to race everyday?" asked Gypsy.

"No," said Sunshine. "But we'll run more then we did at Corpus. We'll still get days off, though."

Placed once again in the starting gate, the bell went off!

Chasing after the lure, Merit's feet slid to the outside as she banked the first turn. In an instant, she slipped, tumbled, and slid right into Sunshine. Sunshine let out a huge and pained yelp.

Joe and Tom ran to Sunshine's aide. As Joe tried to stop, he slipped and fell backward with a loud thud. Tom looked back and asked, "OK?" Joe grunted "Yep." Tom knelt by Sunshine and looked her over; she had stopped crying and was trying to get up. "It's her left front," said Tom flatly. "Looks like it's broken. Let's get her to the vet."

"Can you carry her?" asked Joe. "I'll get the others." As Joe looked Merit over, she spoke softly to Sunshine. "I'm so sorry."

"It's okay," replied Sunshine. "I know it was an accident." As Sunshine was being led away, Gypsy whispered. "Broken?"

"Well Merit," said Joe, "You look no worse for wear." Putting on their leashes and leading him back to the weight room, he then took off their blankets and muzzles. Each of the dogs was hosed down with warm water and towel dried.

Neither Merit nor Gypsy spoke. Merit couldn't even enjoy her rub down. All she could think about was Sunshine's shrill cry, Tom's voice saying "broken" and Sunshine's pained expression. She felt miserable. She wanted to go back home. She wanted to see Isabel and King. She trembled. Joe kept rubbing her down.

"Poor Merit, you got a chill. I'll give you a warm dish when we get back to the kennel. Our time here is about up. We should be heading back." Joe put a comfortable fleece- lined rain slicker on Gypsy and Merit before leading them back to the kennel. Tom was standing by their crates when they returned. "I didn't expect to see you," said Joe.

Tom seemed unsteady. "It doesn't look good. I asked Carol to come for a second opinion."

Joe didn't say anything as he put the dogs away. After he closed the door, he spoke. "I was going to give them a warm dish. Merit's shivering." "I'll come with you," said Tom. As they walked away, Joe asked the question he really didn't want to hear the answer to. "What did the vet say?"

Tom's voice wavered. "He strongly suggested I put her down." Merit started to cry.

"Oh no!" said Gypsy.

Joe opened the door to each crate and set the dishes inside. Neither Gypsy nor Merit made a move toward the food. "When do you expect Carol to be here?" asked Joe.

"Not 'til after midnight," replied Tom. "Vet Evens wants me to page him when she arrives."

"Hey now," Joe snapped at the dogs, "You two have got to eat."

Tom seemed exasperated. "I don't *need* this!" Hearing that, Merit walked up to her dish and took a tentative taste. "Hmmm, this is pretty good." Her stomach rumbled and Gypsy said, "I guess we won't help matters by not eating." "That's a relief!" said Joe, noticing that both dogs had started eating.

"I have to decide what to do without having Sunshine this race season," said Tom. "I think we need to get more dogs. I sold Music. We lost Clark, King and Sunshine, and it'll be too long before Isabel's puppies are old enough to race."

"Yeah, two dogs don't make much of a race kennel," agreed Joe. "Good thing, Merit wasn't hurt."

"Why don't you look around for a couple dogs to buy?" suggested Joe.

"Good idea. I'll keep my eye out."

"Well, might as well go get some rest," said Tom. Merit and Gypsy were still not talking as they drifted off to sleep.

Merit suddenly woke up and looked around. The man from yesterday had returned and was leading dogs out to the paddocks. Merit listened to him, once again calling, "Here doggie! Good doggie!" Joe soon came up and let Merit out of her crate, then gave her a rub down. She looked at Joe. "How is Sunshine?" But as always, Joe didn't listen.

Joe led Gypsy and Merit outside and down by the track. Tom and Carol were standing there waiting. "How's Sunshine?" asked Joe. Carol sighed. "She's heavily sedated right now. Not feeling much of anything. I've set the leg in a cast, but keeping her off it will require a lot of diligence. It will be a long, slow and painful recovery."

"She'll never race again," added Tom. "But Carol's offered to adopt her and see to her recovery and her retirement."

"That's awfully nice of you," said Joe.

"Well," replied Carol, "she's a great dog. Plus, she'll make a good mascot at the hospital, and if I ever need a blood donor, I'll have one."

"What do you mean?" asked Joe.

"Well, a greyhound's blood type allows them to be universal donors. So their blood can be used for any canine blood transfusion."

"Didn't know that," said Joe. "So Sunshine will have a new purpose in life." Merit and Gypsy both breathed a sigh of relief as they were placed in their paddock. "I don't even want to think," said Gypsy, shuddering, "about what would have happened to Sunshine if Tom hadn't called Carol."

Chapter 29

Fire!

Merit had fallen asleep, but woke and inhaled. She lay awake, listening. She stretched and rolled over and fell back to sleep.

Suddenly, Gypsy was shouting.

"*Wake up*, Merit!"

Merit struggled to concentrate. "Merit, you've *got* to wake up! *There's a fire*!"

Merit's mind swirled and she sneezed, sneezed and sneezed. In the distance far away, she heard long, steady howls, almost deafening. Over this was Gypsy's frantic call to action. Merit shook her head and tried to pry open the door to her crate. The latch was hot. She yelped and Gypsy yelled, "*Hurry* Merit!"

It was getting hot and Merit was now having trouble breathing. Deciding she had to bear the pain, she tried her latch one more time. It released. Merit leapt out of her crate and then she opened Gypsy's gate.

"Gypsy, take the dogs around outside, to the entrance gate. You should be safe out there." Merit made fast work of the other crate doors. A few other dogs learned to open crates by watching Merit and helped free the rest of the dogs. By the time Merit got outside, she was coughing badly and couldn't catch her breath. But she was alive.

Gypsy hovered over Merit. "Are you okay? Do you need some water?"

"Yes, please," said Merit, gasping. "What caused the fire?"

"I don't know. It started in the office."

"Thanks for waking me."

"It was hard. You were sound asleep."

"Yeah, I know," said Merit.

Feeling better, Merit looked around at all of the dogs, and watched the fire engulfing their kennel. The sirens grew closer.

"Merit," said Gypsy, "you don't look good."

Merit barely heard her friend. Instead, she watched as fire trucks and cars careened into the parking lot. Among the people she saw running out onto the asphalt were Joe and Tom. "Oh my god, I thought you were dead!" said Joe. "How did you get out?"

Tom wasn't paying attention, he was examining Merit. "Her nose is burnt. Her whiskers and eyelashes are gone."

"Gypsy looks fine," said Joe. The two men looked at each other, puzzled. Other trainers, looking at their dogs in disbelief, started questioning one another. "Who let the dogs out?" one of them asked. No one replied. Eventually, the commotion died down and the men turned and again asked each other how all of the dogs could possibly have come out of their crates. Now, the dogs all turned to gaze at Merit. It was at that moment, for the first time, that the dogs knew that the men understood. One by one, they stammered and mumbled. "Well, I'll be damned. It's not *possible.*"

Tom looked at Merit kindly. "You're a very special dog," he said, stroking her head. All of the men cheered, and Merit coughed. "Come on, Joe," said Tom suddenly. "Let's get Merit to the vet. She needs attention."

Tom was right, Merit did feel terrible. She heard Tom's voice again. "Maybe it will do you good to get you home for a while."

"Home?" thought Merit. Where is my home? Where is it, really? It seemed to her that King and Isabel's home was with Tom. But where was hers? Perhaps, thought Merit, she, too, would someday have a home and family to call her own. Within moments, she was asleep.

When Merit woke, she was not at home, or in any familiar kennel. But from the smell, even before she opened her eyes, she knew she was at the veterinarian's office. Both constrained and sore, Merit tried to lift her paw, but it was no use. She also knew she had something in her nose.

A buzzer sounded and Carol walked in.

"Oh Merit, you're awake! Good! We had to put you on some oxygen because you had smoke inhalation. Lie still, now." With that, Carol patted her on the head. Merit now tried to lick her lips, but her tongue felt thick and dry. Feebly, she lifted her head and looked Carol in the eye, then laid her head back down. "You poor heroine," said Carol. "All I want you to do now is just rest." Quickly, Carol gave Merit a shot that made her mind dull. Drifting in and out of consciousness, she was able to dream. But Merit didn't know how much time had passed when they finally took off the straps holding her down, and gently placed her in a crate.

Tom walked in. "Hey, Carol, is she ready to go home?"

"Yep, she's all set. Here are the antibiotics to prevent any infections. I know she'll probably lick it off, but put this ointment on her nose twice a day."

"Thank god it was just a second-degree burn," said Tom.

"You and Merit are lucky," replied Carol. "But we'll have to monitor her closely. I'm just glad we didn't have to do a skin graft."

"Gosh," said Tom. "The poor dog."

"She should be good as new soon," replied Carol. "Her lungs sound clear, that's a good thing. Hey, as anyone found out yet what started the fire?"

"Yeah," replied Tom. "Cesar left the space heater on in his office."

"Where was Cesar?"

"Working on the other side of the track. He *did* come running when he heard the alarm."

Carol thought a moment. "Good thing the smoke detectors went off."

"Yeah," said Tom, scratching his head. "The fire marshal discovered the sprinkler system wasn't hooked up right. The contractor is in big trouble for the sprinklers failing. There've already been lots of lawsuits filed. Me, I'm tempted to sue for Merit's medical bills." Tom paused.

Carol said, "It is maddening to hear about such negligence."

The really sad thing is when the fire marshal contacted the company; the guys there just said it was only a bunch of dogs, that it really didn't matter."

Carol sighed. "Makes you really question people's integrity."

"Yeah, anything for a fast buck."

"What *is* this world coming to?" replied Carol.

"Well," said Tom, "Guess I should be getting back. It's mayhem with Isabel's new puppies."

"They're so cute!"

"Are you going to come by tonight?"

"Of course," said Carol, smiling.

"See you then." They kissed. "Wow," thought Merit. "I *have* been away a while.

Tom loaded Merit into the truck, and she got to ride in front. "You don't get the window rolled down but this far," he said firmly. "I don't want you sticking your nose out of the window." Merit curled up as best she could on the space next to Tom. It was then that she realized she was no longer a pup but a big dog. As if reading her mind, Tom spoke. "M, you're not as small as the first time you rode with me, are you?" Hearing that, Merit laid her head on Tom's lap, and he stroked her all the way home. The warm truck and the slow rumble of the engine helped Merit feel completely and utterly content.

Chapter 30

Home Again

Merit was almost sad when the ride was over. She craved Tom's attention and gentleness. But looking outside, she saw Gypsy, King, Isabel and Clark, and three of the most adorable puppies she had ever seen. Merit's heart caught in her throat. She had no idea how good it would be to see her friends again. She had missed them, and Tom's home, much more than she realized.

Lunging out of the car, Merit jumped right over the fence. She could hear Tom "M, you never cease to amaze... "

Just then, Joe walked out. "What's going on?"

"Oh, Merit just jumped over the fence."

"No way!"

"Way!" Both men laughed.

The dogs gathered around Merit. "I told them how you saved everyone," said Gypsy.

"I guess it's a good thing I taught you to open gates," added King.

"Definitely," said Merit. "Otherwise, we probably wouldn't be here."

Meanwhile, the puppies timidly smelled Merit. "Come here," said Merit gently, addressing the male with gray and white splotches. "What's your name?

"They call me Patches," he said.

Merit approached a little girl dog who was completely black. "And you?"

"I'm Licorice," she answered.

The smallest pup now spoke. "And I'm Emmy." This one was all blue, and even had blue eyes. She reminds me, thought Merit, of another dog, I just can't remember which one. But no matter how much Merit concentrated, she couldn't make the connection.

"Nice to meet you Patches, Licorice, and Emmy,"

"I'm named after you," blurted out Emmy.

"You are?" asked Merit, but looking at Isabel.

"Yes, it's true," said Isabel. "Her name is really Merit, but we call her Emmy, or M."

"Oh..." This was all Merit could say, stammering.

"Mom told me our name means." continued Emmy solemnly. "It means worthy of praise,"

"We have special names, too," said Patches.

"Yeah, we do," chimed in Licorice.

"Of course you do," said Merit, feeling their envy.

Isabel now looked lovingly at her children. "Come. It's time for a snack and then a nap." She waddled away; Isabel still had the body of a nursing dog.

Gypsy turned to Merit. "Am I ever glad to see *you*."

Clark held out his paw. "It *is* good to see you, Merit. How's your nose?"

"Feels funny. It kind of stings and itches at the same time."

"Did you hear what caused the fire?" asked Gypsy."

"I heard Tom telling Carol about it. What a mess."

"When do you think we'll go back?"

"Pretty soon," said Clark. "From what I've been hearing, they are setting up temporary kennels."

"Oh," said Merit. Walking away, she found a sunny little spot on the grass and stretched out. Merit then rolled over on her back and let her tongue roll out of her mouth, across her nose and onto the grass. Her sleep was quick, deep and without dreams.

She awoke to the familiar sound of Joe's voice. "How could things be so different and still be the same?" thought Merit. "Is it just me who has changed?"

Merit, Gypsy and Clark were put away for the evening. Once they were settled in their crates, Clark had an announcement. "Merit, you were asleep when King came outside," he said. "He told us that three new dogs arrive tomorrow."

"Really," Merit said, her voice trailing off. She didn't know why, but she was feeling blue.

Gypsy was quick to notice. "Merit, are you okay? I mean, you don't seem alright."

"I'm fine," replied Merit. "I guess."

"When you say 'I guess,' it's not very convincing," said Clark.

Merit tried to explain. "I just feel that something is missing. It's strange. I mean, here we all are, but Music and Sunshine are gone. And Isabel and King have those three little adorable puppies, and I…"

"Are you missing your new friend, the one who was talking to you just before we were supposed to race?" interrupted Gypsy. "Maybe that's what's wrong."

"I haven't thought about him at all." She heaved a sigh. "I don't know what's wrong."

"Maybe you're just a little depressed," said Clark. "You have every right to be. You've been through a lot. You were at Carol's for a while, and before that, you were at the track. Get some rest. You'll feel better tomorrow."

"I know *I* won't," said Gypsy. "The thought of new dogs scares me." Clark and Merit chuckled. Gypsy was so predictable.

Chapter 31

Newcomers

Merit woke up a little excited the next day. Today she might make some new friends. As Joe let them out and they walked outside, Isabel joined them. "The van's delayed. The new dogs won't arrive until this afternoon." Joe then brought out their dishes, and they ran over and gulped their fill. Meanwhile, Isabel's puppies were allowed to wander around, but were quickly reminded by all that they were not to get too close to their dishes.

The pups laughed. "Oooooh you're so tough," said Patches teasingly. "I'm so afraid." Merit winked at Clark, knowing that it really was a farce and that none of them would ever hurt the pups. Nonetheless, it did remind them to mind their manners.

After all three dogs ate Joe walked them to the woods. "I never realized," said Merit to Gypsy, "how much I missed nature."

"Yeah," agreed Gypsy. "Being released in a run is not the same as getting to walk in the forest. I like it here, and I like the routine. I wish we could race close to home again."

Merit thought for a moment. "I like the forest and walks and having Joe and Tom's special attention here, too," she said. "But Gulf Park has an energy about it that's much more exciting than the Corpus track."

"It's too big for me," said Gypsy. "And too many dogs. I hate it, hate it, hate it! I hope I don't ever have to go back." The dogs fell silent.

After the walk, they were groomed. First Merit was given a warm bath, then had her nails filed and then had ointment slathered on her nose. She was enjoying all of the pampering, her eyes held a relaxed daze. Joe laughed. "Merit, look at you! You're going to fall over!"

She was leaning over so much she almost lost her balance. As Merit crumpled to the ground, Joe continued to rub her down with the towel. She was now on her back so he could rub and scratch her chest. When Joe finished, Merit waved her paw for more, and he chuckled and rubbed her again. After doing this a few times, Joe said to her, "Enough! I still have to do Gypsy and Clark," he said, chuckling. "Get up."

Merit now went outside where she found a sunny spot on the grass. There, she stretched out and looked at the clouds in the sky. Smelling the air, she tried to focus on each scent. Emmy came over. "What do you smell, Merit?"

Merit smiled. "All kinds of things. I don't know what they all are, but they're familiar and they're good. For a while, all I smelled was smoke."

"I always smell Gypsy when I'm outside," said Emmy. "My mom says that he's got a lot of gas." Merit chuckled. "You should try bunking with him."

"Ugh!" Emmy exclaimed. "Can I lie with you?"

"Of course." As Emmy lay next to her, she once again inhaled deeply. But this time, all Merit could smell was Emmy's wonderful puppy scent. Merit's heart leaped. She was happy to be able to spend some time with these wonderful little pups. Her heart also tugged, although she wasn't sure why. Nuzzling Emmy, Merit let out a contented sigh. "I'm glad we're friends."

"Me too," replied Emmy.

King walked up.

"Oh, there you are Emmy. We couldn't see you. Hi, Merit."

"Hi King."

"What you want, Dad?" said Emmy.

"I need you to come inside now."

"Oh Dad!" Emmy started to protest, but she could sense by Merit's expression, and King's look that disobedience would not be tolerated. So Emmy got up, shook and stretched. Yawning, she turned toward Merit. "I'll see you later."

Merit watched them go into the house. She sniffed the air. Something in the wind smelled bitter and Merit sneezed. Next, she got up to find Clark. It was his turn for grooming, so Merit stood in the doorway. There, she watched Clark with Joe and thought that although Joe was nice to everyone, he didn't seem to have any real sort of relationship with any of the dogs, not like what he had had with Speedy. I wonder, thought Merit, what it was about Speedy that, at least for Joe, all of the other dogs seemed to lack?

Clark suddenly noticed Merit and snarled.

"Hey, what are you looking at?" Clark hated to be groomed, thinking it was too sissy to be all fussed over. Joe started to trim his toenails, but Clark kept pulling his foot away. "Clark," Merit said, "stop testing Joe's patience. Let me remind you what he did to you the time you ran off."

"I remember," said Clark, sulking. Now, he stood quietly, allowing Joe to cut his toenails.

"Good boy," said Merit, walking off. Clark snarled again. "Bug off."

A van drove up.

As the dust settled, a man got out and walked around to the back, where he opened the doors. Merit called out. "They're here!" Tom came out of the house alone, closing the door on the dogs. Then Joe stepped out, but left Clark inside. Merit looked around but she couldn't see Gypsy. Then she spotted him hiding behind the tree. Just like Gypsy, she thought.

"Hi Mr. Hutchins," began Tom. "How was your trip? Find the place okay?"

"Yes," replied the man. "Good directions."

"Would you like anything to eat or drink?"

"Nope, I just stopped a while ago. Just want to drop the dogs off and get heading back so I can make it home before dark. Got a later start than I hoped for. Got a sick dog, you know."

"Mrs. Hutchins told me when she called. Sorry to hear about it," replied Tom.

"Yeah, my best girl. Hopefully the vet will be able to save her. Well, anyway, here they are. You can send me the money." The man turned. "Joy's no Joy. If it don't work out, I'll take her back."

At that, Tom walked over and got the leashes from the man. Merit could only see the legs of the dogs from behind the van's doors as they were unloaded. Hutchins and Tom shook hands and Tom led the dogs around to the side of the van. As the man was getting back inside, Merit saw... *him*. Her admirer, here was here! Gypsy came screaming out from behind the tree. "Merit, it's *him*! Clark, come here!"

Tom next led the dogs into the gate and then let them loose. Merit just stood there, frozen. But Gypsy ran up to perform the usual doggie-greeting dance that dogs do on first encounter. Merit's new friend walked slowly up to her, his head lowered. In response, Merit kept her head down. "Uh-oh," said Joe. "I think we're in for a dog fight."

"Yeah," agreed Tom. "Seems like they're stalking each other." They started to approach.

Merit and the other dog lunged for each other, then stopped nose-to-nose with their tails turned up. Puzzled, Joe and Tom looked at each other. Merit then bowed down and, as the other dog leapt forward, she spun and took off. The two greyhounds were soon running together, nipping and chasing each other.

"Well, I'll be," said Joe. "Do you think they know each other from the track?"

"I'm not sure if they were in the same kennel or raced or what... but I've never seen this behavior before," replied Tom.

Merit stopped running. She was panting and her tongue was hanging out as far as it could. Her new friend was gasping for air. "We'll have to work on getting him more fit," said Joe. "He's winded."

"You're right," said Tom. "But look at Merit. Looks like she smiling."

Merit turned to her friend. "What your name?"

"Von," he said, panting. "My name is Von."

Joe and Tom watched the two of them walk around together. Then Von said, "Come here, I want you to meet my traveling companions. Hank and Joy, this is Merit, she's the dog I told you about."

"Hi," said Joy. "We hear you're fast." Merit didn't know how to reply.

"She's the fastest!" Gypsy said.

"We'll see," said Joy. "You look pretty fast but not everyone wins all the time." With that, she walked off and did her business on the grass.

"Don't go on the grass!" yelled Gypsy. "You're supposed to go in the sandy area." In response, Joy just glared at Gypsy.

Gypsy looked at Merit. "I don't like her," he whispered.

"We don't either," said Hank. Von nodded. "She's mean."

Merit was silent. "Tom will take care of her. I'm sure of that."

"I sure hope so," added Gypsy.

Soon, Joe came out with their dishes. They all ran up, but before they got their food, Joe put muzzles on all of them. Merit, Clark and Gypsy couldn't understand why. "Muzzles?" said Merit. After all, they were all adults now. Clark only shrugged. Joe set down their bowls.

As soon as Joy was done with her dish, she looked around with a face that could only be described as cruel. Noticing that Gypsy was the only dog with any food left, Joy leapt at him and scratched at him with her front paws. Gypsy tumbled over, crying. "Hey what the..."

Joe instantly grabbed Joy. Snarling and clawing and trying to bite him, Joy was not successful: Joe maintained his hold, then carried her into the kennel and threw her into a crate. "Tom, come out here," he yelled.

"Mr. Hutchins was dead-on center about Joy. She is no joy."

"Too aggressive?"

"Yeah. I'm taking her back right now. Okay?"

Tom nodded his assent and went back inside. Merit glanced at Hank, Clark, Gypsy and Von. "I told you." The dogs watched as Joe went into the kennel, took Joy through the gate and put her into a crate in the back of the truck. As the truck roared off, Gypsy yelled at the top of her voice. "Good riddance!"

"*That's* a relief," said Hank. "She's mean and she's nasty. I'm glad she's gone."

"Me, too," echoed Von, "and the fact that she was removed so quickly speaks well of our new owners." He turned to Merit. "So, how's your nose? I see you still have a scab."

"It's healing," replied Merit.

"Well," said Hank, "I hear you're quite the hero."

"Not really. I just know how to open crate doors because King taught me."

"Will you teach me?" asked Hank.

"Maybe," said Merit, a little tease in her voice. "So Hank, where did you race?"

"Florida. I was down there for a couple of years. I guess Tom bought me and had me shipped here. Seems nice."

"It's not bad," said Clark.

But Merit was looking over at Von. She was so busy studying his face that she didn't realize that she was not paying attention. Then she noticed that all of the other dogs were looking at her. Blushing, Merit walked away.

The dogs were still standing, puzzled, when Tom came out and called them all into the kennel for the night. All obeyed, except for Merit, who didn't saunter in until everyone else was bedded down. But Merit had her reasons: she had been waiting to walk by Von's crate. As she did, he whispered softly. "Good night love."

Merit stepped into her crate. "Good night everyone," she said, wishing her voice wasn't so tight and curt. Her head was spinning. She couldn't decide if she liked how Von made her feel. Did she really like having him here? She thought she couldn't sleep with him so close. What if she snored or passed gas? As the night wore on, Merit found it impossible to relax. She wanted to pace, but didn't dare get out of her crate.

Chapter 32

Something's Different

When morning came, Merit wasn't even sure if she had ever gone to sleep. None of the other dogs were having any trouble; she could tell by listening to their steady breathing. She decided to reason with herself. After all, Hank and Von were the ones in a new home, not her. But neither sleep nor peace came to Merit.

Then Joe came in and noticed that Merit was awake. First he let her out into the yard, then looked her in the eye for what seemed to her like a very long time. He nodded. "There *is* something different about you, Merit. Something *definitely* different. At first I thought it was the scar on your nose, but it's in your eyes."

Merit yawned. Boy, she thought, am I tired. She wondered off, did her business and lay down. As she drifted of, she heard the noises of the morning routine. She was comforted by the warmth of the sun and the jingle of the dog's collars. Each dog had its own distinct jingle, she thought. Her mind continued to wander. She noticed that the sound of the kennel had changed with the loss of Music, Speedy and Sunshine, and the addition of Hank and Von.

Merit didn't know where the sound from one particular tag came from. Curious, she lifted an eyelid to see that it was Hank's collar making a tink, tink sound. Von's, noticed Merit, made a deeper, softer and clankier sound. Closing her eye again, Merit listened contentedly to the music of the kennel. Clark's familiar ting, ting sound... Gypsy's infrequent but annoying scratching sound when he moved a certain way. Merit could now remember Gypsy once telling her that he disliked the noise, too. It would be nice, thought Merit, to get Gypsy a new tag. Exhaling deeply, she finally fell asleep.

Merit awoke to the soft tinkle of Isabel's collar

Opening her eyes, Isabel looked concerned. "Merit, are you okay? You've been asleep all day."

Merit sat up, yawned then stretched, shook slowly head to toe, then shook more quickly. She shook again so wildly that this time, her feet flailed out to the sides, her body twisted back and forth from side to side. She shook out all that energy into and out the tip of her tail. Isabel chuckled. "Friend, *you* are some strange dog."

Merit smiled. "I know."

"But to know you is to love you, Merit."

"Thanks, Isabel."

Merit looked around the yard and Isabel spoke again. "Joe took the dogs for a walk, then to the track. He said, 'I'm letting

Merit sleep.' I got worried when you didn't move for hours. Sorry if I woke you."

Merit yawned again. "That okay," she said. "I needed to get up."

"How *are* things, Merit?" asked Isabel.

"Really strange right now."

"I've heard," said Isabel, "that Von is calling you his love."

"He was kenneled with us at Gulf," explained Merit. "He started talking to me one day. But Sunshine didn't like him."

"Do you?"

"I don't know. He seems nice," said Merit. The words tumbled out. "But he makes me feel weird—like I'm not myself. I feel unsure around him. I'm not sure I can act normal around him. At the kennel I tried to ignore him, but I just couldn't. Luckily I never had to race against him."

"I'm surprised you haven't," replied Isabel. "Von is pretty fast. After watching you and him run yesterday, it would be an interesting race. I wonder why you didn't compete at Gulf."

"Well I had just made the A grade. I had to work up. Maybe we would have."

"Yeah."

"Have you heard when we go back?" asked Merit.

"No, not yet. They're waiting to see how Hank and Von adjust to their training schedule. Plus, they want to give your lungs time to heal. You almost died, Merit."

"Really?"

"Do you remember anything?" asked Isabel.

"Just Gypsy yelling, and lots of smoke, fire and pain." At this, Merit eyes welled up and she breathed deeply.

Isabel was silent for a moment. "That was a challenging and heroic thing to do opening all those crates by yourself."

Merit interrupted. "I *didn't*," she said. "I couldn't have. Some other dogs helped, but I didn't know them. I hope they're okay. Who said I did it by myself?"

"Gypsy."

"That figures. I had told him to go outside... anyway." Merit inhaled again.

Isabel thought a moment. "You know it's weird. I mean, one dog can say something, and no matter how far it is from the truth, it *becomes* the truth."

"Yeah well, you won't catch me lying about that," said Merit firmly. "I *didn't* open all of those crates alone. It's wrong to say, and the other dogs who helped will think I'm taking all the credit. I'll have to tell Gypsy." Merit paused. "It's funny," she mused.

"He was there, but he wasn't there. Why is he talking about something he doesn't know for sure?"

"Dogs assume things sometimes that aren't true," offered Isabel.

"Bad practice," replied Merit.

"How do you like racing at Gulf?" Isabel asked.

"It's okay, different from being here. There's no time for rest. You're always defensive and every dog is a competitor, even if they're in a different class, and ..."

Isabel interrupted. "Then it's even worse. A dog should *never* socialize outside its grade. Especially the one beneath them."

"That's the problem with Gulf," said Merit. "It really is no fun, except for the racing. I guess that would be the idea."

"Uh-uh," said Isabel. "I never really thought of it before, but when you're at a track like Gulf, there's real anticipation about the next race. Plus, you learn the stats of the other dogs. You probably weren't there long enough in any grade, but when you've been racing in one grade against the same dog over and over, you start to notice things. Like if they're feeling sore, tired or sick. You watch their routine and notice the cues they give you about how much competition they're going to give you that day, that race."

Isabel paused, then wrinkled her nose. "Some of them even count how often you go to the bathroom. They'll look for anything that might slow you down."

"Why?" said Merit. "It makes no difference to them if I'm hurt. They still have to run."

"It's all about strategy," replied Isabel. "If you know ahead of time who the weaker dog is, you try to get them to yield to you in case there's a jam-up.

"Oh," said Merit. She thought about these points while watching a bird land and sit in the tree. "Hmmm. Has any dog ever faked something, to throw everyone off?"

"Who would think to do that?" said Isabel, laughing. "Merit, you've got some mind."

Just then, Joe came home with the dogs. Merit's heart stopped.

Isabel cocked her head. "Merit, *relax*. You're in love. Enjoy the feeling while it lasts."

"How long *does* it last?"

Isabel shrugged, "As long as it lasts. Time will tell."

Just then, Von walked up to them. "Hi Von," said Isabel. "See ya, Merit," she said, walking away.

Von smiled at Merit. "How are you doing, sleeping beauty?"

"Fine," said Merit, stretching.

"Well," he asked, "what do you feel like doing now?"

"Running!" yelled Merit. As she leapt off, he went tearing after her, barking "No fair! No fair!" Joe stood watching as Tom came out of the house. The two looked at each other. "Uh-oh," said Joe, smiling.

"We got problems," replied Tom. "Boy, do we have a problem."

"Yeah," said Joe. "I think they like each other."

"Take a look at Clark, Hank and Gypsy," said Tom, chuckling. "Don't think they haven't figured out what's gotten into those two."

It was true. Clark, Gypsy and Hank just stood there, watching the two fools chasing each other around and around. "I better put a stop to this," said Tom suddenly. "I mean, before they hurt themselves."

Tom called them over, but they paid no attention. He yelled, loud. "*Merit! Von! Stop*! Come *here*." Joe then tried one of his ear splitting, finger-in-the-mouth whistles, but nothing worked. None of this stopped them. After several minutes, the two dogs finally trotted to a stop. "That's *it*!" Tom yelled. "You'll have to be separated. We can't have you guys exhausting yourselves by running around all the time."

Tom then grabbed Merit by the collar and threw her in her crate. He next got Von, roughly put him in his container, slammed the door, and left the kennel.

"Boy, is he mad," observed Von.

"I've never seen Tom act like that," agreed Merit.

"I thought he was going to beat us," continued Von.

"Tom has never hit us," explained Merit. "But even I was scared he might."

"Always a first time," mused Von.

"I wish I had some water."

Hearing this, Von began lifting the latch to his crate. "No, don't!" said Merit. "If they come back in and…" Suddenly, she stammered. "Where? Where did you learn to open..."

"During the fire, Merit. I watched you."

"You? I let you out?"

"I'm not surprised that you don't remember," said Von. "There was a lot of smoke. I couldn't even see, but I knew it was you by the sound your collar made above the roar of the fire. Then I watched you open the crate next to me, and watched you start on the next. It took me twice as long as you, but I managed to open two."

"Wow," said Merit, slowly shaking her head. "It's just a blur." She was quiet for a moment. "How did you manage to come to Tom's?"

"I'm lucky," said Von, nodding. "Real lucky. Joe came by one day and talked to my owner, and then I was sold. I had no idea

I was coming here or that I'd ever see you again. But voila, I'm here."

Merit gazed at him. He was so confident. "My life has always been like that," continued Von. "Maybe I just *see* it as lucky, so it is. Or maybe I *am* truly lucky; whatever you want to believe."

Merit nodded, she didn't know what to say.

"You're pretty darn fast," said Von. Merit said nothing, but Von kept talking. "I think you may be faster then me," he said, laughed, and then added, "*Not*."

Merit chuckled. She was starting to relax. Maybe Von was someone she could trust. As the afternoon went on, the two talked and learned more about each other. "Have you ever been in a racing accident?" asked Merit.

"Nah," replied Von. "I've been lucky."

"There's that word again!" said Merit, groaning. The two laughed.

"Have you?" asked Von.

"Just once," said Merit, and she told him about the time she accidentally broke Sunshine's leg.

"Sounds serious," said Von. Merit noticed the way his eyebrows furrowed with concern.

"Well, she's retired to Carol's clinic."

"Who's Carol?"

"Our vet and Tom's girlfriend." Merit thought back to the kiss she saw and smiled. The two kept talking and Merit forgot how thirsty she was. Then Tom came in and took her out. He gave her food and water and let her do her business. Merit noticed a new run out in the yard. Tom came and put her into the run.

The isolated confinement did not fit Merit's temperament, she howled. Tom growled back. "Be quiet! *Sssshhh.*"

But Merit continued to protest, so Tom grabbed her and put her back into her crate inside the kennel. Then he took Von out into the yard. After a while, Tom came back in, retrieved Merit and released her in the yard.

Merit saw that Von was in the pen. Merit walked up to him. "You're in jail."

"No worries," replied Von. Hearing this, Merit sat down on the opposite side of the fence from Von. He then lay down as well. The two just looked at each other nose to nose. Joe walked up and laughed. Tom glowered at him. "Well, at least," said Tom, "this will keep them from running each other into the ground."

Joe and Tom went back inside, leaving the door open for the puppies to wander out. The trio—Patches, Licorice and Emmy—were soon sniffing around, not looking where they were going. In a moment, they all ran into the fence and looked up, cross-eyed.

The pups then put their heads down and sniffed single file all along the perimeter of the fence. When they got to Merit, they all piled on her, laughing and barking lightly. Merit kept poking them with her nose. "I'm gonna bite!" she said, giggling. In response, the pups just squealed louder.

"You," said Von, "are going to make a great mom, Merit."

She looked at him. "I hope so."

Von laughed. "We're going to have the best looking puppies. Just you wait." With that, he lay back and fell asleep." Merit played with the pups until it was time for supper. They didn't have muzzles put on, but Von was not let out of the pen. When Joe took Von's dish away, he put Clark and Gypsy in with him. Meanwhile, Merit sat outside the pen and watched them goof around.

Gypsy teased Merit. "Merit and Von are in love! Merit and Von are in love!" Both Clark and Von pounced on Gypsy, rolling him over. When he started to protest, Von and Clark walked away, giving him the cold shoulder. The two dogs whispered to each other while looking over their shoulders at Gypsy.

This was driving Gypsy to distraction. "What are you two talking about?" he whined.

"None of your business," growled Clark. Hearing this, Gypsy lay down on the other side of the fence next to Merit.

"Merit, I don't like having Von here," said Gypsy. "It's too weird. I know you like him, but that's what makes it really weird."

"I know," said Merit, nodding.

Chapter 33

Separated

Just then, Joe came to gather up all of the dogs and put them in their kennels for the night. All fell asleep quickly, and slept soundly. Joe rousted them awake the next morning, first putting Von in the run and then giving the other dogs their dishes. After Merit was finished, Joe put on her leash and caught Hank and Gypsy. First he took them for a walk through the woods, then they went directly to the track.

The dogs ran a few laps and headed back home. After Joe let them in the gate, he took Von and Clark. When they came back, Von was placed in the pen, they were given their dishes, and finally they were put in their crates.

"So, Merit," said Von, "I guess this is the way it will be for us. King told Clark that Tom and Joe aren't going to let us be together."

"Really?" said Merit. "For how long?"

"Forever—at least for now. I'm not sure. I guess we shouldn't have gotten so carried away."

"Yeah," agreed Merit. "We should have stopped when Tom called to us. If not then, at least when Joe whistled."

"I know," replied Von. "Clark said he couldn't believe that noise didn't stop us dead in our tracks. Hank said he's never heard anyone whistle that loud in his life." Von paused. "Anyway, it doesn't matter. They really can't keep us apart."

With that, Von opened his crate door and walked over to Merit's container.

"Von, *no!*" said Merit. "You'll get us into more trouble, and then Tom may actually get rid of one of us."

Von opened her door. "You worry too much," he said softly. "Good night, love."

Before Merit knew it, he had given her a soft, quick kiss, her door was shut, and Von was back in his crate. After he closed his door, Von spoke again. "Merit, you really do worry too much."

"I don't think that's the case," said Clark sternly. "I wouldn't push your luck with Tom. Do you think he and Joe are happy having to accommodate you two lovebirds by building unnecessary pens and having to keep up two different training schedules?" Clark paused. "I'd watch what you do, lover boy." With that pronouncement, Clark stretched and said good night.

The next day, the next and the next after that were all pretty much the same.

Merit was lying in the sun when Isabel walked up. "You're leaving the day after tomorrow. You, Von, Hank and Gypsy are heading back to Gulf. Tom's taking you. Joe's staying here. Then they're going to take turns each week, being away.

"It sounds like you'll be staying there a while."

"I figured it was time," said Merit, sighing. "These last few days were beginning to feel too comfortable. At least I get to look forward to a good grooming tomorrow."

"Ahhh," replied Isabel. "That's always a nice treat, isn't it?" For a minute or two, they watched the pups wrestle around.

"Oh no!" said Merit. "This is probably the last time I'll see your pups!"

"Don't remind me," said Isabel. "I don't think Tom is planning to keep any, now that he's got a full kennel. I mean, they'll have to be 18 months old before they can race. And every time I think of the pups going away, I get a knot in my stomach."

"They'll do well," said Merit. "You and King have done a great job with them."

"They'll be so sad to know you're leaving," said Isabel.

"They don't know yet?" said Merit

"No..."

"Please don't tell them," said Merit. "I don't want to have to say goodbye. It will be too hard."

"But don't you want them to know that this may be the last time they see you?" asked Isabel.

"No I want them to be happy," said Merit. "And I don't want them to worry. If we just leave, it will be easier."

"Yes, Merit, for you it *will* be easier," said Isabel firmly. "But my puppies should be able to say goodbye, especially because you're so special to them."

"I guess you're right," said Merit. "Pups!" she called. "Come over here!"

Hearing Merit's voice, the pups came bounding up, then stopped, all panting. The trio had begun to lose their puppy fat, with their noses and legs becoming long and slender. "Why look at you," marveled Merit. "You're almost all grown. I hadn't noticed. It happened so gradually. Now, I have something to tell you."

Emmy cocked her head, Patches lay down, and Licorice stood panting. Merit chose her words carefully. "I'm leaving tomorrow to go to Gulf Park." The pups nodded.

"The thing is, I don't know when I'll be back. So I just wanted to let you know how much I enjoyed watching you grow, and getting to play with you. And you'll always be friends of mine." Merit felt herself tearing up. "I hope we get to see each other again soon."

"But, we *will* see you soon, right Merit?" asked Patches.

"I hope so," said Merit.

"When?" asked Emmy.

"I don't know." said Merit, her voice trailing off.

"But not too long, right?" said Licorice.

"I don't know, but I'll be gone for a while. So it's just goodbye for now."

"Oh," all of the pups said, sitting very still. "When do you leave?"

"The day after tomorrow," said Isabel gently.

"Clark too?" asked Patches.

"And Gypsy?" asked Licorice. "And Von and Hank, too? *All* of them?" Isabel nodded.

"Ohhhh, it will be sooo boring here with just Mom and Dad." Patches groaned.

"So, said Isabel," you guys better go say your good-byes."

With that, the pups ran off. Isabel looked at Merit fondly. "See, that wasn't so hard now, was it?"

"No, but they don't understand it like I do," replied Merit. "It would be lovely to get to watch them grow up. I bet they'll make fine racers. Look at them. Licorice's right front turns in a bit. May cause her problems, but it's not too bad."

Isabel agreed with her friend. Soon it was time for dinner. Again Von let himself out of his crate and sneaked over for a good night kiss. But other than that, he and Merit followed the rules.

Chapter 34

Merit Works it Out

Merit awoke the next day looking forward to her grooming. Sure enough, Joe and Tom were preparing for the track. She was grateful to Isabel for telling her what would be happening, it helped to prepare Merit. After all, it was much more difficult to adjust to changes in their routine at Gulf since she never knew what to anticipate. No wonder the dogs are more nervous at the track, she thought. It's not the racing or the competition, more, it was the uncertainty.

Joe called to Merit. Tail wagging, she ran over and hopped up and down in front of him. Laughing, he took her to the wash rack and gave her a bath. After she was all done, Joe put her in Von's pen while he let Von wander around the yard. At that point, Tom walked from the house through the yard.

"Looks like our love birds are learning to be apart," said Tom.

Joe agreed. "Yeah, looks like it." He next took Clark in for grooming, then Hank, Gypsy and finally, Von. Still stuck in the pen, Merit began howling, "*Hey*, let me *out*!"

"Sssshhh!" said Joe. Merit did not obey. He then tried to quiet her down by talking softly, then loudly. When neither worked, he grabbed the hose and squirted Merit, but that didn't help either. The howling continued until Joe finally let her out of the pen.

Like magnets, Von and Merit came together nose to nose. Merit bowed down, sprung, and away they went. Joe cussed and Tom ran back into the yard. First the two men ran after Von, who was chasing Merit. Gypsy decided to join in the fun but Hank and Clark sat on the sidelines.

"This isn't good," said Clark said Hank.

"Nope," replied Hank. "This is not going to be pretty."

Luckily, Merit caught the expressions on their faces as she ran by, and stopped dead in her tracks. Von was able to jump over her just in time, but Tom and Joe came crashing down on top of her. At that point, Merit started yelping. Tom got up quickly but Joe was having a hard time. In a few moments, Tom was able to help Joe up, and the two glared at Merit.

Merit stopped yelping. She lay quietly and perfectly still. "Is she breathing?" asked Joe. Panicking, Tom knelt next to Merit; at that point, she looked up and licked his nose. Jumping up, she walked into the kennel and into her crate.

"I'll be!" said Joe. "Well, I never..." added Tom. But Merit knew she was in trouble. She lay down and sighed. Only a few moments went by before Joe came in. He pulled her out of her crate. Merit put her tail between her legs, unable to look him in the eye. He was feeling down her sides and legs when Tom came in.

"Seems okay," said Joe. "But what should we do with these two?"

"Well," replied Tom, "let's just keep them separated until they leave tomorrow. When they get to Gulf, they'll be in different kennels anyway, so they won't be able to see each other."

"Until –" said Joe, drawing in a deep breath, "they race against each other."

"Well, getting them to run shouldn't be a problem."

"That's true," replied Joe. "Should I put her back in her crate after we walk?"

"Yeah," said Tom. "Take her and Hank for a walk. Then rub her down afterwards to make sure nothing's knotted up."

Agreeing, Joe put Merit's leash on, but she still refused to look him in the eye. He next grabbed her nose and stared at her, but she was looking off to the side. "Merit," said Joe softly, "It's... *okay*." She looked at him then. He patted her on the head and they walked out to get Hank.

"So Merit, what's the deal with you and Von?" asked Hank.

"What do you mean?"

"Well, why do you guys have to run crazy like that when you get together?"

"I'm not sure,"

"You know," replied Hank thoughtfully, "you should think about your actions and how they affect other dogs around you. I mean, when you get Joe and Tom angry, it makes it more difficult for the rest of us."

Merit didn't answer. She could hear Hank, but all she could think about how she wouldn't get to see Von at Gulf.

Then Merit spoke. "Hank, you just got here. Who are you to tell me how to behave?"

"I'm just trying to make you aware of the consequences of your behavior," said Hank. "When Tom and Joe are mad, they don't hand out treats or pat us. They just walk around fuming, ignoring us. I think we end up getting punished more than you."

Merit softened. "I hadn't thought of it that way. I'm... I'm sorry, you're right. When they get mad, their mood is so dark they're not nice to any of us." Why in fact, asked Merit to herself, did she behave so poorly? Why had she acted so foolishly, so utterly unlike herself, when she was around Von? She suddenly realized that Von didn't really know her. He couldn't really love her either, a foolish dog that disrespected her owner, her friends, and even herself. Perhaps it wouldn't be a bad thing to not see Von for a while, this way; at least, she could maintain a sense of control.

But, wondered Merit, can I maintain a sense of control around Von? She could and she would. I don't have to be so out of control when I'm around Von, thought Merit. This is not how I want to behave. "I only hope," said Merit, under her breath, "that I get the chance."

Hank interrupted her thoughts.

"I knew this gal once. She gave me the jitters. We were kenneled together and she was really sweet..." Just then, a moth flew in front of Hank. He snapped at it, caught it and ate it. Merit watched, amazed. "I acted like a goof around her," continued Hank. "I realized that she really didn't care for me. Probably because I acted like such a dope around her."

Hank paused, perhaps looking for another bug to eat. "I guess it's part of life. A stage everyone goes through. Hopefully, Merit, you'll realize that it's not working before too much damage is done. Just think if you acted up on the track! You'd be dismissed so quickly, and then what?" Hank was quiet. "We all have to keep an eye on preserving our standing. Keeping what we have. And I know it's a struggle."

Merit suddenly realized how much was a stake for all of the dogs. She had become too comfortable back at the kennel. Did she even have the right mind set to race at Gulf? The bottom line is that she was, at best, ambivalent about the track.

"Are you looking forward to going to Gulf?" asked Merit.

"Not really," replied Hank. "This lifestyle is more to my liking, more relaxed."

"We're sort of on the same schedule with both places. But they're so different, too."

"Your kennel is your *home*," said Hank. "And the track, it's just a place you live until you get to go home."

"How old are you?" Merit asked Hank

"Four."

"Really?" Merit looked at Hank a little closer. Yes, he did have some grey hairs on his nose. "Wow, you've been racing a long time."

"I've been around lots of tracks." The two watched some birds drive a hawk away. "I'm going to miss these walks," he added.

Heading down to the track, the two did some practice drills and laps. Next, Joe quickly rubbed them down, and they walked back to the kennel. Von was in the pen and Merit walked up to him. "If we're ever together again," she said firmly, "I don't want to run around. We can't."

Von stared at her, then smirked.

"I'm serious. If you encourage me to run, I can't be your friend anymore. I *have* to be able to obey Tom and Joe."

"Okay Merit," replied Von. "I respect that. And, I'll behave." He winked at her and Merit rolled her eyes, then walked away over to the water bowl, where she drank her fill.

At that moment, Emmy scampered up. "Hey Merit, want to play?"

Gently, Merit pushed Emmy with her nose, and in response, Emmy jumped all over her. They played until it was dinnertime, then Merit ate and lay down in the yard. It was then that Isabel came walking over.

"Thank you for playing with Emmy all afternoon. She's so sad that you're going."

"Me, too," replied Merit. "I like being around you guys. But I'll be back in a few weeks. If not, I'm sure Tom will see that I'm well taken care of. I have faith in that." Merit paused. "I mean, look what he did for Sunshine. He could have easily saved lots of money by just putting her down, but he wants to do what's best for the dogs. And Isabel, you'll always be my friend, so no big good-byes. Okay?"

Isabel was quiet for a moment. "I just want you to know how much you mean to me, to us."

"I know. I love you, too," said Merit. Quietly, she began to cry, and then Joe called them in for the night.

Chapter 35

Back to the Track

Before morning had even broken, the dogs were loaded up and driven to Gulf. As they were taken out of the truck, Merit noticed that were the old kennel was only a pile of rubble with a bulldozer parked beside it. She could recognize the smell of burnt wood and felt sick to her stomach.

Joe led all the dogs past the rubble and on to another kennel. There, they were offered water and put in their crates. No one said anything. Greyhounds are usually quiet dogs, but today everyone was exceptionally quiet. Again, a man came out saying, "Here doggie," and they were led outside. The sun was bright and it was a beautiful day. A slight breeze blew as well, carrying frequent smells of wonderful food.

Merit's stomach grumbled and Gypsy laughed. "Merit, your stomach is complaining!"

"I know. I'm hungry."

"Me, too!" replied Gypsy. "They'll feed us in a little while."

"I know." With that, Merit stretched and yawned.

"Where's Von?" said Hank suddenly.

"No idea," said Merit. "But he's on a different rotation then our barn, so we probably won't see him." Looking around, they sniffed the air. "No sign of him," added Merit. At this point, Merit decided to walk over to a drinking bowl. She liked the feel of the cool water on her dry tongue. Then, trotting around and sniffing, Merit next lay down and stretched out.

Soon Cesar came and gave them their dishes. Merit got up and stretched, then shook and sprang toward her dish.

Cesar laughed. "You're *that* dog." He patted her on the head. "You're a wonderful girl." He left and Merit ate her fill.

Cesar left and Tom walked up to the pen, and silently looked at them through the fence for a while. He then opened the gate, collected the dogs and led them out to the track. They were once again put into starting boxes. And once again, the doors opened, the dogs then sprung out and chased the lure.

Immediately, Merit knew something was wrong with her.

Her lungs started to burn. She ran as fast as she could, but she couldn't catch a deep breath. As she crossed the finish line, her lungs heaved, she coughed and wheezed. Tom came up, knelt down and stroked her. She slowly caught her breath. "Merit, are you okay?" asked Hank. Merit nodded. "You're still fast," said Gypsy, trying to be reassuring. Tom petted her and then looked at the other dogs. He began to look sad. Finally, he led them off of the track and back to the paddock. There, they were rubbed down and given water. Tom left.

"I wonder what's got Tom so sad," said Merit.

"I wish Isabel was here to tell us," said Gypsy. "She overhears everything that is going on."

"Unfortunately for us, they don't talk much in front of us," said Merit.

Hank interrupted. "My last owner was constantly talking to herself. She never shut up. She was always telling me what we were going to do and how we were going to do it. At the time, I hated constantly hearing her, but at least I knew what was going on."

"It's especially bad since Joe isn't here, too," offered Merit. "Now, Tom has no one to talk to."

The Gulf man came in, once again calling, "Here doggies!" He gathered them up and brought them in for the night. Merit slept soundly.

The next day, the same dog man came. Cesar brought them their food. After eating, all of the dogs lounged out in the paddock.

"Boy," said Merit. "This routine is getting boring."

"I bet we race tonight," said Hank.

"You're probably right," replied Merit. With that, she stretched, laid down, and slept most of the day. Tom then came and took all of the dogs for a long walk around the grounds. After he returned with them, he rubbed them down and trimmed their nails. Cesar brought dinner and the other dog man returned, calling, "Here doggie doggie!"

The dogs were then led into their crates. An hour later, Tom came for Gypsy. Gypsy returned not long after. "How did you do?" asked Merit.

"I got third."

"Good show!" barked Hank.

Tom then placed Gypsy back in his crate and got Merit. Led down the corridor out into the yard, she and Tom walked into the weight room, where Merit was placed on a scale. "Seventy-two pounds!"

Tom then led her away and placed the blanket over her head, pulled it down and gently placed the waistband. A muzzle was fastened over her ears. Tom then handed Merit to the track aide, and from there, she was led in front of the grandstand. Merit noticed that it wasn't that full.

Next, placed in the number three starting gate, Merit crouched down, ready to spring. Finally the door opened, and out she flew. Her feet carried her quickly around the track, kicking up dirt. Her heart pounded, her lungs burned and her eyes watered, but Merit ran as fast as she could. When the race was over, she stopped. She coughed and wheezed, then coughed more. Hearing this, the track aide ran up and called for the track vet. As soon as he got to Merit, Tom jumped over the railing and came running up.

Merit gave one big cough and stopped.

The vet looked her over, mostly listening to her lungs. "She seems fine. Just a little rattle, doesn't sound serious."

"I know," replied Tom. "She was in the fire. She had some damage, but I was told her injuries weren't bad enough to end her career."

"Obviously, you're right," continued the vet. "She not only won that race, she set a new record. I would tell you not to let her overexert herself, but she seems no worse for wear."

"Thanks for looking at her," said Tom.

"Not a problem. When do you plan to race her again?"

"If everything looks good, day after tomorrow."

"See you then," said the vet, beginning to turn away. "I want to check her out before her next race."

Nodding his assent, Tom led her off the track, patted her on the head and removed her muzzle and jersey. He then rubbed her down and gave her a nice warm bath. Next, he put her under a heat lamp. There, he rubbed her dry, filed her nails and brushed her teeth. Finally, he returned her to her kennel.

Gypsy turned to Merit. "I heard you broke another track record."

"Who told you?" said Merit.

"Two guys walked by and Hank and I could tell they were talking about you, especially when they mentioned your cough. They said that the vet has decided to monitor you closely. You might not be allowed to race if you cough."

"Really? They said that?"

"Yep."

"Wow," replied Merit. "I feel fine. I just got a little winded. It's not like I'm walking around the track."

"I know," said Gypsy. "But one of the guys said that he's never seen a dog cough without there being something seriously wrong."

"What does he know?" said Merit. "I feel *fine*." With that, she lay down and sighed.

Chapter 36

The Cough

All of Tom's dogs were out in the paddock the next day when Carol arrived. She came up to Merit and led her outside. She listened to Merit's lungs and then walked her into an examining room and put on an apron. She positioned Merit, told her to stay, and walked around the corner. There was a buzz, and Carol walked back in and moved Merit around. Once again, she told Merit to stay and once again, she walked around the corner. Again was a buzz. Merit stood there as Carol walked up, patted her on the head and offered her a treat. Merit gently took it from her hand.

When Carol took Merit back to the kennel, Tom was there, smiling.

"Hello," he said, softly.

"Hi." The two kissed.

"It's good to see you. It's good to see you, too. I'm, I'm sorry to hear about your mother."

"Yes." Tom's face grew tight and his voice cracked. "It was her time to go. I'm glad she didn't have to suffer anymore."

"Yes, but it's still sad." They hugged.

Merit finally found out why Tom was upset the other day. Oh no wonder he was so sad, Merit thought. After a minute, Merit nudged Tom's leg with her nose. "Can I have some water?"

He smiled and pulled away from Carol. "Did you look at the x-rays?"

"Not yet, just took them and I need to go develop them? Want to come?"

"Sure," said Tom. He placed Merit back into the pen and walked away.

"Where did you go?" asked Gypsy.

"To get some x-rays," said Merit.

"Why?" said Hank.

"For my lungs, I guess," replied Merit. "Did you hear about Tom's mom?"

"Yes," murmured Hank. "How terrible."

"Yeah," added Gypsy.

None of the dogs saw Tom until the next day when it was time to race.

First he took Gypsy to the track and when they returned, Hank and Merit were collected. "Does this mean we're racing together?" asked Hank.

"Maybe," replied Merit.

Led to the weight room, the “Here doggie!” man declared that Hank was 74 pounds.

The track vet approached Merit, Tom and Carol. Carol spoke first. “Hi, here are the x-rays you wanted to take a look at. The two of them walked into an office. Shortly they came out. The man listened to Merit’s lungs. “I don’t hear anything of great concern. Trot her around and see how she breaths. Tom quickly led Merit up the shed row and back. As Merit trotted she concentrated on keeping every breath even and shallow. The vet listened to her lungs again. Merit could feel the tension. The vet finally said I hear some congestion but it doesn’t seem to be deep. After a pause he said Ok, let her race. I’ll check her again afterwards.”

Merit weighed in at 70 pounds. Muzzles and blankets were then placed on them just before they were handed over to the track aides. “Good luck, Hank” called out Merit.

“You, too,” replied Hank.

Merit noticed that the grandstand was not as empty as the day before. It was all becoming routine: the two were placed into their starting boxes and the gate flew open. This time, Merit was caught by surprise and scrambled to get a foothold. The pack was already far ahead, but she still sprinted with all of her might.

Merit passed one dog, then another, and was closing in on a third when he swerved into her path. Merit leaped over him and ran past two others. The race was over, and she had finished in third place.

Merit stopped and began to wheeze. Feeling her body shake with a coming cough, she held it in. Then the track vet walked up to her and she took two deep breaths, struggling to keep her breathing regulated and smooth. As he was listening to her lungs, Tom walked up. "She sounds much better today, than yesterday," said the vet. "She can continue to race." Tom took a deep breath. "Thanks Doc."

After collecting Merit and Hank from the aides, Tom took Merit into the weight room to have her muzzle and blanket removed. She gave two quick deep coughs and Tom just looked at her. Merit could tell he was puzzled. He rubbed them down, gave them their dishes and took them back to their crates.

"What happened, Merit?" asked Hank.

"I couldn't get out of the box."

"That was *you* flying up on us? That was quite a comeback!"

"I tried to catch you," replied Merit, "but I couldn't."

Gypsy interrupted, "What about the vet?"

"Merit's fine," said Hank. "She can race."

"Cool," replied Gypsy. All exhausted, the trio fell fast asleep.

The next day was just like their last day off. First they went for a walk. Then there were rub downs and three meals. The day after that was a race day, and like all of the other race days before.

"All of these races are beginning to feel the same," said Merit. The dogs nodded, it seemed that they had been racing at Gulf now for a long time.

"It's boring around here," agreed Gypsy. "Nothing changes except the weather."

"But things can change at any time without any notice. So we should just enjoy it."

Merit nodded. "Yes, remember to be careful what we wish for." And the race season went on and on and on…

Chapter 37

Indifference

Merit woke up to a hard rain.

Her first thought was once again having to race in cold, wet mud. It was not anything to look forward to. Just then, Gypsy woke. "It's raining *again*?! Man, another day of walking around the indoor arena." Hank awakened next but didn't open his eyes. "I can tell by the sound of the rain hitting the roof *and* by your whining," he said wearily, "that it's raining. So when someone from the track comes, just tell him I've died. That way, I can just lie here."

At that point, Cesar arrived with their food. "Yummy," said Hank. But he didn't get up. Merit and Gypsy did get up and eat. After they were finished, they lay back down, but no one uttered a word. Joe was next to arrive. It was his week at the track and he opened their doors. "At least Joe and Tom get to rotate weeks," said Merit. "It breaks up some of the monotony."

"Yeah," said Hank.

"Whoopee," added Gypsy.

Joe tried to coax the dogs out of their crates, but they wanted nothing to do with such an idea. "Come on dogs, don't you want to go for a walk?" "No," said Hank.

"Yes, if we can walk somewhere *else*," offered Merit.

But Joe wasn't listening. He grabbed each dog and took each out of its crate. "You guys are in a foul mood today," he said, nonetheless offering them each a treat. Each dog gently took the offering, but there was little enthusiasm. "Hmmm," said Joe to himself. He then led them down the shed row, straight outside and into the rain.

Gypsy squealed. "He's a nut! He's not walking us indoors and we'll catch cold." Gypsy started to shiver, but then he noticed the rain was not that chilly. With Joe, the dogs walked through the parking lot, out the front gates and onto the sidewalk. "Where is he taking us?" asked Merit. "Beats me," replied Hank.

The group walked a few blocks one way and a few blocks another way until they were overlooking acres of green grass, lots of trees and a pond with some ducks. No one was around.

"No one's here," said Merit.

"That's because it's raining," replied Hank.

"Hey," said Gypsy. "At least we're away from the track."

Joe led them to the center of the park, through a gate, and let them run loose. Going from bush to bush and tree to tree, the dogs were still exploring when the rain stopped and the sun came out. Merit shook herself and water flew out of her downy coat. Gypsy and Hank followed suit. They continued to sniff and roam until Joe called to them. He put their leashes back on and led them back out the gate, then a few blocks down and a few blocks over, until they were back at Gulf. Returned to the track, they were given warn baths, rubs and hot dishes.

"I'm glad we got to go to the park today," said Merit, beginning to fall asleep for the night. "How nice was that?"

"It was wonderful," said Hank. "It made me feel like a real dog, not just this racing machine. I hope we go again soon." Gypsy and Merit agreed and soon, all three had dozed off. When Joe came and got them that night, preparing to race, they rose quickly and walked out of their crates. Once the evening races were over, Merit realized that she didn't mind the conditions of the track.

"It's kind of fun racing in the mud," she said.

"Really bogs me down," replied Gypsy. "I don't like it."

"It *is* different," said Hank. "Could you imagine what it would be like if we had to race indoors? How boring would that be if the track conditions never changed!"

"Yeah, at least we get *some* unpredictable stuff in our lives," said Merit, yawning. "Good night, everyone."

And the season went on and on until…

It was Merit's turn to race.

She was a trim 72 pounds and had her muzzle and blanket put on her. Tom handed her over to the track aide, who then placed her in the starting block. Merit crouched, waiting to spring. She waited and she waited, noticing that the dog next to her was clawing at the door. "What a fool!" she thought, shaking her head. "How in the world did that dog get into the A grade by pawing at the gate?"

At that moment, the gate opened. Sprinting out, Merit leapt past the pawing dog and looked over her shoulder. It was Von. "Von!" she yelped. "Merit!" he said, as they ran side by side. "Where are you boarded? I'm in the kennel furthest from the track." "We're in the closest," replied Merit. "Better run!" "Go!" replied Von, as the two sprinted past the competition side by side and neck by neck.

The race was over and Merit wasn't sure who had won. "It's a photo finish!" a voice boomed over the loud speaker. With that, the track aides came and collected the dogs. Tom gathered up Merit and Von was lead away by a man Merit had not seen before. As she was being rubbed down and given water and a treat, she could do no more than wonder. Tom then walked Merit around to order to cool her down. Every now and then he would pat her on the head and say tell her what a good girl she was. And, she *did* feel good.

A man passed by Tom. "That was the best race I've ever seen."

"Yeah," replied Tom. "Pretty exciting."

"You got yourself a couple of fast dogs now Tom," continued the man. "What's your secret?"

"I don't have one. I just got some dogs that like to run. Just lucky, I guess."

"When will they race against each other again?"

"Don't know."

"Well," said the man, "Let me know. I want to see it!" As he passed, Tom patted Merit on her head.

As soon as Tom put Merit in her crate, she laid down.

"Good race?" asked Hank.

"I raced against Von."

Gypsy gasped. "*Really?*"

"Yes."

"But how did it *go*?" pressed Hank.

"Well, I'm not sure who won, but everyone says it was a good race."

"Hmmm, a photo finish," nodded Hank.

"You know you won," said Gypsy.

"Not for sure," replied Merit. Sighing, she fell asleep.

Chapter 38

Outdoors

All of the dogs woke up to Joe calling their names. They could tell by the lack of daylight that they were going to the park. "Goody!" said Gypsy. "About time," grumbled Hank. "We need to do something different." "Yeah," said Clark. "I was getting so bored."

Joe looked at Merit and laughed. "Why do you hop around all excited while the rest of them just stand there?"

"Because," explained Merit, "I like adventures." But, as usual, Joe didn't hear her.

"This should be fun," said Clark. "I'm looking forward to our adventure, too."

Setting out, all of the dogs were silent as they took in the new scenery. Merit sniffed the air as she walked, her nose wiggling back and forth, raised high in the air. She took a deep breath and relaxed. The sun was rising, taking away the bite from the morning chill. Everything was quiet; there wasn't even any traffic as they were led down the street.

Coming to the park, Joe took them into the fenced area and let them loose in the field. As they roamed and sniffed, Merit sighed. "Ahhhh, I needed this."

"We all did," said Clark.

"Thank goodness," added Hank, "that Joe does this for us."

"I wonder why Tom doesn't bring us?" questioned Gypsy. "Maybe Joe hasn't told him he brings us here?" replied Merit.

"But why wouldn't he say something?" continued Gypsy.

"I don't know," said Hank. "Maybe he just wants to do this for us and he doesn't want to ask permission."

"Maybe," Clark replied. "We'll never know." "I just wish," said Hank, "that Tom would bring us, too. Then we could come here more often."

"Yep," said Clark. "Of course, we could always come here *ourselves* –" said Gypsy. "Merit could get us out of our crates."

"No way," interrupted Merit. "It would be dangerous for us to come all this way by ourselves."

"We'd get in too much trouble if we got caught," agreed Clark.

The dogs continued to explore and sniff around and around. When Joe called for them, they obediently went up to him. After giving them all water, he led them back to the track.

"It's amazing how good I feel," said Merit, exhaling deeply. "So energized." Joe let them loose in their paddock and then gave them their dishes. They rested most of the day after that.

Merit woke up to Clark talking. "Look at all of these people. Must be a big race day."

"I've never *seen* so many people here," said Hank.

"Look at those little people," added Gypsy.

"Those are children," said Clark.

"Why are all of these people here?" asked Merit. Now, some of those people were stopping in front of their crates.

"Look," said one man. "There's Merit." Merit cocked her head to one side.

"She's pretty," a woman said.

"Look at how muscular she is," observed the man.

"They're all too skinny," another woman chimed in.

Another woman laughed. "I think you're just jealous." The group walked away.

"Hey Merit," said Joe, just walking in. "You're getting to be known." Making his way through all of the people milling around, he collected the dogs and started leading them out to their pen when a man walked up.

"My name is Bryan Jones. I'm a staff writer for *The Telegraph*." Jones handed Joe his business card. "I'd like to ask you a few questions for a story I'm writing about Merit."

Clark chuckled. "Why Merit, you're becoming famous!"

"Famous?" asked Merit. "What does that mean?"

"When people hear about you and then want to know more about you."

"Oh," said Merit, puzzled. "What's good about that?"

"Nothing," replied Hank, "Except that you'll have people around you all the time, just wait and see."

"What's bad about it," added Clark, "is that now people will be around us too all the time. Kiss our walks in the park goodbye. They'll be following you everywhere. I've seen it happen before."

Joe had finished answering the reporter's questions. But as they walked all walked outside, there were more people by their pen. "Excuse me, excuse me," he said, trying to lead the dogs into their pen. No one really moved.

"Is that her?" asked one. "Is that Merit?" asked another. "Can we pet her?" asked a third.

"No", said Joe firmly. "Let her be! Cesar!" he yelled.

Merit, Joe and Clark lay down, but people kept walking by.

"I've never seen so many people," said Merit.

"It's crazy," agreed Gypsy.

It took several minutes, but Joe finally returned with Cesar. "Folks," said Cesar, "this area is closed. Unless you have a pass, you must leave." Looking around, the crowd listened and began to disperse. "Thanks for getting them to leave," said Joe.

"I'll put up the barricades so the general public can't come back here," replied Cesar. "Some dog you've got!" he added, chuckling. "I haven't had to secure this area since Golly Bob raced here."

That night, just as Merit was being weighed and dressed for a race, she saw Von. They looked at each other and nodded their hellos. Merit knew he was going in the number nine starting position, and that she would be in the third position. As Merit was led past the grandstand, she saw it was packed full of people, in fact, she had never seen a crowd this large.

The announcer was booming off their names. "Slaid, Betty Marie, Merit, Guy, Foolish Fancy, Dreamer, Wink, Jewel and Von." The crowd went wild.

Merit was placed in the starting box. She crouched. The gate flew open and out she flew. Her legs pounded hard as she dug in the dirt. Her body nearly folded in half as she sprang out, all legs outstretched. As Merit passed Slaid, he tried to slow her down by getting in her way. But Merit was able to corkscrew her body in mid-air and avoid hitting him. Somehow, she managed to land soundly, and kept on running. Merit then made it safely to the front of the pack and ran until the lure stopped. The crowd was going crazy... throwing things, stomping their feet, yelling and cheering.

Merit began to tremble. When the handler came to get her, Merit discovered that she couldn't move. The handler first tried pulling Merit and then gently coaxing her, but she wouldn't budge. Instead, Merit was frozen, her tail between her legs, visibly shaking.

Just then, Von walked by with his handler. "Merit, it's okay," he said, smiling. "They won't hurt you, I promise. Come along now."

Merit fell in step alongside her love, and the handler was visibly relieved that she had moved. "That was some race," yelled Von over the crowd. "I couldn't even catch you today, Merit. I've never seen you run that fast. I think you may have broken your own record again."

"Oh," replied Merit. As they were led into the room, Merit realized she was glad to be away from the crowd. "I don't like all that noise," she murmured. "It hurts my ears"

"Mine, too," said Von.

Joe came in, handed Hank over to a handler and then came to collect Merit.

"See ya!" Von barked.

"Later!" replied Merit. As she was led out outside, she also turned and barked out good luck to Hank, who nodded. By now, she had cooled down.

The spectator area seemed practically deserted; Merit thought that most of the people must be watching the races from the grandstand. She was also tired and her left hind leg ached. Joe seemed to notice as well. "Merit, are you favoring your leg?" He felt her over, then led her to their office and got some ice out of the freezer. "Hold still, girl. I need to ice your leg, you've got some swelling." Merit obeyed while Joe held the ice pack around her, then watched as he grabbed a towel and wrapped that around the ice pack and placed it against Merit's leg. Merit's leg was getting cold and numb.

Joe patted her head. "You're being a good girl." She wagged her tail, and Joe then meticulously felt her legs, each muscle, tenderly but firmly, his eyes looking into hers to notice any flinch or shadow of pain. As Joe felt her right front foot, he hit a tender spot.

"Ouch!" yelped Merit. Joe probed a little more and then was quiet. "Merit, I think you may have broken a bone." He reached for the desk phone and called Tom. "Yeah, she raced great, but we have a problem, we need to x-ray Merit's foot. I think she may have broken something. There's some clicking of bone." Joe listened and began to speak again. "She did get crossed up when she was passing Slaid. She must have tweaked herself then, because her left hind is swelling and her right front is tender. Uh-uh." There was more talking on the other end. "Yep. Okay, see you then." Joe got out another ice pack and told her to lie down.

Merit quietly whimpered as she lowered herself. "Ouch, ouch, ouch."

Joe wrapped her foot completely in ice, then placed another pack on her back leg. He sat next to her on the floor, stroking her head. After a while he got up, filled a dish with water and put it in front of her. "Want some water, Merit?" Merit drank deeply. When she was done, she looked up at Joe and wagged her tail. He moved the dish and sat down again and Merit put her head in his lap.

With a start, Joe spoke. "Oh my god, Hank! I've got to go. I'll be right back!" As he closed the office door behind him, Merit looked around, then got up and gingerly stretched and shook. She began to look around for food, but saw nothing on the desk or counters, or even in the trashcan. She sniffed more, there was a good smell near the refrigerator, in the cabinet. Merit opened the door.

Pulling boxes out, she out tore open the cardboard on one. Merit sniffed, What was this? She tasted it, and it was so good that she stuck her nose inside and tried to take a bigger bite.

When her mouth was full, she tried to pull her head out from the box but couldn't.

Using her front paws to grab the box didn't work either. Now she swung her head madly from side to side, but still couldn't get the cardboard off her head. Merit couldn't see and she couldn't breathe. It was panic time: Merit flailed, bumping into the desk. The pain caused her to suck in her breath and, she choked on the food. Trying as hard as she could, she couldn't catch her breath or get the box off of her head.

Merit collapsed.

Chapter 39

Predicament

"What happened?!" Joe dropped Hank's leash and ran up to Merit, then pulled the box off her nose. "Merit! Merit! Merit!" Grabbing her head, Joe listened to her chest, then grabbed her jaws and pulled them apart, then took his finger and cleared away the food. He blew into her nose and mouth, again and again.

Letting out a cough, Merit gasped for breath. "Thank god," said Joe. "Thank god." He gazed at Merit. "Merit, you're too smart for your own good."

Hank had stayed on the sidelines. "Are you okay, Merit?"

"Yes... but it's a good thing you guys came in when you did." She was shaking.

"You must have been scared, Merit. You're shaking."

"I didn't know what to do," said Merit, gulping her breaths. "I'd tried everything I could think of. I would have died if you hadn't come in."

Joe picked up the shreds of cardboard and swept up the food. He gave both dogs some water. "Okay, let's take Hank to his crate." As they were led to their boxes, Hank spoke.

"Merit, where are you going?"

"Not sure," replied Merit.

"Did you hurt yourself? You're limping."

"Yeah," said Merit. "Got tangled up in the race. How was your race?"

"Frustrating!" said Hank with a snarl. "I got boxed in behind Dolly and Simon and I couldn't get by. Got third."

"Bummer," said Merit.

Placed in his crate, Hank turned toward Merit. "Take it easy."

"You, too," replied Merit. With Joe, she was led to the track vet's office. "Hi Joe. Bring her around back here." The vet looked her over in the examining room while Merit lay quietly, first touched and then x-rayed. "Definitely fractured," said the vet, returning with Merit's film. She broke this bone in her foot," he said, pointing at the picture. "Bad break, hard to heal. Your best bet is to probably put a pin in her foot."

Joe sighed. "Let's call Tom."

The men left the room. Merit stood at the door, whimpering and shaking. She was hurting, and she was scared.

"Shhh, Merit," said Joe, coming back in. "It's okay. You're going to have little surgery to put a pin in your foot. I promise, it will be okay." At that moment, a woman came through the door.

"Hi Joe. I'm Cathleen and I'm here to prep Merit. When was the last time she ate?"

As Joe answered her questions, he stroked Merit's head. She was not as scared as she had been. The woman stood up and quietly led Merit out the back door and into a kennel, where she was placed in a crate. After a few hours, Merit was let outside to do her business, then brought back in and placed on a cold steel table. Next, Merit felt a shot, and she slept. When Merit woke up, she was back in her crate and had a bandage around her foot. Her head was dizzy: she tried to stand, but she was too groggy. So she lowered her head and went back to sleep.

Joe was calling out.

"Merit, Merit, wake up." Lifting her head up, she wagged her tail. "Come on, girl. Let's go." He led out of the track hospital and back to her kennel, Tom was on the phone.

"How is she?"

"Looks sound."

"Good. Thanks for taking care of things.

"No problem," said Joe. "I'll call you when I get home."

"Okay."

With that, Joe grabbed a bag and led Merit out into the parking lot. Merit was so excited she hopped and barked, "I'm going home! I can't wait to see Isabel!"

Joe looked down at her. "Get in front, Merit. Step up. Slowly. I don't want you jumping."

Chapter 40

Alone

The drive seemed to take forever. They stopped for gas, then food, and then bathroom breaks. Merit was growing impatient. If Tom was driving, she thought, they'd be home already.

When they reached the kennel, Merit got out of the truck and looked around. It was the same, but different. It was strange, thought Merit, that there were no dogs in the yard. "Where is everyone?" Merit asked Joe. But as usual, he didn't say anything. Instead, Joe led her into the yard and, instead of taking her to the kennel, took her inside the house.

There was another surprise: there were no dogs they're waiting to greet her. Merit's heart fell as Joe led her to Isabel's bed and told her to lie down. He picked up the phone. "Hi it's me. We're here. No. Yes. Uh-uh. Doing good. You take care, too." After hanging up, Joe gave Merit a dish, sat on the couch and turned on the television. Merit sighed.

For days, Merit and Joe lived together, alone. Merit found herself becoming sadder and sadder because she didn't know what had happened to all of her friends. Joe gave no clues. All he said was "Come, sit, stay, eat." She was bored, lonely and sad; the days dragged on and on.

One day, Joe took her for short walk and when they returned, a van was in the driveway. Merit looked around, but could neither see nor smell her old friends. A man got out. "Hey Joe! I brought King back. Nice dog."

"We like him," replied Joe.

The man opened the back of the van and King came out. "King!" said Merit, wagging her tail.

"Merit!" exclaimed King. "When did *you* get here?"

"A while ago... but... but... where have you been? And where is Isabel?"

King gazed at Merit sadly and then spoke softly. "Oh, you don't know. How could you have known?"

Merit's eyes closed. "How?"

"I think her heart just gave out. She was running around and she just... dropped."

Merit began to cry. "It's good to see you Merit," continued King. "What brings you back?"

"Oh, I had surgery on my toe. But where were you, King?"

"I went to another kennel to breed with their dogs."

"Oh," was all Merit could think to say. Joe put the two old friends into the yard and they lay down together. Merit kept expecting Isabel to come out the door. King looked steadily at Merit. "I'm haunted by her. Every time I do anything, I can feel her with me. It's a wonderful feeling, but it's the greatest loss I've ever felt. She still feels so close and so real, but I can't touch her, talk to her or hear her. Oh Merit, what am I going to do?" Merit could only shake her head. She, too, felt an enormous loss.

Now, it was three living together, and for the first time, Merit realized that she had no set routine. Everyday was different, nothing was as it was. Joe left and Tom returned, but their routine did not. She was not walked everyday and was allowed to come and go into the house as she pleased. Perhaps, thought Merit, I'm retired. Maybe I won't get to race anymore.

"Am I retired now?" Merit asked King. He shrugged his shoulders listlessly. "I don't know. What do I know?" Merit tried to hang around, maybe she could learn something, but the people were preoccupied by something called a wedding. So Merit just moped.

One day Joe returned from Gulf with Clark, Gypsy, Hank and Von. Merit's heart leapt.

Running up to the fence, she barked loudly. "I'm so glad you're here!"

"Merit!" they sang back. "We didn't know what had happened to you."

"I had surgery. I've been retired, I think"

Clark laughed. "No you haven't. When we go back to Gulf, you and Von will be racing."

Gypsy interrupted. "Yeah, it's being called The Race of the Century!" He howled with laughter.

Merit looked at Von, puzzled.

"Yep, Merit, we're in this hyped up race. That we *do* know." Clark agreed and Merit broke into a grin. "Great! I was getting so bored here." With that, Joe put Von in his special pen in the yard and Merit lay down in front of him. Clark, Gypsy and Hank lay down next to Merit.

It had to be brought up. Merit asked if they had heard about Isabel.

"No –"

"She died. She's not here anymore." A tear slid down Merit's cheek as she softly sobbed.

"Wow," said Clark. "It's so unexpected."

"That's so sad, offered Gypsy.

"She was so nice," said Merit. "When I first got here... she... she took care of me."

"How is King taking it?" asked Von.

"He doesn't seem the same," said Merit, softly.

"I'm having trouble believing it myself." Clark said.

"It's just not the same here without her," said Merit, sighing.

"Me, I expect her to walk out of that door over there," added Gypsy.

The door opened and King walked up. "Hey guys!" he yelled. "I'm glad to see you."

King walked over and lay down with the group. "It was really lonely here after the pups and... ah... Is... Isa... Isabel left...it's good to have you back."

"It's good to be back," said Clark.

Merit had some questions of her own. "Have you guys been racing a lot?"

"Yeah," replied Von. "The pace has picked up. I'm racing five days a week now."

"I raced five last week," added Hank.

"What have you been doing, Merit?" asked Gypsy.

"Nothing since I broke my foot. Things are so different now. I get to sleep in the house."

"Not for long if you keep getting into the trash," said King.

"Merit!" scolded Hank. "Haven't you learned your lesson?" He then told everyone about the cardboard box incident.

"You'd better watch out," said Clark sternly. "Or you'll end up dead." As the sun was setting, Clark lowered his voice. "Wow, things have gotten so relaxed here."

"Well," offered Merit, "Tom and Carol are planning a wedding. I don't know what it is, but it's all they talk about." "When is it?" asked Clark. "I don't know," replied Merit.

Long after dark, the dogs were fed dinner and brought into their crates. As usual under the new rules, Merit and King got to sleep in the house. Merit heard Tom talking on the phone when she woke up.

"In a couple of weeks, this will all be over and we'll be on a beach in the Bahamas. … I know, but Joe needs a vacation, too." Tom paused, then spoke again. "Do you want to come over tonight for dinner? Okay, see you." As soon as Tom hung up, Merit got up, shook and stretched, then asked to be let out. Tom leaned over and opened the door for her, and Merit saw that the rest of the dogs were already in the yard.

After a few hours, Tom came out and gave them their breakfast.

"I don't know how much more of this I can take," said Clark, gulping his food. "Breakfast at noon."

"I don't think you have a choice," replied Hank.

"I think they call it brunch," said King.

"You won't hear me complaining," offered Gypsy. "I hate schedules."

"I have some news," said Merit. "I heard Tom on the phone. *This* schedule will last for a couple of weeks. Joe is on vacation this week and then Tom goes. Then, it will probably back to normal."

Gypsy sighed. "Ugh!"

Chapter 41

Vacation

For next few days, the dogs were fed whenever they were fed, and there were no walks. "It's funny," observed Clark, glancing at Merit and Von. "The only thing Tom really *does* take care of these days is separating the two of you."

"Very funny," replied Merit sarcastically.

"But true," added Von.

Eventually, Joe returned, and took them all for walks in the forest. "At least he's taking us out," said Von. "I got so bored lying around the yard day in and day out."

"We haven't even walked that far and I'm already winded," added Hank.

"How do they expect us to race if we're not in condition?" said Clark.

Merit didn't answer the question. "Well, personally, I'm glad for this break in the routine. For the first time I feel like a real dog, not some racing machine. Do you remember how bad it got at the track before Joe would sneak us to the park?"

"Yes," said Gypsy. "Dullsville."

Hank had a bit of wisdom to share. "We should enjoy today because who knows what tomorrow holds."

"And *that*," offered Clark, "is what my friend Sunshine would say."

Joe was a little better about keeping to the schedule and they got their daily walks. Merit and the other dogs were sunbathing when Tom and Carol returned. The dogs ran to the gate to greet them. Joe walked out of the house. "Did you have a good time?"

"Yes, it was so wonderful," replied Carol.

"Great weather!" added Tom. "And the dogs look good." Carol bent down and inspected Merit's paw. "This looks good, too." She fixed her gaze on Joe. "How has Merit been moving?"

"She seems to be 100 percent sound. Never seen her take an off-step."

"Good sign," said Tom, chuckling. Scratching Clark's head, he said, "I didn't realize how much I would miss these dogs."

Joe nodded.

"I guess where all so used to having animals around that need our care," added Carol. "It's a huge change not to have to worry about walking or feeding anything, and walking alone is foreign."

"I just like having animals around," said Joe. "While I was on vacation I went to Sea World and the wild animal park, just to check out some animals. I saw a caracal; a fascinating cat."

"They're so cool," agreed Carol. "I love their eyes."

Von caught everyone's attention by howling. "Hey! Over here." Carol laughed. "You want some attention, too!" She went over to the gate, opened it and went to step in. But Von leapt past her, ripping the gate from her grip and knocking her over. She fell with a thud. "Oh!"

Paying no attention, Von ran past her and started to run toward Tom and the rest of the dogs. But when he saw the expression on Tom's face, he stopped in his tracks and put his head down and his tail between his legs. He then looked slowly from side to side.

"Are you alright?" Tom asked Carol, helping her up.

"Yes –" she murmured, brushing off her clothes. Tom then walked up to Von—but Von turned around and walked to Carol and then nudged her with his nose. As Tom approached, Von started to tremble.

"It's okay, Von," said Carol, petting him. Sighing, Von buried his head into her side.

"What's with Von?" asked Tom.

"He thinks you're going to beat him," replied Carol.

Tom called out softly. "Von, it's okay." Reaching out to pet the skittish animal, Von flinched and moved, but Tom stood in one spot while Carol kept reassuring the dog. It took a few minutes, but Von slowly pulled his head away from Carol and looked up. "You're okay," said Tom, slowly holding out one hand to him. Von looked away.

"Hm. It's obvious that Von has been beaten," said Carol.

Tom looked at Von. "Poor guy."

Merit needed to comfort her special friend as well, so she walked up to Von and began to sniff him. "Uh-oh," said Tom, grabbing Merit's collar. "Last thing we need is you two running loose and hurting yourselves, and knocking other dogs down."

Joe spoke up. "I'll start unloading the truck, so I can get it ready to take to the track."

"Let me help you," replied Tom, handing Merit to Carol.

She led Merit into Von's pen and closed the gate. "You can stay in here for a while."

It felt good, Merit lay down and Von did the same, but on opposite sides. Joe laughed. "I guess it doesn't really matter if they're together if all they do is lie across from each other anyway."

Carol laughed as well. "So I see."

Merit and Von watched Tom, Joe and Carol go from the truck and back into the house several times. "Well," said Von lazily, "I guess we're ready to head back to the track." Merit stretched and rolled over onto her back. "I'm not sure I want to go back." Von yawned. "I don't think we have a choice. You know, the big race and all."

Gypsy walked up and lay down next to the two, then watched a bug crawling in the grass. First he snapped at it, then muttered "Yuck!"

Von shook his head and Merit wiggled back and forth. Joe and Tom were putting their crates and other race items in the truck. When they were through, they once again disappeared into the house. After a while Joe came out. "Dishes everyone!" Joe made sure that Merit was led out of the pen.

The dogs were hungry and got up quickly to eat. After finishing, Merit walked up to Von, but Joe grabbed her collar and put her back in the pen. "Noooo," she howled. "Let me *out*!" Even though Joe told her to quiet down, she refused to obey. Finally, Joe left her in the pen and went back inside the house, but Merit continued to complain.

"Merit, C'mon now, be quiet," said Von.

"Yes, it's a pain," said Clark. "It hurts my ears."

Gypsy was less tactful. "Merit, shut up!"

This last comment got Merit even madder, "No, *you* be quiet! I want *out* of here. Let me *out* of here. "

"Let yourself out," said Gypsy.

So Merit did, as she lifted the latch, she said, "I will." After that, she got a drink of water and then lay down. Von followed her and lay down beside her. It was then that Joe came back out of the house.

"Good girl! Look, I have treats!" But his face dropped when he noticed the gate open and Merit with Von. "Merit!" he shouted. Merit wanted to show that she was not really a troublesome dog, she trotted up to Joe, wagging her tail. Hoping for a treat, Von and the rest of the dogs came over as well.

Tom and Carol were out of the house. "Well, Carol, you were right," said a bemused Tom. "You said Merit would eventually stop howling. Of course, it was after she let herself out of the pen!" With that, he handed all the dogs a treat, including Merit. After gobbling their goodies, Von and Merit were looking at each other nose to nose. Tom tried to grab Merit's collar, but she pulled away and ran, and Von chased her. Merit stopped by the tree. Von did, too. She stretched and lay back down. Von did, too.

"Do you think we can let them be together?" asked Carol.

"I don't know," replied Tom. "They're very competitive. If one of them starts running, the other will give a good chase."

"Yeah," added Joe, "but they're certainly not as bad as they were when they first got together. Maybe they're mellowing."

"Maybe," said Tom. "But I don't think we can take chances." With that, Tom grabbed Von and put him in his pen. "However, maybe we can start having them boarded in the same kennel."

"It would make things a whole lot easier," replied Joe.

"Just one thing more –" said Tom. "Joe, you've got to promise me that the first time they act up, you'll send Von off to Mike."

"Will do."

Merit got up and and then sat across the fence from her love. Clark laughed. "You two amuse me to no end."

Hank gave a low chuckle. "Makes me sick, how you're so inseparable. Get a life!"

Neither Von nor Merit said anything. Gypsy spoke next. "When do you think we're leaving?"

"Soon," said Clark. "Very soon."

As Tom, Carol and Joe went into the house one more time, King sauntered out. "I guess you guys are leaving. It was good seeing all of you and good luck."

"What will you be doing?" asked Gypsy.

"Don't know," said King, shrugging his shoulders.

"You're one lucky dog," said Clark. "You get to hang out here with Carol. She'll take good care of you."

Merit chimed in. “King, I want to thank you for all of the things you taught me, like how to open latches and how to spring from the starting gate. I’m glad we became friends.”

“Me too,” said King. “I’ll miss all of you. It’ll be too quiet here with everyone gone.”

Joe, Tom and Carol came out of the house for the final time. “Come on dogs,” said Joe. “Load up!” commanded Tom. With that, Carol petted each dog and whispered ‘good luck.” She then closed and latched each of their crate doors. After that, Joe got into the truck, started up the engine and waved. “See you on Saturday.”

The dogs knew it was going to be a long drive, so they settled in.

Chapter 42

Back to Work

A surprise awaited them at Gulf: they would be in Von's kennel.

"Not that it matters," said Clark. "They're all the same anyway." "You're right," agreed Hank. "Well," said Gypsy, sniffing carefully, "this one smells different. What is that odor?" Clark also put his nose in the air. "Maybe a flower."

Cesar walked up to the group. "Hey Joe. How've you been?"

"Good, and you?"

"Good here, too."

"I see you found your new home. Need anything?"

Joe scratched his head. "Actually, Cesar, there is. Can you make sure that Von and Merit are not turned out together? Von will be going in with Mike's dogs."

"Okay, I'll see to it," replied Cesar. As he walked away, Joe turned to his charges, rubbed them down then and put them in their crates.

A young man came and let them out a few hours later, just as dawn as breaking. He called to each dog by name. "Come Faith, here Stormy, mornin' Topper. Daisy, how are you?" When he got to Merit, he opened her crate, put a leash on her and then led her out. He next reached down to read her collar. "Merit. And who do we have here? Hank. Gypsy. Clark and Von." Now, he led them all out into the paddock area and put all of them in one pen. As he walked back inside to get the rest of the dogs, Merit was puzzled and turned to Von.

"He put us together?"

"Well, then," said Von, smiling, "do you want to run?"

"No," replied Merit firmly.

"Me neither." Instead, the two walked and sniffed.

Joe came into the area and quickly noticed all of his dogs together. Opening the gate, he called to Von and then Joe yelled for Cesar. The young man who had led the dogs out came scurrying back. "Is there something I can help you with, sir? Cesar is taking care of an emergency in kennel five."

"Did you turn my dogs out?" The man nodded.

Joe's mouth had tightened. "I can't have Merit and Von turned out together. They run around too much."

The man looked around. "Uh, which one do you want removed?"

"Please put Von in with Mike's dogs." The young man began to comply.

"See ya, Von," murmured Merit.

Hank, Gypsy and Clark added their good-byes.

"Hey, I'll just be next door," said Von with a chuckle. With that, he was placed into the kennel next to his friends, but seemed to know everyone here as well. "Hi Faith, Stormy, Topper. Looks like I'm stuck with you, again."

"Hi Von," said all of the new dogs together. "Where have you been?" asked Stormy.

"Just on a vacation," said Von.

"We were wondering what became of all of you," said Topper. "We heard Tom and Carol were getting married and the next thing we knew, all of your guys were gone.

We thought Tom might be done with racing for good."

"Nah," replied Von. "We just got to go back to our kennel for a while."

"Well, it's good to have you back," said Topper. "It's been dull without you."

"They moved everyone around after you left," added Faith. "To make room for, *them*... and to build a security fence." She now looked at Merit, Clark and Gypsy. "Is the brindle Merit?" she now asked.

"That's her," replied Von.

"She looks so strong," said Faith. "Look at those muscles."

"No wonder she's so fast," offered Stormy.

"It's not right for a female to be so big," added Topper. "She must be on steroids."

"She's not," said Von firmly. "She's just how she is. She's always been fast. It's just the way she's built."

"Still," argued Topper, "*I* don't think it's normal." Von only stared at Topper and then walked over to the fence separating Merit and him.

"Hey Merit," he said.

"Hi," she replied, walking up to Von. Merit stretched, as did Von, and then they laid down nose to nose. Merit rested her head on the paws and sighed while Von rolled over on his side. "The sun feels good," said Merit. "It's starting to warm up." Clark, Hank and Gypsy trotted up to the couple.

"Hey, Von and Merit," said Gypsy. "We're guessing when we're going to race next and whoever is closest, or even exactly right, gets a treat from everyone's dish. Wanna play?"

"Sure," said Merit. "I think I'll race tonight after dark."

Gypsy turned to Hank. "What about you?"

"Bet it'll be late this afternoon, when it's the hottest," Hank replied.

It was Gypsy's turn. "For me, I'll say I race as the sun goes down and the lights come on."

"I'll race this afternoon, after Gypsy but before Hank," added Clark.

"Hmmm." Von smiled. "I'm going to race with Merit."

"Do you think so?" asked Merit.

"It won't happen," said Clark firmly. "This isn't the day of the big race. There's nobody around and there's no hype."

"So," asked Von, looking over his shoulder toward Stormy. "When is the big race?"

"Tonight!" barked Stormy.

"See," said Von. "There you go. We're the last race of the day."

"It'll be getting cold," said Merit. "I don't like to run then."

"Ah, it shouldn't be too bad," said Clark.

Joe returned, fed the dogs breakfast and then began the track grooming routine. As Joe was putting Merit down from the table, she gave him a kiss. "Thanks, Joe. That was lovely."

Joe laughed. "I got a greyhound kiss and that's very rare indeed." He reached out to pat Merit on the head. "You're a special dog." Joe then put Merit back in the pen, where she stretched out and slept.

Later that afternoon, Joe came and led all the dogs out. As soon as they walked through the gate of the fence that surrounded their kennel, they could see hundreds of people. Once again, some tried to pet the dogs or talk to Joe.

He barked back at them. "Please, *do not* touch the dogs. Excuse me. Let me through." Finally, Joe and the dogs made it out the front gate and into the parking lot, and once there, Joe led them down the street.

"Where are we going?" asked Gypsy. "The park?"

"We've never gone this late in the day," said Clark.

"Guess we'll just have to wait and see," said Von.

Sure enough, Joe led the group into the park. "But there are people around," observed Gypsy. "I don't think we'll be let off of our leashes."

"Probably not," agreed Hank. "But at least there aren't so many people as at the track."

"I've never seen so many," said Merit. "The noise will be horrible."

Ever the practical dog, Clark added his thoughts. "It will all be over after tonight. Everything will be back to normal by tomorrow." The dogs nodded. After leading them through the park, Joe now steered the group back toward Gulf. "That was nice," said Merit. "I needed that," added Clark.

"How is your foot?" asked Von suddenly.

"Fine," said Merit. "Mine, too," added Clark.

"Look at all those cars!" exclaimed Hank suddenly. "I've never seen this parking lot full." Clark agreed. "Yeah, *tons* of cars!" exclaimed Gypsy. "Think all of the people driving those cars and all those passengers squeezed inside."

"And we," added Merit, "have to walk through them."

"The sea of people," Clark said. "Noisy. Fat. Smelly... people." Gypsy added, "Boney. Annoying. Touchy... people." Clark was not as strident. "I just hate crowds," he murmured.

As the dogs were led through the people, they touched, poked, and grabbed. "Let us *through*!" said Joe loudly. "Ouch!" yelped Merit, as someone stepped on her bad foot. Joe wheeled around angrily. "*Leave the damn dogs alone! Let us pass*!" Startled, the crowd parted as best they could. Joe was then able to lead the dogs to the security fence. He opened the lock and led them through.

"Oh no," Joe said to Merit. "You're limping." He knelt down and took her foot into his hand and rubbed it gently. He then gently put it down and shook his head. "Shoot, what do I do now? Damn them all. What am I going to do - now?"

Merit did her best not to limp. Clark spoke softly. "Merit, if it hurts, respect the pain. You don't want to make it worse."

"But look at Joe. He was nice enough to take us for a walk and now I'm hurt... and there's the race, and..."

"Uh-oh," said Von. "Look." Tom was at the dog's pen. "What's going to happen now?"

Tom roared. "What happened to Merit's paw? Where have you *been*? Gypsy's race is set to go off in a few minutes."

"Uh," said Joe, stammering.

"Give them to me and get Gypsy ready to race, commanded Tom. Joe didn't move.

"Go *now*!" yelled Tom. With that, Joe left with Gypsy.

Chapter 43

Trouble

Tom looked at Merit's foot. He felt around and was fuming. "How could he have let this *happen*?" Tom fumed.

Merit could only put her tail between her legs and look away.

"It's okay, girl, it's okay. I'm not mad at *you*." Just then, Carol came up. "Merit's foot is hurt," said Tom.

"Hi to you, too," she replied. Tom looked at her as if he wanted to say something else, but she interrupted. "It's okay. Let me take a look."

Carol went over the foot carefully. "Well it's tender. But it doesn't feel broke. Let's put some ice on it. Maybe it's just sore. What happened?"

"I have no idea!" Tom snapped. "I mean, I show up, and Joe and the dogs are gone, nowhere to be found. I looked everywhere, and when he does show up, Merit's lame."

"Where's Joe now?"

"With Gypsy. He's racing."

"I know her foot looks bad," said Carol softly. "But let's give it an hour and then reassess the situation."

"I just know that I need to get away," replied Tom. "I'm so mad at Joe right now that I'm likely to say something I'll regret."

"Then go," said Carol gently. "Why don't you go take a walk and get us something to eat? I'm starving. Don't worry. I'll stay here with the dogs."

"Thanks." Tom kissed her and walked away.

Shortly thereafter, Joe returned. "Hi Carol. Where's Tom?"

"He went to get something for us to eat."

"Is he still mad?" Joe asked. "I've never seen him that angry."

"Well," offered Carol. "He's upset, but I don't think it's about you. He's just worried about Merit and the big race tonight. He knows you take excellent care of the dogs. By the way, what *did* happen to Merit?"

"I took them for a walk," explained Joe. "It seems to help them before a race. When I came back, there was such a huge crowd that I had trouble getting back here. I think someone stepped Merit's foot."

"My god, you had to lead them through that mob?" Carol motioned.

"Sure did. Anyway, Tom should be happy to learn that Gypsy won his first race tonight."

"Congratulations Gypsy!" Carol let out a little cheer.

"It was the least I could do for Joe," explained Gypsy. "I mean, seeing how he risked so much to take us to the park and all."

Just then, Tom returned with sandwiches and drinks. He and Joe and Carol all took turns holding ice on Merit's foot. No one spoke. Tom finally broke the silence.

"How did Gypsy do?"

"He won," said Joe. "Really?" "Yup, he actually broke a track record."

Tom's face softened. "Well, *that* calls for a celebration!" With that, Tom got up and left, but when he returned, he had treats for all of the dogs.

"Yum!" said Merit. "Thanks for the treat, Gypsy."

"Thanks!" added Hank, Von and Clark.

At this point, Carol encouraged Merit to get up and walk around. "She looks better, Tom." Hearing this, Joe breathed a sigh of relief. "You think we should race her?" Carol took a moment to answer. Instead, she first led Merit around, then had her walk, jog and run this way and that. "I don't see why not," she said finally. With that, the dogs were left alone in their pen, where they all stretched out in the sun.

"I'm glad I get to race," said Merit.

"As long as you're up to it, Merit," said Von tenderly. "You don't want to tweak it worse."

"I know," replied Merit. With that, she fell asleep.

An hour or so later, the dogs were brought inside and fed, and then placed in their crates. Joe and Tom arrived next, and Tom got Merit while Joe got Von. The two were led around the warm-up arena and given to the handlers, who weighed them. As they lined up preparing to be paraded before the grandstands, Joe walked up.

"Can you put these in?" he said, handing a small bundle to Merit's handler. The handler put something—Merit didn't know what—in her ears. Merit turned around and saw that Von was getting them as well. Merit could also tell that Von was saying something, but she couldn't hear him. They were then led in front of the grandstand. Merit noticed that she could see people clapping and stomping; she could also tell they were yelling. But now, she only heard muffled noises. The quieter sounds, she thought, were welcome.

Merit knew the drill by now: she was placed in her starting box and she crouched down. She waited and waited... and waited. Then, with a sudden burst, the door flew open and Merit ran, ran, ran, and ran. Her solitary focus was on the lure. She heard nothing. She smelled nothing. As the lure stopped, Merit slowed, then, her handler retrieved her. As Merit was being led back down in front of the stands, she was thankful she had whatever was in her ears.

Catching up with Von in the changing room, she watched their handler give Von to Tom, and then give her to Tom. Quickly, Tom reached down and removed the plugs from both her and Von's ears. Everything was suddenly very loud, and Merit shook her head and pawed at her ears. Tom then led the two dogs outside. A huge crowd had gathered by the door and they cheered as Merit and Von walked by. "Be quiet!" yelled Von. "You're hurting my ears!" This only made the crowd roar louder, with laughter. Tom asked everyone to let them through, and when they finally reached their kennel, the two were cooled down and rubbed down, given dishes and then turned in for the night.

Cesar came to let them out in their pens the next morning.

Merit, however, was so tired that she only wanted to nap. Gypsy walked over to her. "Can I join you?" That was fine with Merit, so Gypsy lay down, then spoke slowly.

"When you were racing last night... I heard Carol. She... she told Joe that they had sold King."

"Oh," replied Merit. "Well, I'm not surprised since he was the only one left. Do you know where he went?"

"They gave him to a rescue group for adoption."

"Really? He didn't go to a breeding farm?"

"Nope. Carol said that 'King deserved to be loved as a pet.' I guess someone called and wanted to take him in."

Merit sighed. "Good for him." The two dogs then fell asleep. Joe was getting Clark when they awoke.

"Hey," said Hank. "Remember, you have to share your dish. You didn't race yesterday when you said you would."

"I know," said Clark with a sneer.

"I can't wait," said Gypsy with a chuckle. In response, Clark shot both of them a nasty look.

Chapter 44

Florida

Merit didn't race for a couple of days. On the third day, she woke up knowing immediately today would be a race day. When Joe came and got her, he led her out to the track. "Hmm," thought Merit. "I must be racing the first race of the day." She was then handed over to Tom, and with Joe, they walked her into the grandstand. Now Merit was not sure where they were going after all, instinctively she tucked her tail between her legs and held her head down.

The next thing she knew, Merit was led up a ramp toward a group of people who were all standing under bright lights.

A woman looked down. "This must be Merit." She patted Merit on the head, but Merit looked away. A man said, "Are you ready?"

"Yes," replied the woman.

Tom and Joe and Merit then joined the man who was in front of the lights. "Five, four, three, two, *one*!" said another man.

The woman spoke again. "Hi Ted. Yes, I'm here with the trainers of the fastest greyhound ever. Meet Tom Coal and Joe Rivera. Tell me Tom, how have you managed to build the fastest kennel to come out of Texas?"

"I've been lucky. And, Merit's mother is True to Form," said Tom. "True actually held many of the records that Merit is now breaking," said the woman. Tom nodded.

"Well," replied the man. "It must be more than luck. I say that because you've taken some of your other dogs, who don't have the best pedigrees, and you turned them into champions. Gypsy won his first race the other day. But many trainers would have retired him long ago."

"Well," said Tom, pausing, "he always placed respectably. Gypsy is sound. I think he just needed some time to become comfortable with racing. He didn't take to it right from the start like Merit did. She's a natural."

The woman spoke. "So how did you motivate Gypsy?"

"We just worked with him consistently," said Tom. "And now, he seems to have figured it out."

Joe spoke up. "He was always fairly competitive. This told us that he had potential."

Merit was growing bored listening to the questions and answers, until Tom spoke again. "Florida will certainly provide more challenges for Merit. Although I love Texas, this is my home, where I was born and raised, but the opportunity to race at the Hollywood track is too good to pass up." Merit perked her ears up.

"Do you expect to return to Texas in the future?" the woman asked.

"At some point, yes," replied Tom. "Corpus and Gulf are great tracks, and without the experience I gained working with the local trainers and owners I wouldn't have been able to graduate to a track like Hollywood."

The man began to wind down the interview. "We wish you and Merit all the best." "Yes," added the woman. The man then turned to the camera. "We'll continue to bring you stories of this amazing dog and her next big race, Ted."

The man who had given the number countdown yelled out. "Cut!"

"Thanks for talking to us, Tom and Joe," said the woman. "Well, thanks for your interest in Merit," replied Tom. With that, Tom shook hands with the man and woman and then led Merit away.

After Merit was put in her pen, she quickly walked up to Gypsy, Hank and Clark.

"Have you heard anything about going to Florida?" None of them had and now Merit asked Von the same question.

"Not a word," he said, walking up to the fence "What's going on?"

"I'm not sure," said Merit slowly. "But, but, Tom just led me over to a group of people in the stands and they asked him all sorts of questions. I wasn't really listening until I heard him say something about me racing in Florida."

"Well," said Clark matter-of-factly. "It *is* where the fastest dogs end up racing" Gypsy looked at Clark. "You used to race there," he said. Clark sighed. "Yeah, I did. But when I started going down in grades my owner sold me to Tom. He knew that Tom was racing 'slower' tracks in Texas."

"Huh?" said Gypsy.

"Maybe not really slower," replied Clark. "Just less competition because not that many great dogs race in Texas. See, the best dogs end up racing in Florida where there are bigger purses."

"So, are we all moving to Florida?" asked Hank.

"That I don't know," offered Merit.

"Only time will tell," mused Von.

"Well, I wouldn't mind going back to Florida," said Clark. "It's a nice track, although it's probably more humid than here."

"What do you mean by 'humid?'" asked Gypsy.

"When it's hot out, but it's cloudy and feels like rain, but it doesn't rain. It just gets hotter. That's humid."

"If any of you hear anything more, let me know." The dogs all agreed and with that, Merit walked away and lay down to take a nap.

Chapter 45

The Next Adventure

Hank was talking when Merit woke a little while later.

"I should probably wake Merit," he was saying. "She'll want to know."

Merit shook herself up. "Want to know what?"

"Well, you'll be going to Florida with Tom and Carol, and Joe will be staying here. You're going to join a kennel that Tom will be training. Sounds like you'll be there for a long time; Carol's even moving her vet practice."

Merit couldn't think of what to say at first. "Wow... but when do I leave?"

"I'm not sure yet," continued Hank. "Well, I heard Joe and Tom talking earlier," added Gypsy. "And they said you were going to race tomorrow night."

"But you don't know that for sure," interrupted Clark. "Things are *always* subject to change, without notice."

"Yes," said Merit with a tiny sigh. "You're right." Slowly, she shook herself, letting her body wave from side to side like a slithering snake. "No use worrying about when or what event will happen when you have absolutely no control."

"That's right," said Von. "Plus, Merit, you're a good racer. You've been pretty lucky. You shouldn't worry about Florida."

"I'm not," replied Merit. "But I don't like the thought of going alone. I'd feel a lot better if one of you came along."

"Don't worry Merit. You'll manage to make friends with someone," said Clark. Gypsy barked softly. "I'll miss having you around."

Now Von and Merit looked at each other, but neither of them spoke.

Von sighed and lay down while Merit sniffed around the pen. "What are you thinking about, Merit?" asked Gypsy.

"My next big adventure..."

"Should be an interesting one," said Clark. "At least you'll get away from the monotony of this place."

"Oh no!" said Merit suddenly. She groaned. "If Joe is staying here, I'll *never* get to walk out into nature."

"Tom might take you to the beach," offered Von.

"Is Hollywood close to the beach?"

"Sure is." Clark called out.

"Good," said Merit. "Because I like the beach and I don't get to go nearly enough."

"Well, maybe you'll go more often now," said Gypsy. "You've earned the right to enjoy yourself."

At that, Cesar came and turned all of the dogs in for the night. Joe came later that evening and got Hank and Clark ready for racing. When they returned, Merit asked again if they had heard anything more. They hadn't, and Merit then asked how they had placed in their last race. "Third," said Clark.

Hank grumbled. "Fifth."

"Ouch," said Merit. "Yeah, I know, I know," mumbled Hank. He lay down and put his heads between his paws. Merit knew Hank was upset. But she didn't know what to say.

Merit was the only dog let out the next morning.

First Joe gave her a dish and then walked her around the grounds. She was then placed in a crate and given a pill to swallow. It only took a minute to work, Merit laid down, felt awfully sleepy and then fell fast asleep. When she woke up, she was thirsty and still in her crate, but couldn't tell where her crate was.

It was dark and cool. Merit smelled the air. Still, she couldn't place the odors she was sniffing. She cocked her head and listened to a loud, low rumble and thought she might be in the back of a truck. Her head felt fuzzy and her tummy rumbled. She noticed something intriguing: a bottle hanging from the side of her crate. Licking the spout, water came out. Ahh, thought Merit, as she lapped the water. She quickly dozed back to sleep.

Bright lights and lots of noise suddenly flooded her senses. Quickly jumping to a standing position, she looked out her crate. She couldn't see anything familiar—just a sea of legs. There were a lot of people, walking, passing—what seemed to be an army of people.

Merit whimpered. "Where am I?"

Carol looked inside and spoke. "Tom, she's awake. "Hi, M."

"Hey girl," said Tom, looking into her crate. "Want to stretch your legs?" Nodding yes, Merit got out and shook herself. Many people stopped and asked if Merit was a greyhound and Tom told them she was. Tom led Merit out of the busy building, through more mazes of legs, and finally, toward the back of a car. "Get in," he said. After Merit obeyed, Tom put her crate in beside her.

Merit stood on the back seat while Tom and Carol got in front. Tom started up the car and then told Merit to lie down. Merit curled up as she heard Tom thank Carol for getting the car.

"Where do we go?" he asked her.

"Take the first exit."

Meanwhile, Merit looked out the window. She was so happy that she started to squeal.

"I see the ocean! I see the beach!" "I think that Merit wants to go down to the ocean," said Tom.

"Well then, let's take her," said Carol. Merit let out an even bigger yelp. "Yippee!"

Walking toward the beach, Merit began to tug on her leash. She only wanted to be let go.

"Knock it off Merit," said Tom, tugging right back. "If you don't heel, we'll go back to the car." Merit could tell by the tone of Tom's voice that he was serious, so she stopped her shenanigans.

Carol spoke to Merit gently. "We just can't risk you getting hurt."

"Oh, if she got hurt now," said Tom, "I'd be finished."

"No you wouldn't," replied Carol. "You worry too much," she said, laughing. Tom stared at Carol, his face serious and cold. They walked in silence.

"Should we turn around?" asked Tom suddenly. Carol looked behind her.

"I didn't realize that we'd walked so far." "Yup," agreed Tom. "Looks like a long way." With that, Merit, Tom and Carol headed back.

"What's the game plan now?" asked Carol.

"Well," said Tom, "I thought we could take Merit to the track, get her situated, and then go to the hotel and order room service."

"It's too expensive!" exclaimed Carol.

"Let me worry about that," replied Tom. "That's my job." Carol laughed softly.

"Okay."

The car pulled into the track's parking lot.

Merit was led out into the lot, then through a gate and to the kennel area. "Stay here," Tom told Carol. "I'll go find out where we need to go." After walking into a building, he soon came out with a man.

"Paul, this is my wife Carol."

"Nice to meet you, Paul."

"How was your flight? How did Merit fare?"

"She slept the whole way," said Tom. "I don't even think she realized that she was in a plane," added Carol.

"Good," replied Paul. "We wouldn't want anything to happen to our star." At this point, he motioned over to a small grassy area. "I have you set up over here." Merit saw there was a shed and a small run connected to that. She was placed inside. She stood there and pawed at the door.

"No," said Tom firmly. "Stay." Merit turned and walked through the shed and out into the pen, then watched the group all walk away.

"It's all I could do," she heard Paul say. "We're full right now, but as soon as something opens up, we'll move her."

Merit decided to lie down. There were no other dogs around, so she stood up and sniffed, then began to howl. Merit howled and howled and howled, but no one came. Finally, she lay back down.

Chapter 46

What's a Cat?

A moment later, Merit noticed movement in the shadows.

"Is something there?" asked Merit. She heard nothing, but saw something again, and heard a slight swishing noise. "Who's there?" barked Merit.

"Shhhh," a voice purred. "Be quiet or I'll come over there and *slice* you."

"What are you talking about?"

At that moment, a gray cat slicked out of the shadows. Looking at Merit with green-gold eyes, she rubbed on the corner of the fence.

"What are you?" asked Merit.

"I am a cat."

"What is your name?"

"I have no name, she hissed. "I am the barn cat. You are not allowed to talk to me."

"Why not?"

"Because all dogs want to chase and kill me."

Merit laughed. "I don't. I race all the time, so I wouldn't want to chase you. And I certainly wouldn't like to *kill* you. I believe in peace."

"You're just trying to fool me," the cat said matter-of-factly. "So then, when I let my guard down... you can *get* me."

"I wouldn't, but think what you want." Merit shrugged her shoulders.

The cat was now busy watching a fly buzz around and leapt for it. She missed the fly, which then buzzed over by Merit. Merit snapped, caught the insect and then spit it out. "See," said the cat. "You will treat me just like that fly. I know all about dogs." Merit shrugged again. "Whatever."

Merit lay down again, and the cat swished by and walked away. Soon, a young women approached her and then led Merit out of her pen.

"Hi Merit! My name is Molly and I'll be one of your handlers." First Molly looked Merit over, feeling along her legs, feet, back and tail. "Merit, I hope you like walks." Hearing this, Merit jumped up and down. Molly laughed. "I can tell you're a good dog."

Then Molly patted Merit's head and led her around the grounds, explaining how the track worked. "There's the weight room and there's where we'll be grooming you and…" Paul walked by and laughed. "Molly, are you talking to those dogs again? You really think they understand, don't you?"

"I *know* they do," replied Molly. " Hearing this, Merit wagged her tail hard, she was lucky Molly was her handler.

As Merit was led down to the track, she spoke to Molly. "I like sand. I'm glad to see this is a sand track." Molly looked down at Merit. "You like sand, don't ya girl?" Walking Merit by the starting gate, then all around its perimeter, Molly then took Merit back to her temporary shelter and gave her food and water. "See ya later," Molly stated, waving at Merit as she walked away. After Merit finished eating she lay down. As she was falling off to sleep, she heard the barn cat swishing past her. This time, Merit didn't open her eyes.

"Hey Swish," she said softly. "Do you mind if I call you that?"

"Yes, I do," said the cat. "*You* are not supposed to talk to me. *You're* to ignore me."

"But why?"

The cat made a low growl. "Because I am a *cat*!" With that, she sprung over to where Merit lay, then swiped at Merit's nose with her paw. Merit's nose had scratches and oozing blood. Merit yelped, then jumped up and yelled.

"Ouch! What was *that* for?! I was just lying here!"

"Because," said the cat with a hiss, "you did not *respect* me. And remember: *I* am a cat. *You* are a dog. We cannot be friends." With that, the cat once again swished away.

Merit tried to wipe the blood away and ease the sting with her paw. Molly returned and noticed Merit's nose.

"Looks like you've met the barn cat, the meanest cat I know." She took Merit into the kennel. Merit winced, the hot stuffy barn smelled like urine. She looked at all the poor dogs stuck in their small crates. Merit and Molly kept walking, down the shed row, into a room the leading off to the left. Molly went up to the sink and began cleaning Merits nose. Just then, Merit saw Carol walk in.

"Hi, Molly. Is that Merit?"

"Sure is. I walked by to check on her and noticed her nose was bleeding. I think she got into it with the barn cat."

"Oh, that cat is nasty!" replied Carol. "She approached me all sweet and when I went to pet her, she bit me and ran off."

"I'm surprised you got close enough for her to bite you, or Merit, for that matter. I can't say I blame her, she's afraid of the greyhounds because she's been chased so many times."

"I would think so," said Carol, laughing. "She must be a fast cat."

"Not really. But she's learned to stand her ground, and that's why she's still alive."

"Amazing that a cat that small would stand up to a greyhound."

"Especially one that can run 30 miles an hour."

"I think I kind of admire that cat now," replied Carol. "Ornery little thing that she is."

"Well," said Molly, "Merit's nose is clean now. I've got some other dogs to tend to."

"Thanks," replied Carol. "I just came in to get some more vaccinations. I'll be in kennel four if you need me."

"Come on Merit," said Molly. Leading her back to her pen, she told Merit to stay away from the barn cat. That was fine with Merit, she lay in the sun and fell asleep. When she heard Swish approach, Merit opened her eyes and spoke evenly.

"Swish, you really don't have to attack me when I haven't done anything. I'm not interested in you. So leave me alone."

Swish didn't seem to hear what Merit had said. "Do you know that this is a goat pen? Baaa, baaa."

"Well," replied Merit, "I'd rather be outside than inside."

"Yeah, but I'm free," taunted Swish. "And you're in a goat pen, baa baa baaa. Goaty the greyhound, Goaty the greyhound. Baaa, baaa, baaa." Swish jumped and danced around. Merit stood up.

"You're boring me," said Merit. She yawned. "Go away."

"*No!*" snarled Swish. "I'm free and you're a trapped goat! Baa baa baa!" With that, Swish jumped up on the fence and walked back and forth. "I'm going to get you, I'm going to get you." The cat waved her paw, nails extended, back and forth."

Determined to ignore Swish, Merit walked through the yard into the pen. "Looking for goat food? Baaa, baaa –" Swish kept up her taunts. Merit waited. Finally, Swish's curiosity peaked and she walked over to the entryway and looked inside. There, she saw Merit stretched out in a sunny spot on the straw. Swish jumped down and Merit growled.

"Don't touch me." Swish ignored Merit: instead, she reached out and swiped Merit's thigh with her paw. Merit yelped and Swish ran away.

Merit got up and looked at the fresh wound. She walked over and opened the latch on her gate and slowly and silently she, followed Swish. Merit hid in the shadows and kept a safe distance while observing Swish, who had no idea she was being stalked.

When Swish became completely absorbed in watching a cricket hop in the grass, Merit sneaked up close, then pounced. Pinning the cat down. Swish was so startled she started to cry. Merit was so surprised that she didn't have to fight him after all, she quickly let go of Swish. The cat curled up into a ball. Puzzled, Merit just looked at the cat.

After a few seconds Swish uncurled and looked up. "You're... you're not going to eat me?"

"No," said Merit. "I've already had my breakfast. What are you so afraid of?"

"I've seen cats chased down and ripped to shreds."

"Really?" said Merit. "I've never seen that."

"Yeah, but before me, had you ever seen a cat?"

"No, but will you stop scratching me, or do I *have* to kill you?" Merit mustered her most ferocious look. Swish laughed.

"Okay, Merit. Truce."

Just then, Tom came walking up. "There you are Merit. I've been looking all over for you. You've got to get ready to race." He looked at Merit and the cat together, watching Swish's tail whoosh back and forth. Shaking his head, he grabbed Merit and led her off.

"You found her!" said Carol. "Where was she?"

"Out by the warm up, with a cat."

"Really? That's strange. That cat *hates* dogs."

"They were just sitting there," replied Tom. "And I talked to Molly about Merit's escape. She's going to install a second safety latch."

Chapter 47

Fame

"Oh," said Carol. "I forgot to tell you that there's some kind of bug going around kennel number four. There may be an opening for Merit, but I think it would be better to keep Merit outside. I had no idea how closed in all of these kennels are. It's a welcoming environment for respiratory illness."

Tom led Merit down to the weight room. Today, she was 72 pounds. She looked at all of the other dogs and all of the people. Everyone was minding their own business and no one was friendly or made eye contact. Molly grabbed Merit and rubbed her down.

"You feel solid," she said. "You should do well today." In response, Merit wagged her tail.

Molly next led Merit down to the starting gate. "You like racing, don't you?" she said with a laugh. Molly put her in the starting gate and the race began. It was now pure instinct: Merit flew out of the starting box and ran and ran. She was so happy, and she crossed the finish line easily. After the lure stopped, Merit slowly came to a walk, panting heavily, her tongue hanging out. Molly ran up to her.

"You're so fast!" Next, Molly collected Merit and led her around the track. For the first time, Merit noticed both the noise and the size of the crowd, and started to tremble.

"It's okay, girl," said Molly. "They're all just applauding your performance. They're showing you how much they like you." Merit cocked her head. She could make out chanting, "Mer-*it*! Mer-*it*! Mer-*it*! " Realizing no one meant her any harm, Merit stopped shaking. "That's a girl," said Molly. She then led Merit off the track into the pen. There, Merit had a urine sample collected and after that, Molly led Merit into the grooming area.

Merit, could not believe how well Molly was treating her. She got rubbed down head to toe, down to every little muscle and joint. Merit's eyes rolled back in her head, completely relaxed in the pleasure, her tongue lolling out of her mouth as well. When Molly completed the special treatment, Merit shook slowly from nose to tail, then stretched as long as her body would allow. She then pulled each leg out behind her and did one fast, hard shake. After this, Molly led Merit back to her pen and gave her a dish and fresh water. While Merit ate, she fluffed up Merits straw bedding. As she left, she turned around.

"Goodnight Merit. I'll see you in a few hours."

Just as Merit was drifting off, Swish seemed to appear out of nowhere.

"Merit," she purred, "Everyone is talking about you. You're famous."

"I don't care. Please let me sleep. I'm tired." Merit yawned.

When Merit woke a little later, she smelled a cat odor and could feel warm, soft fuzz against her fur. She opened one eye, Swish was curled up next to her in the straw. Merit yawned and went back to sleep.

When Merit woke, Swish was gone and Molly was walking into her pen. She gave Merit a pill and a treat, made sure she had water and left. Merit walked out into the yard. It was night, but Merit could still hear races going on.

The next morning, Molly took Merit for a walk. She raced that afternoon. As night set in, she realized she hadn't seen Swish all day. Had something happened to her new feline friend? It wasn't until late the next day that Swish appeared. "Where have you been?" asked Merit, concern in her voice.

"Around," hissed Swish. "Why do you ask?"

"Because you're my friend."

"I've told you, cats and dogs can't be friends."

"What are you talking about?" replied Merit.

"*Look*," said Swish, showing Merit her tail. It was bandaged.

"One of your fellow canines did this to me because I got it too close to his mouth."

"Well," said Merit thoughtfully, "you taunt the dogs too much. You practically ask for it, Swish. Look how you treated me. I'm telling you, if you want the dogs to leave you alone, try leaving *them* alone. Some dogs may really be out to get you and I'm sure you have to be careful," continued Merit. "But don't go picking fights with dogs who wouldn't be interested if you didn't provoke them."

Swish only hissed and walked away. That night, just as Merit was falling drifting off, Swish nestled into her body to sleep with her. Merit smiled. "I like it when you hang out with me." Swish hissed back. "Ssshuuussshhh, I'm trying to sleep."

Chapter 48

Burnout

She didn't know why, but Merit realized that she was racing later and later in the day. She also realized that she wasn't really training anymore, yet she was racing almost every day. She was also not sure how long she had been in Florida.

One day, Swish was sitting in her pen, and Merit pounced. "Hey Merit, what's the deal?" she said with a hiss.

"I'm bored," barked Merit. "I want out of here." Merit howled and kept howling and howling. Swish looked at her friend, jumped over the fence and ran off. Just then, Molly came up.

"I wonder what Swish was up to?" said Molly. "And Merit, what's wrong?"

Merit howled. "I want to go some place! I can't stand the boredom! I want to have some *fun*!" Molly nodded, opened the gate and led Merit out. Once outside, they found Tom working with some dogs at the track.

"Tom," said Molly firmly. "We need to get Merit out of here. She's going stir crazy. I think we should cancel the races until the Hollywood Futurity."

"That long?" he said. "That's not until January."

"She needs time to regenerate," continued Molly. "We've been asking a lot from her and we can't afford for her not to be in top form for the Futurity."

"You're right. What should we do with her?"

I know of this place, in Dania. A woman named Joanne Wilson owns it. It's kind of a retreat for racing greyhounds."

"I've heard of her. She has a good reputation," said Tom thoughtfully. "Okay, let's see if she'll take Merit."

"I'll go call her."

"If it's a go, I can take her over this afternoon after I'm done training," said Tom.

Later, Merit was loaded into a truck. The drive wasn't very long. They pulled into a driveway and after a gate automatically opened, they drove down a long brick driveway until they reached a barn. As they got out a woman greeted them.

"Hi Tom, I'm Joanne."

"Nice to meet you."

"Let me show you around. First, here's the kennel." They walked into a beautiful barn with huge kennels "Each kennel has its own individual run," continued Joanne. "There's no common fencing and all of the dogs are exercised four times a day.

"Each walk is different," she went on. The first one is short, 20 minutes around the lake. The second walk one comes mid-morning, two miles through a forest preserve. After lunch, all of the dogs get another 20-minute walk. Then in the late afternoon they get a one and a half mile trot-walk combination around the track."

"What kind of food will Merit get?" asked Tom.

"We make our own feed here. It's rice with chicken, or lamb mixed with apples and carrots. I've never had a dog not eat it, and it helps keep them fit while they're not racing. By the way, how long will Merit be with us?"

"Until January," replied Tom. "How many dogs do you have here anyway?"

"About 50." Joanne laughed. "And about 30 are mine. I never met a greyhound I didn't like... guess I'm pretty much a sucker for those soft brown eyes." She patted Merit on the head. "You're free to visit Merit any time, day or night. Don't bother calling first, unless you want assistance with something. Then I prefer normal business hours."

"Thanks," said Tom. "I can't imagine why I'd want to come in the middle of the night, but it's nice to know that if I want to I can."

"I like to be flexible," replied Joanne.

"Well... thanks for showing us around. I've got to get back."

"Here," she said "let me take her."

As Tom walked off, Joanne led Merit back into the barn. "Come on girl, let's show you where you go." Placed into a kennel; Merit walked outside into her run. On her left was a big black and white dog, laying down, for a moment, it made Merit think of King. "Hi."

"Hi back." Then the dog went to sleep.

She now looked on the other side of her kennel at a black and tan brindle.

"Hi."

He just looked at her and nodded. "Friendly bunch," muttered Merit, now stretching out in the sun. Still, it was nice to know she wouldn't have to race for a while.

Chapter 49

Time Passes

One day a new dog was placed next to Merit. This greyhound greeted her. Merit ignored her and let out a deep sigh –realizing the new routine had quickly grown stale and she was looking forward to returning to the track. She had not seen Tom or Molly since she had been here and the dogs that were originally next to her had left and been replaced several times. Once she realized her kennel companions would be temporary, she had stopped trying to make any friends.

But Merit had never been without manners.

"I'm sorry," she said, suddenly realizing her rudeness. "Did you say something?"

"I said 'Hi,'" replied the dog, now timidly.

"Hi! My name is Merit. What's yours?"

"Lilly," the dog stammered.

Merit looked Lilly over. "You're pretty. You have beautiful eyes."

"Thank you," whispered Lilly, looking at her feet.

"Why are you so uncomfortable with my compliment?"

"Because... because I don't want you thinking that I think I'm better then you."

"Why would I think that?"

Lilly's voice could barely be heard. "Other dogs have said to me that I think I'm better than everyone else because I'm beautiful, and I know it."

"Well," said Merit, "the same has been said of me because I'm fast, and I know it."

"Why are you here?" asked Lilly.

"I'm resting for the Futurity race."

"Me too!" said Lilly.

"Do you know when it is?" asked Merit.

"We qualify in two weeks."

"Oh," said Merit, sighing deeper. "That's a long time."

"Not really," "It'll be here before we know it, and then it'll be back to the grueling schedule of the track and all of those qualifying races and training." Lilly paused. "You must have already been here a long time to be that eager to get back to the track."

"I *like* racing," replied Merit.

"Really?" replied Lilly. "I can take or leave it. Actually, if I could, I'd leave it. Your muscles get all sore. But I like the training, the rubdowns and the walks, so it's not all bad. But I don't like having to go up against the other dogs. Too nerve racking."

"Hmm," said Merit, thinking before she answered. "I like running with other dogs. It's more interesting, more challenging."

"Have you already raced at Hollywood?" asked Lilly. "What kennel where you in?"

"I've raced there, but I wasn't kept in the kennels. I had my own pen."

"Oh," said Lilly. "I wish I had my own. The kennels at Hollywood are too smelly and dark." Lilly stretched out and Merit sighed.

"I wish there was more variety in my life," said Merit. "I'm gotten so bored with everything."

"Just wait," said Lilly. "Change is bound to happen, and when it does, you'll look back and wish things were like they are right now. You'll regret wishing that things would change and not be so boring."

"Yeah," nodded Merit. "Things could be a *lot* worse, I guess." Merit was glad that she had finally found someone to help her pass the time.

Chapter 50

Beach Day

One morning Tom and Carol came. Merit ran up to the gate, wagging not just her tail, but her whole body.

"Hey Merit!" said Lilly. "You have visitors. How exciting!"

"These are my people," replied Merit. "Tom and Carol."

"Hey Merit," said Tom. "You look *great.*" Tom opened her gate and put Merit's leash on as Carol knelt down and petted her. "Come on," said Tom. "Let's go." As they led her away, Merit turned around to say her good byes to Lilly.

Where are you going?" Lilly asked. "Don't know," replied Merit. "Bye."

Lilly looked fondly at Merit. "I hope I see you again."

Merit stopped, it seemed as if her whole life had been making new friends... and then, being taken away from them. She looked sadly at Lilly. "I hope so, too."

After Merit was led to Tom's truck and jumping into the crate, Tom and Carol got in. As the truck roared to life and started to move, Merit lay down. Soon, though, the truck stopped. When Tom came to get Merit, she could smell salt in the air. "Thought you might like to walk on the beach, ol' girl."

Merit barked with joy. "Yippee!" As Merit jumped around, Carol laughed. "Boy, you weren't kidding when you said Merit liked the beach. I'm glad you suggested bringing Merit with us."

"Actually, it was Joe who made the suggestion," said Tom. "I told him this morning that you and I were taking the day off to go to the beach and he said, 'You should take Merit.' And speaking of Merit, can you take her so I can carry the rest of this stuff?"

"Sure," replied Carol. "You don't want me to carry anything?"

"No, just take Miz M, I've got the rest of the gear."

The threesome walked down to the beach, where Merit had a wonderful time walking in the warm sand and watching the waves roll in and out. There was a little breeze that brought in smells of the ocean. After walking a few minutes, they stopped and Tom spread out a blanket.

"Merit," he said. "Down." Dutifully, Merit obeyed and watched the birds run after the waves, looking for food. She stretched out and sighed and Carol scratched her belly.

"Do you want anything to eat?" asked Tom.

"Not yet, but I could use a drink." As Tom gave Carol a can of soda, he gazed at Merit. "Bet M would like some water."

She did, eagerly lapping up the bowl of cool liquid he brought over. "I guess she was really thirsty," said Carol. "Would you like some more Merit?" asked Tom. He refilled the bowl, but Merit didn't drink any more. Instead, they all quietly watched the waves. Carol then took out a book and Tom lay beside Merit.

"Hey girls," said Tom. "You want to go into the water?"

"Sounds good," said Carol. "I'm getting warm. Do you think Merit will go in?"

"Don't know," replied Tom. "Let's just go in and if she comes in behind us." After they let her off her leash, Merit followed them into the water she stopped when she was chest deep. She barked, then turned around, then ran and ran down the shoreline. Then, she turned around and ran back as fast as she could. Playfully splashing Tom and Carol, she ran through the waves, then out onto the shore and down the beach once again.

Racing felt great: Merit's heart was pounding and she was panting. When she finally thought to turn around, she saw that Tom and Carol were mere specks in the distance. Stopping to catch her breath; she slowly started walking toward them. After a few minutes, she started to trot back. When Merit finally reached them, they looked serious. Tom called her over and she went up to him; he then put on her leash.

"I should have known better," said Tom, shaking his head.

"We're lucky she came back," said Carol. "Can you imagine chasing a greyhound all the way to Miami?" She laughed and Tom joined in. Merit was glad she wasn't in too much trouble. Once again, they led her to their blanket and asked her to lie down. Tom and Carol started eating and Merit whined. "I'd like some, too!"

Carol laughed and gave Merit part of her sandwich. Tom shot Carol a look.

"Don't worry, a little people food won't hurt." Merit wagged her tail and after lunch, they took her for a long walk up and down the beach. Merit was sad as she watched them packing everything up.

"Time to head back," said Tom.

"It's been a nice day," said Carol. "A nice break." They kissed and Merit weaseled herself in between them. The two separated and laughed. "Merit is something else," said Carol. "So much personality." Tom nodded his head.

As Carol led Merit back up to the truck, Tom carried all of their beach stuff. They took Merit back to Joanne's place and put her in her pen. Gently, Carol and Tom petted her and said good-bye. "See ya."

Lilly was waiting. "Where did you go?"

"To the beach."

"What's a beach?"

Merit tried to explain and Lilly cocked her head. "I think I may have *seen* one, but I've never actually *been* there. You're sooooo lucky, Merit."

"I guess I am," said Merit, stretching out. "I'm so tired now," she said, yawning. As the sun set, Merit fell into a contented sleep.

Chapter 51

— Friends Come and Friends Go —

Lilly was collected the next day. "Where are you going?" asked Merit.

"No idea," replied Lilly.

"Well, hopefully you're going to the beach and I'll see you this evening."

"That'd be cool," said Lilly. The two said their farewells.

But that night Lilly did not come back, or the next. Lilly had been right: Merit was lonely and things had changed for the worse. Pacing in and out of her kennel and back and forth around the pen, she felt the dirt become soft under her toes as she wore away the grass. Just as her agitation began really growing, Joanne's helper Ben walked up with a new dog.

Merit was shocked. "Hank!" she called out.

"Hey M!" he yipped, jumping up on his hind feet. Merit noticed that Hank had a large bandage around his left paw. Ben laughed. "Down boy! Could this be your girlfriend?" With that, he led Hank into Lilly's old pen.

"How are you doing?" asked Merit. "And what happened to your foot?"

"Oh, I'm fine," replied Hank. "Just a sprain. They want me confined and rested for a few weeks. Hey, I thought I'd be bored, and now look, you're here."

"Well, where have you been?" asked Merit.

"I started racing at Hollywood three weeks ago," replied Hank. "We hadn't seen or heard about you, Merit. We didn't know what to think, but here you are." Hank was talking so rapidly that Merit had to concentrate. "It's sooooo good to see you."

"It's good to see you, too, Hank. Who else is at Hollywood?"

"Everyone now."

"Even Von?" asked Merit, her heart pounding.

"Yup," replied Hank. "Even Von." He continued talking, but Merit had stopped listening.

"Oh joy!" thought Merit, her heart fluttering with a mix of excitement, relief, apprehension and anticipation. "I can't wait to see him." She tried to focus on what Hank was saying.

"He's been breaking records left and right, he's the favorite to win the Futurity. By the way, Merit, why are you here?"

"Tom and Carol brought me here to rest until the Futurity." She laughed softly. "I *was* the favorite."

"Sounds like you two will be going neck to neck." Merit laughed because it was just like old times.

Merit had another question. "Well, how did everyone end up in Florida?"

"It was all because of Joe," began Hank. "He was in the kennel and went to lift a sack of food. He hurt his back and couldn't move. He lay flat on his back yelling for help for a couple of hours before someone finally walked past the gate and heard him. We were outside and we couldn't get to him." Hank paused. "And we were afraid to make any noise, because that might cover up his calls for help. We all felt pretty worthless."

"Sounds awful," said Merit, nodding.

"Well, Von kept trying to get the door to open, but he couldn't. Poor guy. We heard Joe has to have some surgery and a long rest, we all flew here the other day."

"Poor Joe," said Merit, wondering how Hank could say so much and speak so quickly without taking so much as a breath or a pause. Merit stretched and Hank continued. "And here you are. Looking good and fit."

Merit looked at Hank steadily. He looked the same, but she could sense something was different, Hank was older. He had a few gray hairs on his muzzle and as he lay down, she could hear his joints crack and pop. Merit lay next to him and suddenly noticed her own limbs creaking and grinding. Was her nose turning gray as well? How old was she anyway? She wasn't sure just how much time was passing. She sighed heavily.

Hank was still talking. "I guess you'll be going back to the track soon. I mean, the race is less then a week away."

"Really? I wonder why they haven't brought me back to the kennel."

"Probably because of Von," said Hank, rolling his eyes.

Just then, one of the men Merit had seen around, Carlos, walked up and gathered Merit.

"See you later," she said to Hank. Hank nodded. Carlos led Merit around Joanne's property, then rubbed her down and groomed her, then took her on a route she had not gone to before. At the end of the drive, they turned left. The blacktop was warm on her feet and the sunshine was bright. It was nearly blinding Merit. She decided to keep her head down in order to keep the sun out of her eyes. Next, Carlos led Merit off the asphalt and onto some cool dirt. They stopped in the shade.

Merit looked up, and saw a racetrack in front of her.

The glistening sandy track was cut out of a wonderfully grassy field. "Oh! Joy!" Merit grunted and leaped forward, springing loose from Carlos, her leash flopping behind her. She ran and her legs found their rhythm. But then her hind leg reached forward and caught her leash. She somersaulted and then rolled, ending upside down, her neck between the fence and ground.

She could neither breathe nor move.

Merit could hear Carlos running over to her, yelling. Bending down, he pulled her shoulders and stretched her lifeless body on the track. "Oh god, oh god, oh god," muttered Carlos. "Merit, breathe!" He blew into her nose and mouth. Merit tried to obey, but couldn't. Carlos didn't give up, instead, he kept breathing into Merit's nose.

Suddenly, Merit gasped. She didn't know how, but she had finally caught her breath but kept gasping. Carlos looked at her, grinned and breathed a huge sigh of relief." Oh thank god!" he said.

"Man oh man, you just about ruined my career. Thank god you're not dead. Are you okay, girl?"

Carlos carefully looked Merit over and noticed a tear on her back, close to her spine. "Oh man," murmured Carlos. "They're not going to like this. Okay, let's head back."

Merit looked at her wound and tried to clean it. Carlos snapped. "*No! Don't!*" All the way back he talked to himself. "Oh man, I'm going to get fired..." Merit limped along, feeling light-headed and sore. Carlos called Joanne on a walkie-talkie he was carrying. "Joanne, Merit got away from me. She's okay, but she's bleeding."

Merit could hear Joanne's reply. "Bring her to the hospital barn. I'll call the vet."

Both Carol and Joanne were waiting for them when they arrived. "Poor Merit," said Carol. "Come now." Leading Merit into a very clean room that smelled of antiseptic, Carol first inspected the wound, then grabbed some cotton balls and cleaned the cut.

"Hmmm," murmured Carol "Don't think I can really stitch this... it's a puncture wound... it's pretty deep and it's so close to her spine..." Carol looked up at Carlos.

"What happened?"

Carlos stammered. "Uh... she... she ran away, and she, uh, she got, uh, tripped up, and uh, it was her leash and she uh, she... she hit the fence."

Carol inspected Merit more closely. Standing next to Joanne, Carlos was close by, motionless and hardly breathing. His lips were closed tight and only his eyes shifted.

Looking up, Carol fixed her gaze on Carlos. "I think she'll be okay."

He exhaled deeply. "Thank god."

Joanne turned to Carlos. "Why don't you go tend to the others? We'll finish up here." Carlos nodded, turned, and then bolted out the door. Joanne shook her head. "What are you going to do? He's usually my best guy."

"Well," replied Carol, "I guess he's learned a lesson. You could tell he was worried. Bet it'll be a long time before another dog gets by him."

Joanne nodded. "Sometimes things just happen."

Merit kept standing and Carol petted her and kissed her muzzle. Merit leaned into her when she scratched her back. "Put this ointment on twice a day for two days and then put this stuff on once a day," instructed Carol. "Just put on a thin coat so it'll absorb quickly. Oh, and make sure you watch Merit for a few minutes to make sure she doesn't lick the stuff off."

Carol pulled something out of her pants pocket. "And give Merit one of these pills for three days, with some food. She should be all set by then. She can even continue with her training. Then," she said with a little frown, "see how the wound is healing. If it pulls too much we may want to cut back. Let us know."

"Thanks for coming so quickly," said Joanne, walking her to the door.

"No problem, I can't believe I was around the corner when you called, but I have to get back. I have to examine the dogs before race time. I'll see you later."

Joanne looked down at Merit. "Well girl, you didn't get out of training. Let's go." Now it was Joanne who took Merit down the drive that led to the track. Merit sighed, yawned when they stopped, and then shook herself from head to tail. "Careful," cautioned Joanne. "You're sore." Merit felt no pain; she only wanted to be off the leash. She only wanted to run. Joanne put her in the starting gate, the bell rang and the gate opened. It was, once again, pure instinct: Merit flew out after the lure. When Merit trotted back up, Joanne was laughing. "Well Merit, you certainly haven't lost any speed!"

With that, she led Merit down around the walking trail to cool down and then placed her back inside the crate. Merit realized that she was enjoying being in training again. "I feel sorry for you," she said to Hank after she returned. "You had to lie around all day. You couldn't run."

"Don't you feel sorry for me, Merit," Hank said, beginning to ramble again. "I enjoyed my day immensely. I got to rest my aching foot and lie in the sun. Do you really like getting all cut up?"

"No," said Merit. "Of course not."

"Then why do you run away and put yourself in that kind of danger." He chuckled, "I heard what happened. You're lucky you're okay."

"Oh!" replied Merit. "It's just a cut." However, Merit realized that she was sore and tired. As she lay down, her hip made a loud pop. Hank looked over.

"Did that hurt? I heard it all the way over here."

"No, of course not." Merit then yawned and put her head down. But now, she noticed that when she stretched, she could feel every joint and muscle. "I just need to rest," she thought.

Chapter 52

Aging Gracefully

The sun was beginning to set when Merit jolted awake. She tried to stand up, but found that she couldn't get her hind legs underneath her. She lay for a moment, did some little stretches and was finally able to move her legs. "I must have slept funny," she thought, now struggling to stand.

"Merit," asked Hank, "why are you standing all crooked?"

"Just can't get my left hind leg to move. It's numb."

"Huh, you must have slept on it the wrong way," replied Hank. "Happened to me once. I slept funny with my neck all bent and when I woke up I couldn't move it for days. It still locks up every now and then. Not much I can do about it. Maybe when you get your rubdown today, it'll get straightened out."

As her friend rambled on, Merit was playing with her leg to see if she could get it to move. First she forced it forward and her hip gave a loud pop as something moved back into place. Hank stopped talking and looked at her.

"My friend, something is wrong. I've never heard anything pop that loudly, ever."

Nonetheless, Merit realized she could put weight on her back leg without any pain.

"Well," interrupting Merit with a shrug, "I fixed it."

"Still," murmured Hank, "it can't be good."

Carlos arrived to put the two in the kennel for the evening. Merit woke up shivering before dawn. She was so cold. She stood up and her joints creaked. She rearranged her blanket, walked a couple of circles and lay down again. Now a little warmer, she fell back to sleep.

Merit woke up a few hours later and listened to the morning. She could hear birds singing and squawking, someone hosing off the walkway outside, and Hank taking a deep stretch in his crate.

"Good morning," he said. "Did you sleep well? Any good dreams?"

Merit ignored the questions. Hank continued without pause, "I had a great one about how we're all too old to race and we get to stay here and retire here. It was fabulous. Ahhh, wouldn't *that* be great."

Merit yawned in response. "If we get to go to the beach. Only if we get to go to the beach." She stretched and shook, and then Carlos arrived and took them outside. There, he put Hank in his run and took Merit on a walk. As they approached the track, Carlos gathered up the slack in the leash and Merit could sense his grip tightening. She behaved herself and did what she was supposed to do.

After the walk, Carlos returned Merit to her run. She was drinking from her bowl when Tom and Carol approached.

"Hey Merit! Hey Hank!" called Carol. Merit looked up. "Hi M," said Tom, opening her run and bringing her out.

"Whoa Merit, *that* is a nasty tear."

Carol nodded. "But it shouldn't slow her down any."

"No," agreed Tom. "Especially considering how well she did this morning and yesterday. Come on now, girl."

While Tom was with Merit, Carol went into Hank's pen and looked at his paw. "I think we need to give it more time, but it looks okay." She patted Hank on the head.

"Let's head out," announced Tom suddenly. "We want to beat the traffic."

"Bye Hank," said Merit.

"Good luck and don't you know..." Hank was still talking as Merit was led away.

Put in a crate in the back of the truck, Merit hoped they might stop at the beach. In her heart, though, Merit knew it wasn't going to happen. Instead, she had a feeling she would be qualifying for racing tonight or tomorrow. When Merit saw the track parking lot jammed with cars, Merit realized that the race was probably going to be that night.

"I wonder... I wonder when I'll see Von," she thought. Merit's heart leapt but she quickly buried her excitement. Instead, she knew that her energy was better spent focusing on what she actually had control over than what she did not.

Carol and Tom got out of the truck and led Merit to her old pen. Just as they left, Swish appeared. "Oh Merit! It's so good to see you!"

"It's good to see you, too, Swish." Merit sniffed the air.

"Smelling for something?" inquired Swish.

"Uh, no," stammered Merit. "Have you heard anything about the race?"

"No," spat Swish. "You know I don't care about such things."

Swish looked at her friend and noticed that Merit seemed unsettled.

"Why?" hissed Swish.

"Oh, just wondering when it is and who'll be in it."

"Uh-uh," replied Swish, curiously eyeing her friend. She waited and watched Merit become more flustered. "I could maybe, probably, go find out, if you need me to."

"Oh, please!" barked Merit, which caused Swish to jump.

"Okay, okay, I'll go."

"Thanks," Merit called out after her. Merit was pacing back and forth when Molly walked up. "Hey M, why are you so worked up? The vacation was supposed to relax you. It's time to go." But Merit wanted to wait for Swish and refused to go to Molly. Molly waited a moment and then walked in, grabbing Merit and pulling at her until she followed.

Merit could tell she was getting prepped for race. Led into the washroom, Molly gave Merit a warm bath and a rub down then trimmed her nails. It was so relaxing that Merit was beginning to forget both about the race and Von.

"Good girl," murmured Molly. "That's it. Relax."

Now though, as the race blanket and muzzle were placed on Merit, she became excited and her lip started trembling. Tom walked in. "How's it going Molly?"

"Well, Merit is not her normal self. She's worked up."

"I can tell."

"I don't know why," said Molly. "She was very reserved when I went to get her this afternoon. In fact, she wouldn't come to me."

"That's not like her," said Tom.

"Maybe she's just had enough of racing."

"Merit," asked Tom. "Wanna run?" Merit hopped up and down, her lip quivering

"I guess she is excited," said Molly with a shrug.

"Dogs can't talk so we'll never know for sure what they want, except for food," replied Tom. "Anyway, keep her in here until about 10 O'clock."

"Gotcha." As soon as Tom left, Merit began to whimper. Molly petted her gently. "It's okay, girl. We'll go in a couple of minutes." Molly finally led Merit to be weighed and then headed out with her to the starting gate. As they passed in front of the grandstands, Merit stopped and smelled the breeze. She neither saw nor smelled Von.

With a gentle pull of her leash, Molly gently pulled on Merit to remind her they needed to be going. It was then that Merit spotted Von behind her. She stopped. Molly tugged more firmly and practically dragged Merit the remaining steps to her starting box. Merit refused to go in. In response, Molly grabbed both

Merit's back end and head and shoved her in. She then shut the door, and Merit could hear Molly breathe a sigh of relief.

Sitting in the dark box, Merit could only think about getting to see Von after the race. Would he be happy to see her? Merit was pulled out of her thoughts when the gate door flew open. She had a late start but was now running as fast as she could. Looking first left and then right, Merit saw that Von was out in front. Dodging other dogs along the way, Merit was gaining on Von.

Suddenly, the greyhound that Von was running alongside plowed into him, running him sidelong into the fence. It caused a chain reaction: now the dog directly in front of Merit ran directly into Von. Merit then stopped, and a dog behind her plowed into her, knocking her down. Merit could hear a loud commotion in the stands and knew that the wreck was spectacular.

She could now feel more dogs careening and piling into her. She struggled to breathe. Other dogs were yelping and barking.

"Get off of me!"

"You ran into me!"

"Ouch, my paw!"

Merit could now hear voices and began to black out. Someone lifted the dogs off of Merit and she could breathe again. As she struggled and struggled to stand Tom arrived and scooped up her hind end and helped her to stand.

"Oh Merit! Hold still!"

Tom looked over to where Von lay. Carol knelt over him. Shaking her head, her teary eyes said everything. Merit collapsed.

She could barely hear Tom scream. "Merit, Merit! Oh my god Merit. Carol, come here!"

Everything went black and Merit floated off.

Chapter 53

The Great Depression

As soon as Merit woke up, the smells told her she was at the vet's office. She couldn't remember anything except standing in the starting box and thinking about Von. Merit's hind end ached and she could barely move. Von, she thought, something, something about Von. But Merit's mind was all fuzzy and she couldn't remember anything more.

Merit took a deep breath. Her sides ached. Maybe she had been in some sort of wreck? Slowly and gently she shook her head, and then heard her neck pop. Merit tried to stand, but the fierce pain made her give up. She sighed. Von. Something about Von. Why couldn't she remember? She put her head down. As she inhaled, a memory appeared through the fog. Von was laying on the track. Carol was crying. Now Merit sobbed, the intense pain making her mournful cries shallow and soft.

Eventually Carol walked in and opened the crate door.

"Oh Merit! You're awake. How are you feeling, girl?" Kneeling down, she gently petted Merit. "Let me look at your stitches." Carol lifted Merit's hind leg and for the first time, the dog saw stitches running from her abdomen down her left leg. She was in shock.

"It's a superficial tear, Merit," said Carol. "It just looks bad. Luckily, nothing was broken or torn, but you must be sore. Here, take this pill. It will help with the pain." Carol opened Merit's mouth and placed the pill at the back of her tongue. As Merit tried to spit it out, Carol closed the dog's mouth and rubbed her throat, forcing her to swallow the pill. Carol offered Merit some water. "I'm going to call Tom and tell him you're awake. You rest and we'll get you out for a few minutes this evening."

Tom and Carol returned in a little while and opened Merit's crate.

"I don't know if we should encourage her to stand," said Carol. "She took quite a beating."

"Well, if nothing is broken she should be able to get up so we can look at her."

Carol stood up. "Merit's your dog. You do what you think is best."

Merit sighed and put her head down. "Merit," said Tom, "do you want to come out?" Merit didn't move.

"I did give her a pill," said Carol. "Maybe she's a little too sedated to get up."

"What'd you give her?"

"Just a pain pill to relax her."

"Well, that's shouldn't be enough to put her in this sort of, of stupor," replied Tom. "Merit?" Tom pulled Merit's head to his so they were looking eye to eye, but Merit looked away. "Merit," said Tom again, but she ignored him. He petted her head and gently stroked her side. She noticed that Tom was breathing funny. She looked at him, and saw tears streaming down Tom's face.

"What have I done to you… to Von? Poor Merit."

Carol knelt down, "It's not your fault. It's not your fault. These things happen."

"Merit, oh my beautiful girl, my beautiful girl."

"Tom," said Carol. "What are you talking about?

"Look, I took the greatest animal in the world and I made her a lifeless cripple."

"You're being too hard on yourself. Life happened to Merit. You always treated this dog better than many people treat their own children. She's raced a lot of races. She's four years old. You know that most dogs don't race nearly this long."

"I've known this dog almost her whole life and I never seen her, so… so unresponsive. You can tell. I took the life out of her."

"*You* didn't. Life did."

"What do I do now? To breed her would be inhumane."

Carol nodded. "You're right. Her hind end couldn't withstand the strain." They were silent and Tom gently cried and stroked his dog.

"What do you want for her?" asked Carol. The question went unanswered for several moments.

Tom finally spoke slowly. "To be loved and well taken care of. To be warm and included. And I want her to be able to go to the beach. That's what I want for her."

"Can't you give her that?"

"No, you know I can't. I've got too much on my plate, too many other dogs... and with our baby coming, I don't think..."

Hearing this, Merit yanked her head away from Tom and curled up as small as she could, despite her pain. Merit never felt so sad and so lost. She hated them. How could they treat her like this?

"I'll ask around," said Carol softly. "I'm sure we can find someone who'll take care of Merit. She's a great dog. Anybody would be lucky to have her." Tom stood up.

"I've got to get back to the track." He blew his nose and left. Carol squatted down and reached in to pat Merit.

"It'll be okay, girl. You'll see." Merit could tell she was crying.

Merit was crying too, inside, where it really counts.

Merit was not sure how many days passed. She ignored everyone and every dish. Carol had started giving her intravenous fluids but still Merit sulked, moped and cried the days away. She vaguely recognized that she was healing and getting better, but she would not make eye contact with anyone. Her lifeless body had to be practically dragged outside for exercise. All she really wanted to do was sleep, and to be left alone.

Chapter 54

Road Trip

One day, a man Merit didn't recognize came and put her in a crate inside a van. She neither cared nor thought about where she was going. She slept, dreaming of better things... Von, her mother, Isabel and her puppies, especially Emmy... Every once in a while, the man would stop, then open the door and try to get Merit to come out. She did as she was told, but kept her head down and her tail between her legs. Then it was back in the van.

The trip seemed to go on for days.

The van stopped and as usual, the man got out. After what seemed a longer then normal time, he finally let Merit out. They were greeted by a woman. "Well, here she is," said the man. "Let me know if it don't work out. This one seems really depressed."

"Yes," said the woman. "They told me." Kneeling down, the woman looked at Merit, but Merit avoided looking into her eyes. "Merit," the women said softly. "You're home now."

Something in this woman's voice made Merit decide to return her gaze.

She was a pretty woman in an ordinary way, but Merit could tell she had that something that makes you believe that they understand dogs. Just like Molly. Merit cocked her head. "Want to come live with me?" Merit allowed the women to lead her. "I hear you like the beach." The women led Merit up the few stairs to the front door, Merit hesitantly took each one slowly. "Not familiar with stairs, huh? But here, Merit, look!"

Merit looked straight through the house and outside. Spread before her was the most wonderful white sandy beach and the most magnificent blue ocean she'd ever seen. Merit, jumped up and whimpered. "Let's go! Let's go!" The woman led Merit to the beach.

Merit hit the sand and took off running. She ran and she ran. When she got winded, she stopped and turned back. Soon, Merit came across some people sitting on a blanket. Walking up to them, they petted her. The little girl gave her some bread. Merit ate it. Thanking the child with a quick kiss, Merit trotted off. When she came back to the woman, she was laughing and then patted Merit. "I'm glad you came back."

Merit lifted her head up, put her nose in the air and sniffed. Her ears perked up and flapped in the breeze. The women stroked her. They stood together. "You're such a nice girl," said the woman. "Your fur is so soft." Merit smiled, realizing that while she was with this woman, she would be well taken care of. "That's it, girl."

The woman sat down in the sand and Merit cuddled next to her. . The woman stroked Merit's head. "You have fur of silk, your so soft M." They both sat there for some time watching the sunset, Merit's stomach rumbled "Let's go get you a dish." Merit was led into the house that sat right on the beach. Merit sighed.

As they walked inside the women explained, "Here is your bed, these are your toys and this is your dish!" It had been a long time, but Merit's heart leapt. She shook her body back to life, twisting from head to toe, her legs nearly flailing completely out from under her. When she stopped, her tongue was sticking out of the side of her mouth. The woman laughed.

Merit quickly composed herself, and went back to her reserved, well-mannered self.

The woman smiled. "Merit you are a special dog."